JACK FINEGAN, Professor of New Testament History and Archeology at the Pacific School of Religion, is an internationally known biblical archeologist. He has written more than twenty-five nonfiction and fiction books, including *The Archeology of the New Testament, The Archeology of World Religions,* and *Handbook of Biblical Chronology.*

His *Light from the Ancient Past* has been the standard introduction to archeology for more than twenty years. It has been recorded for the blind and has also been translated into Japanese. Other books of his have been translated into German, Italian, and Spanish.

Dr. Finegan's travels have taken him around the world five times. He has conducted archeological study tours to Central and South America, the Middle East, and Asia. As hobbies he enjoys flying, yachting, and mountain climbing.

X

MARK OF THE TAW

MARK
OF THE
TAW

by Jack Finegan

JOHN KNOX PRESS
Richmond, Virginia

Library of Congress Cataloging in Publication Data

Finegan, Jack, 1908-
    Mark of the taw.

    Includes bibliographical references.
    1. Mark, Saint—Fiction. I. Title.
PZ4.F495Mar [PS3556.I466]   813'.5'4   72–1762
ISBN 0–8042–1951–6

MARK
OF THE
TAW

48645

Prologue

Swaying slightly amidst the clouds of incense the black-robed priest intoned:

ΣΤΩΜΕΝ ΚΑΛΩΣ:
ΣΤΩΜΕΝ ΕΥΛΑΒΩΣ:
ΣΤΩΜΕΝ ΕΚΤΕΝΩΣ:
ΣΤΩΜΕΝ ΕΝ ΕΙΡΗΝΗ:
ΣΤΩΜΕΝ ΜΕΤΑ ΦΟΒΟΥ ΘΕΟΥ:
ΚΑΙ ΤΡΟΜΟΥ ΚΑΙ ΚΑΤΑΝΥΞΕΩΣ.[1]

I was surprised to find myself translating:

Let us stand nobly,
Let us stand piously,
Let us stand earnestly,
Let us stand in peace,
Let us stand with fear of God,
and with trembling and contrition.

"How is it, Father Mina," I asked afterward, "that I can understand part of your liturgy when I do not know Coptic?"

"Ours is the ancient Egyptian language," he said proudly, "but we write it in Greek characters, plus a few Egyptian signs, and it contains many Greek words."

Then he concluded flatteringly: "The Greek, of course, you understand perfectly."

"*Danke sehr.*" I fell back into German to cover my confusion over the compliment. Like myself, Father Mina had at one time been a student at a German university, and we often found that our best medium of communication was the language we had each learned in student days. So when Father Mina's English faltered, as it occasionally did, and my Coptic was insufficient, as it always was, being limited to the Greek components of that language, we still could talk with each other.

I was in Alexandria on government business. As an archeologist I was reputed to have a good acquaintance with the Middle East and, in a time of international tension, it was thought that I could serve as an inconspicuous listening post in a troubled area. Egypt was being wooed by both the East and the West. Ostensibly occupied with whatever particular archeological investigation I wanted to take up next, I was to collect any information I could on any maneuvers by the Eastern power.

The assignment promised to mingle the spice of contemporary adventure with my customary preoccupation with the dust of the ancient past, and I accepted the work with interest. But as far as I could tell, at least in Alexandria, the post to which I was sent, nothing was happening at all.

Every morning I was awakened by the high-pitched, wavering call from the modern loudspeaker on the minaret of the Mosque of the Prophet Daniel, near which I lived:

> Prayer is better than sleep.
> Come to prayer.

Every day I mingled with the throngs on the streets, and kept up some appearance of professional work in the Greco-Roman Museum.

Every evening I went out for dinner to some crowded place,

whether an international hotel on the waterfront or an exotic restaurant on a back street.

Nowhere did I pick up any whisper of the intrigue which was presumably swirling all about. Perhaps Alexandria was in a back eddy of whatever was going on in the land as a whole. Perhaps I had not yet learned how to listen.

Partly in order to break the monotony, it must be admitted, I went every Sunday to the Church of St. Mark. At first, the chanted liturgy seemed repetitious and unexciting to me. But when I began to understand parts of it, and also struck up the acquaintance with the Coptic priest to which I have alluded, it became more interesting.

One day I caught in the liturgy, in a memorial prayer, these words: ΑΓΙΟΣ ΜΑΡΚΟΣ . . . ΑΠΟΣΤΟΛΟΣ . . . ΕΥΑΓΓΕΛΙΣΤΗΣ . . . ΜΑΡΤΥΡΟΣ,[2] Saint Mark . . . Apostle . . . Evangelist . . . Martyr.

"Why do you single out Mark for special mention?" I asked Father Mina when opportunity offered. In a way it was what you might call a loaded question. I knew that the Copts claimed that Mark had founded the Christian church in Egypt. I also knew that my professors in Germany and the United States had always scoffed at the idea whenever it came up.

To display the small amount of knowledge I had been painfully acquiring by reading and questioning, I went on: "The prayer also mentions Pachomius and Shenute. I know about them. Pachomius founded your first common-life monastery about A.D. 320. Shenute became head of your White Monastery sixty-five years later. You would call him the founder of Coptic Christianity. But what about Mark? Why is he so important here?"

"Mark was the first to preach Christianity in our land," replied Father Mina. "He was buried here." Then he scowled with disgust. "Only, later the Venetians came and carried away the holy bones."

My mind went back to my earlier studies in New Testament and primitive church history in the famous schools and universities

which I had attended in the United States and Germany. I could
almost see myself as I sat in the classrooms in those days, and
I visualized once more the great scholars to whose lectures I had
listened. I recalled the critical arguments they had presented when
they discussed the topics of John Mark and the early history of
the church in Egypt.

"Gentlemen," my American professor began, "the
following facts are found in the New Testament concerning John
Mark:

"He had a Hebrew name, Johanan, which means 'The Lord
is gracious,' and a Roman surname, Marcus, which signifies a large
hammer. He was the son of Mary, and it was in her house in
Jerusalem that the early church met.[3]

"One year near the Passover the apostle Peter was put in
prison by King Herod. He was miraculously delivered, and went
straight to Mary's house. Then he departed and went to another
place. That is the point where John Mark is mentioned by name
for the first time. This king was Herod Agrippa I, grandson of
Herod the Great, and he reigned in A.D. 41-44. Since the narrative
continues to tell of Herod's death, which took place at Caesarea
in 44, I have usually placed Peter's imprisonment and release in
the spring of 44, but I recognize that it could actually have been
in any earlier springtime of Herod's reign as well, and, in fact, in
his *Chronicle* Eusebius places it in the second year of Claudius,
or A.D. 42, which may well be correct.[4]

"Later Peter calls Mark his 'son,' so we may suppose that
Peter was not only a good friend of Mary but probably also baptized John Mark, which would have made him his 'son' in a
spiritual sense. In the same context Peter says that 'she who is at
Babylon' sends greetings, and we may suppose that by this he
refers to the church at Rome.[5]

"As to the connection between John Mark and Peter, it is
also interesting to note the report of Papias preserved by Eusebius.
Papias was a bishop in Hierapolis in Asia Minor shortly before

the middle of the second century. He said that the Elder, probably meaning the Elder John, used to say that Mark was not a personal follower of Jesus but followed Peter, became his interpreter, and wrote down what he heard him say. Since Peter adapted his teachings to the needs of the moment, what Mark wrote down was not a very connected account, but it was written with care for accuracy. In this statement Papias was doubtless referring to what we know as the Gospel according to Mark.[6]

"You also remember the Muratorian Fragment, of which we have spoken in other connections." The professor paused momentarily, and glanced around the classroom to see if he detected even a glimmer of recognition of something familiar among his students. I followed his glance, and realized that what he saw were two students who were sound asleep, another who was writing a letter under the guise of taking notes, and several who were making an effort to look interested but who were actually, in their thoughts, far away. Strangely enough, I myself, who was often enough in a like condition in some of my other classes, found the facts which were being presented very fascinating, and waited for what was to come next almost as if it were another clue in a detective story.

"This document," the professor went on, with a trace of weariness in his voice, "is found in an eighth-century Latin manuscript, but is probably translated from the Greek. The original must have dated about the middle of the second century, thus was only a little later than Papias, of whom we were just speaking. It was a list of the accepted books of the New Testament, and must have begun with the four Gospels, Matthew, Mark, Luke, and John. Now, however, the beginning is lost, and the first words of the Fragment are '. . . but at some he was present, and so he set them down.'

"Immediately after that, the Fragment speaks of the third book of the Gospels, that according to Luke, and then of the fourth of the Gospels, which is John's. Therefore, the opening statement must have been part of an account concerning the Gospel according to Mark.

"But what does it mean?" The slight edge of weariness which

was still to be detected in the professor's voice now seemed to be related not to the sleepiness of his students, but to the difficulties inherent in the materials with which he had to wrestle and which he had to present.

"Taking our clue from what Papias said about Mark's hearing of Peter and his writing down of what he heard him say, we might think the Fragment means that '. . . at some [of Peter's lectures] he was present, and so he set them down.'

"On the other hand, it could mean that '. . . at some [of the events in the life of Jesus] he was present, and so he set them down.' "

As he made the latter statement, there almost seemed to be a touch of excitement in the professor's voice, replacing the weariness. For myself, I made another one of those resolutions which I did not always keep, namely, that I would read the Gospel according to Mark again and try to see if I could recognize any places where it would seem that I could tell that the author was reporting something that Peter had told, or something that he himself had experienced.

At this juncture, as I remembered it, the class session was interrupted by the bell for the intermission. When we resumed a few minutes later, the professor continued his normally straight-forward presentation.

"John Mark," he said, "was also a relative of Barnabas."[7]

Here the professor walked over to the blackboard and wrote the word ἀνεψιός in Greek.

"This is the Greek word," he explained, "by which Mark is described in his relationship to Barnabas. It ordinarily means 'cousin,' and is usually so translated in the New Testament. It may be noted, however, that it is very similar to the Latin *nepos*"— now he wrote this word on the board, too—"and one of the meanings of the latter is 'nephew.' Therefore it is just possible that Mark was a nephew of Barnabas.

"At any rate Barnabas is described as a Levite who came

from Cyprus and became a member of the early church in Jerusalem, where he was distinguished by his generosity. It is said that his name was Joseph originally, and that he was called Barnabas by the apostles, meaning 'Son of encouragement.'[8] As far as I can see, the name Barnabas does not quite have that meaning, but it is rather close to the Aramaic *bar-newaha,* which means 'son of refreshment,' so I suspect his original full name was Joseph Barnabas, and the apostles made a slightly farfetched play on words to arrive at the complimentary interpretation of 'Son of encouragement' for this fine man.

"Later Barnabas went to Antioch and, in the time of the great famine in the reign of Claudius, he and Saul came down from there to Jerusalem with some help for the poor.[9] Claudius reigned in A.D. 41-54, and Josephus mentions a great famine in Judea when Tiberius Alexander was procurator, which was about A.D. 46-48, so we may date this 'famine visit' of Barnabas and Saul to Jerusalem at about A.D. 46.[10] When they went back from Jerusalem to Antioch, Barnabas and Saul took John Mark with them.[11] When they proceeded on what we commonly call the 'first missionary journey' (about A.D. 47-48), Barnabas and Saul had John Mark as ὑπηρέτης."[12]

Again the professor went to the blackboard and wrote the Greek word he had just pronounced. "Since an ἐρέτης is a 'rower,' " he explained, "this word means literally an 'under rower,' and so it is used to describe servants of various kinds. Accordingly, it may mean only that Barnabas and Saul had Mark along with them as a servant to assist them. But there is a possibility, which should at least be mentioned, that the word may mean a great deal more than that. In ancient papyri the word occurs frequently to designate a public official who is in charge of documents, and it probably corresponds to the Hebrew *hazzan,* which was the title of an officer in the Jewish synagogue. The same word occurs at the beginning of the Gospel according to Luke, where it may mean not just 'ministers of the word' in the general sense as it is usually translated, but may refer in a far more specific way to those who 'served as officers of the message,' that is, it may mean that they furnished and were in charge of the documents of the Christian mission. If this should be the clue to the way the word is applied to John Mark in his connection with Barnabas and Saul at the beginning of the 'first missionary journey,' then we could consider that he was the member of the party who handled a written memorandum about Jesus which was used in the mission. That this written memorandum was substantially what we know as the Gospel according to Mark would be a further possible conclusion."[13]

The professor had been speaking more rapidly and with more animation than usual. Then he seemed to catch himself and return with an effort to his customary dry, restrained manner. "Of course, the conclusion I have just mentioned is open to various critical objections, and would itself do violence to the commonly accepted critical dogmas"—again he caught himself— "I mean critical judgments, concerning the origin of the Gospels.

"At any rate"—now the professor moved steadily on with his lecture—"Mark returned from Perga in Pamphylia to Jerusalem before the 'first missionary journey' was over.[14] When the time came to start out again on the 'second missionary journey,' Paul asked Barnabas to go with him but declined to invite Mark because he felt that Mark had failed them on the earlier occasion. Thereupon Barnabas and Mark sailed away to Cyprus, and Paul chose another companion and went off in another direction.[15] Later, perhaps ten or twelve years later, when Paul was writing letters from prison, perhaps from prison in Rome, Mark was with him again, at least temporarily, and Paul speaks of him in all friendliness.[16] Still later, Paul's friend Timothy is requested to bring Mark with him.[17] Since both Paul and Peter probably died in Rome under Nero in A.D. 64, any references that either of them made to Mark would have had to have been earlier than that.

"Those, gentlemen," the professor wound up his lecture, "are the New Testament references to John Mark. Beyond that we have only romantic inference, apocryphal legend, and ecclesiastical fantasy."

It was evident that the professor had no intention of going on into such profitless areas, but a student put up a hand of interrogation. "What would be an example of romantic inference in this connection?"

"The chief example," replied the professor, with a touch of weariness in his voice again, "is based on a passage near the end of the Gospel according to Mark. Jesus was in the Garden of Gethsemane, and was captured by his enemies. After all of his own disciples fled, a young man followed him. The young man was wearing only a piece or garment of linen. When the captors of Jesus seized the young man too, he slipped out of the linen and fled naked.[18] The usual Greek word for 'young man' is νεανίας" —again the professor went to the blackboard and wrote the words as he explained them—"and it is found in contexts suggesting a person from about the twenty-fourth to the fortieth year in age; here in the Gospel we have the diminutive form of the same word, νεανίσκος, which may suggest a somewhat younger person. The σινδών which the young man was wearing was a 'fine linen cloth.' Herodotus uses this word both for the cloth which was wrapped around the body of the dead, and also for the cloth in which a man wrapped himself to sleep.[19]

"Since the event was naturally of interest to the person to whom it happened, but since it would hardly have even been known to the disciples who had fled and was hardly edifying in itself, it has been suggested that the person involved was probably none other than the author of the Gospel himself, that is, presumably John Mark, and that he included the item in his Gospel in much the same way that a painter has sometimes painted a small picture of himself in the corner of his canvas.

"That, of course, is sheer romanticism"—and the professor accompanied the words with an expulsion of the breath that sounded much like a sigh.

"Why," he added, "some have even gone on to declare that the lower classes would not wear 'fine linen cloth,' and to conclude that this young man was therefore probably nothing less than the son of the owner of the Garden of Gethsemane. Perhaps he was spending the night in a watchtower in the garden. Perhaps he heard voices and rose to see what was taking place. Perhaps he came upon Jesus and heard his prayer of anguish. Perhaps he tried to provide some consolation to him. Perhaps some of the more distant disciples saw him in his white garment and imagined they saw an angel. That could account for the statement which is in some manuscripts of the Gospel according to Luke that there appeared to Jesus an angel from heaven strengthening him.[20] Then, when Jesus' captors came, they almost took the young man too, and he barely escaped naked."

As he told this imaginary account it seemed to me that the professor's voice almost trembled with excitement. Then I realized that he ended with his pun about the young man who "barely escaped naked" in order to cover any emotion he may have felt, and to restore himself to his customary pose of slightly amused disdain for anything other than what the prevailing school of scholarship thought.

I had to admit that he was thorough, however, for he went on to complete his report on what he called "romantic inference."

"If the young man in the Garden were the son of the owner, and were concerned with the operation of the Garden, and if this young man were John Mark and the author of the Second Gospel, then it might also be supposed that it would be possible to detect signs of his gardening interest in that Gospel. So some have investigated the Gospel with a particular view to noting if there are any such signs in it. They argue that, in fact, there are such. Note these items: Where the Gospel according to Matthew says that a man dug a wine press, the Gospel according to Mark states that he dug a pit for the wine press, and uses a word that occurs only here in the New Testament.[21] When Mark tells about the Feeding

of the Five Thousand, he relates that the people sat down in, literally, 'garden plots,' again a word occurring only here in the New
Testament, and a word the picturesque character of which you
may quite miss in the usual translation, which says only that they
sat in 'groups.'[22] In the Parable of the Mustard Seed, Matthew
and Luke say that the seed becomes a tree, which, strictly speaking,
is incorrect, since the mustard plant is only a herb, but Mark says
instead only that it puts forth large branches or, as it should perhaps be translated, large twigs.[23] In the account of the Withering
of the Fig Tree, only Mark explains that it was not the season for
figs.[24] In the report of the Triumphal Entry, Matthew uses the
ordinary word for branches or twigs, but Mark employs a tech-
nical agricultural term and speaks, literally, of layers of leaves.[25]
Note also that of all the parables of Jesus, Mark gives only four,
and all four have to do with garden and fields.[26] Of these, one is
preserved by Mark alone, and it is about the Seed Growing Secretly.
In it he tells how the seed grows and lengthens, and he describes
the three stages of growth, 'first the blade, then the ear, then the
full grain in the ear,'[27] and it certainly sounds like a gardener
speaking."[28]

As the professor finished this extended statement I hardly
knew if he were expressing his own opinion or reporting that of
someone else. I was quickly reminded that he was only giving a
scholarly report on "romantic inferences" about John Mark.

"Oh, there is one further ramification of the romantic interpretation," he said. "In the account of the empty tomb of Jesus
in the Gospel according to Mark, the women find in the tomb a
young man dressed in a white robe who tells them that Jesus has
risen.[29] The word for the 'young man' is the same somewhat unusual word which was used for the person in the Garden of Gethsemane." The professor pointed again to the term he had previously
written on the blackboard. "So, you see, the romanticist can declare
that this is the same young man as the one who was almost captured in the Garden."

For a moment it seemed as if the professor were going to add some scathing comment. Then, as if once and for all to dissociate himself from such follies of the imagination, he simply shrugged his shoulders.

He had also referred to "apocryphal legend" and "ecclesiastical fantasy." All of us in the class seemed disposed to let the matter of "apocryphal legend" pass, although I could hardly say that any of us had any firsthand acquaintance with the kind of material the professor had in mind.

I, however, really wanted to know what he meant by "ecclesiastical fantasy" with respect to John Mark, so I put up my hand and asked the question.

Although his answer was brief, it was so precise that I was sure he must have prepared in advance in anticipation that someone would make the interrogation and give him a springboard for the disquisition.

"According to the church historians Eusebius and Socrates," he began, "the apostles of Christ went forth by lot among the nations. Thomas went to Parthia, Andrew to Scythia, John to Asia, Peter and Paul to Rome, Matthew to Ethiopia, and Bartholomew to India.[30] Naturally, therefore, the church at Rome claimed to have back of it in a special way the authority of Peter and Paul, the church in Asia the authority of John, and so on. But what about a great land such as Egypt which was quite left out of these lists? Naturally they wanted to lay claim to some impressive founder, too. Most of the apostles were already spoken for in other parts of the world, so the next best thing to do was to think of some apostolic person, that is, a person who, although not one of the twelve apostles, had at least been personally associated with the twelve apostles. Of such persons, who was a more impressive figure than John Mark, who had been personally associated with both Peter and Paul? So the church in Egypt claimed him for its founder. That is what I mean by an 'ecclesiastical fantasy.' "

"Do you have any explanation as to why it was that particular person that Egypt claimed . . . ?" I had just begun this further question when the bell rang and abruptly terminated the class session.

That was the lecture by my American professor as I gradually recalled it to mind while I was walking up and down the streets of Alexandria. I went over the salient points again. There was evidence for the relationships of John Mark with Peter, Barnabas, and Paul. There were clues as to some chronological points. John Mark was first mentioned by name in connection with the house of his mother, Mary, to which Peter came when he got out of Herod's prison; that was obviously within Herod's reign, A.D. 41-44, and probably in A.D. 42. Mark went with Barnabas and Saul to Antioch around the time of the great famine, A.D. 46; he went with them on a mission about A.D. 47-48. He was mentioned by Paul in letters from prison, probably ten or twelve years later, and by Peter too, in a letter the date of which might be debatable, but which must, at least, have been written before Peter died, probably in A.D. 64, which was probably the date of Paul's death too.

Well, that was it. Those were the facts. In them all there was nothing about Egypt.

I was almost ready to write *finis* to my train of thought and dismiss the problem from further consideration—yet something at the back of my mind was asking a question which could not quite be silenced: "Yes, those are the facts, and those are the established chronological points. But are there no interstices between the facts, and no gaps between the chronological points?" Yes, I had to admit, what the known points cover is covered, but what they do not cover is not covered. What is not covered is certainly a considerable amount of time all together; it could also allow for a considerable amount of movement in space; therefore, one cannot say positively that Mark never went to any other places and never did any other things than those explicitly mentioned in the Book of Acts. So I vacillated in my thinking.

Also I recalled the lecture by my professor in Germany on the earliest history of the church in Egypt.

The several hundred of us who were in the famous lecturer's class had found our ways to our respective seats. The attendant at the door suddenly straightened to attention. The professor's two young assistants entered and took their places at either side of the lecture platform. A perceptible interval ensued, then the professor strode in, placed his hat on the table beside the lectern, opened his lecture notes, and began.

"Meine Herren," he said, studiously neglecting the several women who were scattered among the many men of the class, "we set forth first today what is known of the earliest history of Christianity in Egypt. Unfortunately it is not much. It is only with the episcopate of Demetrius of Alexandria in A.D. 189-231 that the church in Egypt appears in the daylight of history. At that time it was a splendid church. Attached to it was a school of higher learning, the fame of which was carried far and wide. The famous heads of this school, contemporary with Demetrius, were Pantaenus, Clement, and Origen. At least from the last two, we still have voluminous and erudite writings.

"But"—at this juncture the professor inclined his powerful head slightly to one side in what might have been a gesture of regret at the inevitable limitations in his discipline—"prior to Demetrius we know virtually nothing. This, our almost total ignorance of what was happening in Egypt, is the worst gap in all our knowledge of early church history.

"All that we know up to the time of Demetrius may be summed up in the following eight items."

Now the professor flipped a page in his lecture notes and began to follow more closely what he had written out. Lest we should become confused by the multiplicity of items, he carefully gave the number of each item as he proceeded.

"Item one. There was a local Gospel which Clement of Alexandria called 'The Gospel according to the Egyptians.' By the time Clement mentions this Gospel it was probably considered heretical by the orthodox Christians, but originally it was probably read by everybody. There was also a work called 'The Gospel according to the Hebrews.' The contrast in the names may imply that the Gospel according to the Egyptians was read by the Gentile Christians of Egypt, the Gospel according to the Hebrews by the local Jewish Christians.

"Item two. The heretic Basilides worked in Egypt. Epiphanius says that he spent some time in Egypt, and visited various places, including Alexandria.[31] Basilides flourished in the first half of the second century.

"Item three. The heretic Valentinus began his work in Egypt. Epiphanius writes: 'Some said he was born at Phrebonitis in Egypt, and educated after the Greek fashion in Alexandria.' In another passage the same author declares: 'He preached in Egypt. And one result is that his brood still survives in that country, like the remains of a viper's bones.'[32] Valentinus was contemporary with Basilides.

"Item four. Justin Martyr, writing before A.D. 165, argues that promiscuous intercourse is not one of the 'mysteries' of Christianity, by citing the case of a young Alexandrian Christian who had recently asked the governor Felix for permission to be made a eunuch by surgical procedure. The permission was refused, and the youth then chose to remain single.[33]

"Item five. A council was held in Palestine about A.D. 198 to discuss the question of whether the paschal communion should be held on the fourteenth day of the Jewish month Nisan, regardless of what day of the week it fell on (as the 'Quartodecimans' of Asia held), or only on the resurrection day which was the Sunday after that, and could be defined as the first Sunday after the first full moon after the vernal equinox (as the church at Rome taught). As was at last almost everywhere agreed to, except in the province of Asia, the Palestinian assembly decided for the second alternative. They then wrote a letter on the subject, from which Eusebius quotes a paragraph.[34] In this we learn that the church in Palestine had been for some time in correspondence with the church in Alexandria on the subject, and the two were in agreement in keeping the feast on the same day."

Up to this point the professor had been adhering closely to the written notes that he had in front of him, and thus making steady progress through the sequence of items which he wished to present, all of which, one had to admit, were documented with the precision for which he was famous. At this point, however, he lifted his eyes and made an apparently spontaneous comment.

"It was well, I would say, that the Palestinian church chose to keep in touch with the Alexandrian church on the matter of chronology. With respect to the calendar, and astronomy on which it depends, Alexandria was supreme. You may remember that already in the third century B.C., Eratosthenes, librarian at Alexandria, had employed astronomical observations to measure the earth and had fixed its diameter at 7,850 miles, which is only fifty miles short of the modern figure. Further, the 'Alexandrian Year' was so accurate that the 'Julian' was based on it which we still use today. It is no wonder that the bishop of Alexandria was depended upon to fix the date of Easter for the whole church. That this was so is attested by Dionysius of Alexandria in the middle of the third century, and the custom may go back at least as early as to Demetrius."

After this interesting digression, which was in harmony with the professor's well-known interest and competence in matters of chronology, he brought himself rigorously back to his notes and his sequence of items.

"Item six. Upon one occasion Irenaeus, who was active about A.D. 180, wrote a letter to an Alexandrian Christian, and fragments of this epistle are extant in an Armenian translation.[35]

"Item seven. Eusebius introduces with the words 'they say' an interesting statement to the effect that Mark, a follower of Peter and the one whose Gospel is extant, was the first that was sent to Egypt, and that he proclaimed the Gospel which he had written, and first established churches in Alexandria. In a later passage Eusebius also states that a certain Annianus succeeded Mark as the leader of the Alexandrian church in the eighth year of Nero (A.D. 62), and thus implies that Mark probably died in that year.[36]

"Item eight. A list of the bishops of the church of Alexandria is incorporated in the *Chronicle* of Eusebius and was almost certainly derived by him from the *Chronographies* of Julius Africanus. Julius Africanus lived much of his life in Palestine but corresponded with Origen and on one occasion went to Alexandria on account of the fame of Heraclas. The latter was a pupil of Origen who became head of the catechetical school after Origen went to Caesarea (A.D. 231) and, a year later, also became bishop of Alexandria. So Julius Africanus could no doubt have had access, on that visit, to such records as were preserved in the school and church in Alexandria. The list of bishops of the Alexandrian church which can be reconstructed from Julius Africanus and Eusebius contains eleven names. It begins with Annianus, who took office in the eighth year of Nero and continued for twenty-two years. It continues with Avilus and others down to Demetrius, who entered the position in the tenth year of Commodus (A.D. 189)."[37]

With the completion of his eight items, the professor paused as if to think back over what he had just said. I also thought back quickly over what I had just heard him say, as I had the outline of it before me in my notes.

It was his basic affirmation that we know almost nothing of the church in Alexandria and Egypt until the time of Demetrius, i.e., until only shortly before A.D. 200.

My eye ran rapidly back over my transcript of his eight items. It was true. The first six items fell at the earliest in the second century, items seven and eight drew upon Julius Africanus and Eusebius who lived into the third and fourth centuries respectively.

And yet—now my mind toyed with a different possible assessment of the evidence—Julius Africanus and Eusebius were careful historians and chronographers, and what they reported had to do with events as early as the first century. They both believed that they were transmitting an authentic list of the heads of the Alexandrian church, a list that came on down from Annianus who took office in A.D. 62. Before Annianus, wrote Eusebius—and he reported this as something that "they say," i.e., he was here too transmitting information derived from an earlier source—it was none other than Mark who had first established churches in Alexandria.

Along that line of thought, I waited with some fresh interest for what the professor would say next. Would he proceed to analyze the tradition in Julius Africanus and Eusebius? Would he discuss the position of Annianus? Would he speak of actual evidence for a chapter in the life of John Mark which my American professor had dismissed as "ecclesiastical fantasy"?

My mildly hopeful expectation of an exciting conclusion was not fulfilled.

The professor simply said: "Eight items. The sum total of our knowledge concerning the history of early Christianity in Alexandria and Egypt."

Then he went on to the next topic in his syllabus.

I would have thought I were a young theological student again, preparing for my next examination, as I went over in my mind the lectures by my professors. Instead I was, reputedly, an archeologist, walking up and down the streets of modern Alexandria, going, on weekdays, to the Greco-Roman Museum in the Rue du Musée and, on Sundays, to the Church of St. Mark in the Rue de l'Eglise Copte.

As I have said, it was my visits to the church and my measure of acquaintance with the priest there, Father Mina, that had brought back to mind the theological lectures I had heard years before. There, on the one hand, were my esteemed theological professors who had said that we know virtually nothing about earliest Christianity in Egypt and nothing about John Mark except his associations with Peter and Paul and Barnabas on the other side of the Mediterranean, and here, on the other hand, was Father Mina who said with perfect assurance: "Mark was the first to preach Christianity in our land. He was buried here."

Father Mina was, in fact, exercising a considerable influence upon me. He was indeed a rather impressive person. Although relatively short in height, he was deep chested and powerfully built, and he also conveyed in some intangible fashion a sense of great depth of character. He moved quickly when there was work to be done, but there was also a certain serenity about him, almost as if he knew that everything that was to be would be. He was, I thought, of approximately middle age, yet some sense of timelessness clung to him too.

Some of these matters were, of course, intangible factors which I could only say that I felt, rather than that I could point to them to demonstrate them to anyone else. At any rate some of Father Mina's features were obvious to all: a long nose, raised eyebrows, beautiful brown eyes, a bald forehead, and a heavy beard—on the whole a handsome man and probably even handsomer when younger, I thought.

The nose made me think he was of Semitic extraction, but then I recalled that he was, of course, a Copt, and the Copts claimed descent from the ancient Egyptians. A proud heritage!

One other feature in the personal appearance of Father Mina I noticed only upon the first occasion when, after rather long acquaintance—for he was reserved in anything of the emotions —he extended his hand to shake hands. Since he ordinarily wore a robe with flowing sleeves, his hands had generally been hidden from sight. Now, when he shook my hand, I realized that his fingers were abnormally short.

"Curt-fingered," I said to myself, recalling a term I had heard somewhere, then wondered what the term really meant.

Latin *curtus* means both "shortened" and "mutilated," I puzzled it out to myself. Was this, then, a mutilated hand or just one stunted in its growth? Someone had told me, I remembered, that such a malformation could come about in rare instances due to an acute dietary deficiency in early childhood. Later, at his services in the church, I managed to catch sight of both of Father Mina's hands. Both were equally short in the fingers. Abnormally stunted, but compact and strong, not mutilated, I concluded, and forgot about the matter.

But I did not forget about Father Mina's serene declaration: "Mark was the first to preach Christianity in our land." The statement contrasted so sharply with what I had learned at school that I could not accept it, yet I could not put it out of mind. Every Sunday the memorial liturgy spoke of the matter again: "We remember Saint Mark, our apostle, evangelist, and martyr."

I decided to see if I could learn anything more about the matter, all by myself and for myself.

At least for a beginning, the library of the Greco-Roman Museum appeared adequate. I obtained the *Church History* of Eusebius. After some searching I found the passages to which my German professor had referred, as I remembered.

"And they say that this Mark was the first that was sent to Egypt, and that he proclaimed the Gospel which he had written, and first established churches in Alexandria."[38]

"When Nero was in the eighth year of his reign, Annianus succeeded Mark the evangelist in the administration of the parish of Alexandria."[39]

The precision of the chronological reference in the last paragraph reminded me of the *Chronicle* of Eusebius, to which my professor in Germany had also made reference, and for which he claimed that the *Chronographies* of Julius Africanus were an earlier source.

As I puzzled my way through the tables of the *Chronicle*, I was amazed at the learning of the ancient scholars. In the left-hand column of the *Chronicle* were the Years of Abraham, as if the patriarch had continued to live on, and one were giving the years of his life. In the Year 1240 of Abraham was noted the first of the Greek Olympiads, and from there on the years of Abraham and the Olympiads of the Greeks provided double notation for each successive year. Alongside these Hebrew and Greek reference points were also the years of the pagan kings and, in the period in which I was interested, these were the Roman emperors. Opposite these, in turn, were the rulers of the Jews, each with his successive years listed parallel to the other notations. Flanked on either side by these items of chronological framework was a central column of sacred history.

Incredible, I thought, and how precise! We know, for example, that Claudius reigned A.D. 41-54, Nero A.D. 54-68—I looked up the dates in a reference work to be sure that my memory was correct—and so on, down through the successive emperors. But in this very example, what is meant by Anno Domini 54? Is it the last year of Claudius or the first year of Nero? And when you say the eighth year of Nero, what do you count from and what do you mean?

Well—I reasoned it out as I tried to understand how the years of the *Chronicle* were arranged—Claudius was poisoned on October 12, A.D. 54, and Nero was made emperor on October 13. So Nero began to reign in the latter part of A.D. 54, and the calendar year A.D. 55 was his first full year of reign, so obviously his eighth year of reign was A.D. 62.

Obviously, I say! Such fine points of chronological detail are hardly obvious in the usual sources. But when one checks the exact events sufficiently to know what Eusebius is referring to, and then runs one's finger down the columns of his *Chronicle,* one can see at a glance the successive years and recognize the exact points in question.

So I tried to become familiar with the *Chronicle*, and then I found the items for which I was looking.

There they were, and I copied them out exactly as in the *Chronicle*, adding only for my own convenient reference the years according to the Christian era.

Year of Abraham 2058, Olympiad 205 Year 2, Claudius Year 2, Anno Domini 42: Peter the apostle, having first founded the church of Antioch, is sent to Rome.

Year of Abraham 2059, Olympiad 205 Year 3, Claudius Year 3, Anno Domini 43: Mark the evangelist and interpreter of Peter preaches Christ in Egypt and Alexandria.

Year of Abraham 2078, Olympiad 210 Year 2, Nero Year 8, Anno Domini 62: After Mark the evangelist, Annianus was ordained the first bishop of the church of Alexandria.[40]

So that was the chronological framework, according to Eusebius, and probably according to Julius Africanus, and Julius Africanus had been to Alexandria and could have seen the original records in the great catechetical school!

"I have been reading the *History* and the *Chronicle* of Eusebius," I said, when I saw Father Mina the next time, "and I am greatly impressed by the evident precision of his references to the work of Mark in Alexandria."

"Yes," said the priest, as a slight smile lightened his face. "And there is more," he added, but did not elaborate further.

I redoubled my efforts. The manuscript of the *Chronicle* of Eusebius which I had been using was actually a Latin translation of the work by Jerome. I was reminded that Jerome had written the lives of the illustrious men of the early Christian movement. I looked to see if he had anything to say about Mark. As I half suspected would be the case he added only a little to what Eusebius had told, and one could suppose that it was indeed from Eusebius that he had learned most of what he had to tell. Nevertheless it was a little additional bit of information. The gist of it was this:

"Mark the disciple and interpreter of Peter wrote a short gospel at the request of the brethren at Rome embodying what he had heard Peter tell. When Peter heard this, he approved it and published it. . . . So, taking the gospel which he himself composed, Mark went to Egypt, and first preaching Christ at Alexandria, he formed a church so admirable in doctrine and continence of living that he constrained all followers of Christ to his example. . . . He died in the eighth year of Nero and was buried at Alexandria, Annianus succeeding him."[41]

". . . and was buried at Alexandria"—I read the words over to myself again. Why, that was exactly what Father Mina had said so quietly when we had first discussed the subject. Could it really be true? I wondered and wondered.

Two more references I managed to find for myself, one in Epiphanius, and one in Hippolytus. My professor in Germany had often cited Epiphanius, and I had looked him up and ascertained that he lived in the fourth century, first in Palestine, then in Cyprus. In connection with my present interest, I thought it significant to have an authority on the island of Cyprus, because at one point the Book of Acts told how John Mark went off to Cyprus with Barnabas, who was from that place. The statement which I found after a long search in the voluminous writings of Epiphanius did not, however, it seemed to me, add very much to what I had learned already.

Epiphanius said: "After Mark wrote the gospel he was sent by the holy Peter to the land of the Egyptians."[42]

The second reference was so brief that I almost missed it. But when I found it, it startled me greatly. This was in the writings of Hippolytus, and I knew that he lived and worked in Rome from the beginning of the third century, which made him a relatively early authority. In connection with a mention of the Gospel according to Mark, these words leaped out at me: Μάρκος ὁ κολοβοδάκτυλος.[43]

It was the name of Mark, followed by a descriptive term which took me some little time to puzzle out. The last part, δάκτυλος, I recognized at once, for it was the ordinary Greek word for "finger." The first part of the term sent me to my Greek dictionary. κολοβός, I found, was the Greek equivalent of the Latin *curtus,* which meant either "short" or "mutilated."

That was the point at which I was really startled. *Curtus*— that was the word I had puzzled over when I had inadvertently used a vaguely-remembered term, "curt-fingered," to describe my friend Father Mina to myself, on the occasion when I had first noticed the abnormal abbreviation of his fingers. Now, here was Hippolytus, who lived at Rome where John Mark undoubtedly had often been, describing Mark as the "curt-fingered" one. "Short" or "mutilated," I thought to myself, and found myself hoping that Mark's fingers were short only by some strange phenomenon of growth, not by some harsh mutilation, even as I had concluded that the same was probably true of Father Mina.

Father Mina was in the small library room of the Church of St. Mark when I saw him the next time. We exchanged greetings, and then I opened again the subject which, I must confess, was becoming almost a scholarly obsession with me.

"I have been doing some more studying about Mark. Jerome says Mark was at Rome with Peter, then came and preached Christ at Alexandria. Epiphanius says Peter sent him to the land of the Egyptians.

"And," I added as casually as I could, "Hippolytus of Rome mentions him too, so I suppose he had heard a lot about him right there in the great city."

For fear of embarrassing my friend, I did not mention the "curt-fingered" term which Hippolytus had applied to Mark, and which I thought applied equally well to Father Mina himself. I hoped that he did not notice the almost fascinated glances which I could not help directing toward his hands whenever they were to be seen under the flowing sleeves of his robe. His fingers were as short as I had remembered, but certainly also powerful to match his powerful arms.

For his part, Father Mina seemed appreciative of my interest in the apostolic man whom he claimed so calmly as the founder of the church in which he served.

"There is more," he said, using the same words as on an earlier occasion when I had told him what I had found all by myself in the *History* and the *Chronicle* of Eusebius.

This time he did not drop the matter at that point, as he had done on the previous occasion. Perhaps it was because he was now persuaded of my genuine interest. Stepping quickly to a shelf, he took down one volume from a row of volumes which appeared all to belong to a single work.

I saw at once that the text of the volume was in Arabic, then noted that it was a scholarly edition with a translation in French paralleling the Arabic.

"This," said Father Mina, "is the *Universal History* of Agapius, whom we know also as Mahboub."

"I never heard of him," I said, "but seeing that he wrote in Arabic, that is perhaps not surprising."

"No, it is not surprising," replied the priest. "Agapius is quite unknown in the West, but we consider him the first Arab-Christian historian. He was bishop of Menbidj, and flourished in the tenth century. By that time, of course," he added, "Arabic was the prevailing language in our land, as it is today."

Father Mina opened the volume he had taken down, and the pages seemed to part naturally at an obviously often-consulted place. He pointed to a particular passage and read off an English translation at sight, while my eyes followed along on the French.

"Mark wrote the Gospel in Latin for the inhabitants of the great city of Rome."

The priest flipped over half a dozen pages to another well-worn place. He searched for a moment for the lines he wanted, then read again.

"Peter Cephas sent Mark the Evangelist to Alexandria and made him bishop of that city; he sojourned there for two years and died. He had for successor Annianus, whose episcopate lasted twenty-two years."[44]

"The scribe who copied the manuscript made a mistake," Father Mina explained, "when he wrote that Mark was here for two years and died. Actually, it was twenty all together, although he was away in other places part of that time." The priest spoke so naturally that it seemed to me he might have been speaking of a close acquaintance and of an event which was only just past.

Afterward I consulted my notes from my researches in the *Chronicle* of Eusebius.

> Year 2059 of Abraham. Mark preaches Christ in Alexandria.
> Year 2078 of Abraham. After Mark, Annianus was ordained bishop.

Counting inclusively, it was indeed exactly twenty years!

But on the day I am telling about when Father Mina and I were together in the library of the Church of St. Mark, he was already pulling down another volume. Again it was evidently only one volume out of the many volumes of an encyclopedic work, and again the text was in Arabic, with French translation provided by the editor.

"It is the calendar of Abou' l-Barakât," said my friend. "It forms the twenty-second chapter of his great work called *The Lamp of Darkness*."

Finding here too a passage which had probably been consulted many times, he pointed a finger at an entry.

Without waiting for his rendering from the Arabic, I read at once from the French.

"Barmoudah 30. Mark, evangelist, apostle." [45]

I was glad I had studied under the professor in Germany who had specialized in the calendars of antiquity. Barmoudah must be the form in Arabic of the name of a month in the ancient

Egyptian calendar which I had often heard the professor mention, namely, Pharmuthi. Somewhere in my notes I should be able to look it up.

Father Mina saved me the trouble. Glancing, I thought, at some faint pencil notations in the margin of the volume before him, he said:

"Barmoudah is, in Arabic, the Egyptian month Pharmuthi. It would be the same as from March 27 to April 25 in your calendar."

"Then Barmoudah 30 would be Pharmuthi 30, and that would be April 25?" I asked.

"Yes," he said. "To the ancient Egyptians it was the birthday festival of the god Serapis. But to us it is the birthday festival of Saint Mark."

"Birthday?" I asked.

"Yes," Father Mina replied gently. "It was the day of his martyrdom—that was his birthday in eternity.

"By the same way of thinking," he added, "we consider that the terrible persecution of Diocletian was the birthday of our church, so we reckon by the Era of Diocletian and say *anno martyrum,* 'in the year of the martyrs,' as you say *anno Domini,* 'in the year of the Lord.' "

Our conversation had now reached a point of such solemnity, and my friend was obviously so moved, although deeply calm as always, that I thought it best to take my departure.

I confess that my curiosity as to what else the little library at the Church of St. Mark might contain was such that, as occasion permitted, I came back a number of times. It was only after several returns, however, that once again I found the library room open and Father Mina there.

He knew my interest well enough by now, and easily read the eagerness in my eyes as I looked over the book-filled shelves. This time he stepped into a small alcove and returned with a very large volume.

"It is," he said, "the *History of the Patriarchs of the Coptic Church of Alexandria.*"

I was very excited to have this book actually lying open before me. In my own attempts at research I had concluded that the ancient church of Alexandria must have kept a list of its leaders, that Julius Africanus must have consulted the list when he visited the catechetical school, and that in turn this must be where the names and the dates had come from that were presented by Eusebius. Yet I was, it must be admitted, somewhat disappointed to find that the work now in front of me was in Arabic, which meant it must date from after the seventh-century Arab conquest.

Father Mina clarified the situation.

"The *History,* written here in Arabic, was compiled by Severus ibn al-Muqaffa', an Upper Egyptian bishop of the tenth century. He states however that he found histories written in Greek and Coptic and, with the assistance of qualified Christian brethren, translated these into the Arabic tongue, inasmuch as this was then current among the Egyptian people."

This information about earlier Greek and Coptic sources made the work seem much more important after all, but I was still disappointed that the text was in Arabic for another reason— although I had by then picked up a little of the language, I knew that I would never be able to read the book for myself.

Father Mina understood this too. Handling the book as if with the greatest respect, he opened it carefully near the beginning and read off a free translation.

"The first biography of the history of the holy Church. The history of Saint Mark, the disciple and evangelist, archbishop of the great city of Alexandria, and first of its bishops."[46]

This statement seemed to me something of an exaggeration or, one might say, a foreshortening of the historical perspective. In the other sources I had read it was only said that Mark was the first to preach in Alexandria, and that after him Annianus was consecrated as the first bishop. Here, now, Mark himself was called the first of the bishops, and even the archbishop, of the city. That, however, was only a minor matter for which I could make allowance. What I eagerly desired was to know what sort of narrative followed.

Father Mina was now closing the book, however, and I was afraid that our interview was at an end. Instead, he disappeared into the same small alcove and came back with another volume of some size. Now I felt more at home, for I saw that this was a Greek codex.

I read the title aloud, and my own translation of it: "ΜΑΡ-ΤΥΡΙΟΝ ΤΟΥ ΑΓΙΟΥ ΑΠΟΣΤΟΛΟΥ ΚΑΙ ΕΥΑΓΓΕΛΙΣΤΟΥ ΜΑΡ-ΚΟΥ ΑΛΕΞΑΝΔΡΕΙΑΣ,[47] Martyrdom of the Holy Apostle and Evangelist Mark of Alexandria."

"That is correct," said Father Mina. "It is the same work that is often called the *Acts of Mark* for short. But we like to speak more fully of the 'Evangelist Mark of Alexandria,' because it was he who first brought the evangel to our great city."

"How old is this work?" I asked.

"This particular manuscript was copied in the eleventh century. The work itself, however, was written in Alexandria in the middle of the fourth century.[48]

"And, of course," he added, "it embodies the still earlier traditions of the church in this place."

The two volumes which my friend had brought out of the alcove were now lying side by side on the large table of the library room. I was almost afraid to ask him if he would allow me to study them further, and in any event I was in despair as to being able to make out much of the Arabic text in the first volume.

Father Mina understood and, without my asking, smoothed the way for me.

"If you would like," he said, "I shall be glad for you to have access to these volumes here. When you read the Greek you will see that it provides much of the material which is also in the Arabic.

"For the Arabic"—he spared me the embarrassment of having to ask—"my assistant will help you."

So began a period of time which I enjoyed very much, even though I found myself working again as hard as in my student days. On every day it was possible, I was at the small library. The assistant of Father Mina would give me the gist of a section of the Arabic text of the *History of the Patriarchs of the Coptic Church of Alexandria* in his rather halting and broken English, and I smoothed it out in a consecutive English text. I worked on my own on the Greek text of the *Acts of Mark,* writing out an English rendering.

One doubt, of course, continued to assail me. Was I reading only what my professor in the United States had called "apocryphal legends"? Some of the material did sound legendary to me. But underneath it, was there a substratum of old tradition, long handed down in the Alexandrian church and actually preserving some authentic remembrance of the presence and preaching there of John Mark?

Without telling at this point all that I found in these two sources, I will mention one item which startled me thoroughly. In the *Acts of Mark* I found that there was at the end an additional section written in Latin. I had learned that the *Acts* existed not only in Greek, which I was reading, but also in Latin, Arabic, and Ethiopic, so I concluded that at this point the Greek lacked something which was preserved in the Latin, and the Latin had therefore been copied in here at the end of the Greek manuscript.

Anyway, as I say, I was startled to find this section. But what startled me was not nearly so much the language of the section as its contents. In content the section consisted in a description of John Mark. That there should be such a description did not strike me as surprising, but the nature of the description startled me greatly.

"John Mark had a long nose, raised eyebrows, beautiful eyes, a bald forehead, and a heavy beard. He was of middle age, but still quick in action. He was continent in affection, and full of the grace of God."

That was the gist of the description of John Mark in the section incorporated in the *Acts* in Latin. The first part of it was almost word for word the way I had long since formulated my own description of Father Mina, while the last part I was certainly prepared to recognize as applicable too.

Add to that the fact that the fingers of Father Mina's hands were abnormally short—"curt-fingered" I had called them when I had first noticed them as they came momentarily into view from the long sleeves of his robe—and that I had found that very term (in a Greek form) applied to John Mark in an ancient source.

All together the correspondences were uncanny. How often, too, I had been struck by a sort of timeless depth in the eyes of Father Mina. Yet, of course, I told myself, these things are all just coincidences. At any rate I would never dare to mention the matter to Father Mina, and I never did.

One day, however, I did approach Father Mina with a different sort of question. His assistant and I were approaching the end of our time of reading together. When the priest came in I said to him:

"Father Mina, I have deeply appreciated the privilege of reading in these most valued records which you have so kindly opened for my perusal. It is a stirring account which they provide of the heroic life and death of him whom you name as the founder of your venerable church. But you know that I have a strong archeological interest. From the point of view of archeology we always seek to find along with literary testimony some tangible remains which tie in in a convincing way with what is written. Is there anything of this sort, in connection with what I have been studying?"

I could not help looking wistfully toward a door which I had never seen opened, but which I had come to understand gave entrance to a subterranean crypt of the church. I knew that the

Church of St. Mark was a relatively modern building. Its appearance made that evident. But perhaps far underneath there was something much older, something that would be of great interest if one might ever be permitted to go down to see.

My hopes soared momentarily, as Father Mina rose to his feet and said, "Come." But instead of leading me to the door and into the crypt, he preceded me up twisting stairs which led to the very top of the tower of the church building.

It was a striking view we now had. Beneath were the crowded streets of the city, and not far away was the curving shore of the Eastern Harbor. Nowadays the Western Harbor has the major piers, and most of the ocean vessels come into it. Anciently, however, the Eastern Harbor was the more important. Between the two harbors I looked down upon a broad strip of land which runs out to a point called Ras el-Tin. On the point is an Arab fort called Qait Bay, after the Mameluke sultan who built it in A.D. 1480. As the proud citizens of Alexandria had often told me, the point used to be an island named Pharos on which, in the approximate location of the present fort, was the famous lighthouse which was one of the Seven Wonders of the World. Between the shore and the island, and separating the Eastern Harbor from the Western, was a dike called Heptastadion (meaning "seven stadia" long), and this gradually became silted up to make the strip of land that I was looking down upon.

Father Mina, however, was not looking now toward Ras el-Tin and the Qait Bay Fort. Instead he was looking along the shore eastward. There, at the eastern side of the Eastern Harbor, the smaller Point Silsileh projected outward a relatively short distance. Beyond, on the coast of the turquoise Mediterranean, was the suburb of Chatby, lying, I had been told, in what was the principal Jewish area of ancient Alexandria.

"Many people," Father Mina began, "think that this church where we are now was the original Church of St. Mark, and that St. Mark was buried here. But it is not so.

"Look!" He gestured toward the coast just beyond Point Silsileh.

"All the coast yonder has subsided, and the sea has encroached inland. Beneath those waters lies what you would like to see. There by the sea at the east gate of the city"—the priest was speaking now as if he saw it all in his mind's eye—"wɔ the quarter called Bucolia. It meant 'pasture.' It took its name from the herd of cattle which used to graze on some open grassy slopes. There on the grass the idol-worshipers killed St. Mark. There the brethren buried him, and put a simple memorial over his grave. There was the original Church of St. Mark. It was often known as βουκολὶς ἐκκλησία, the Pastoral Church. In his time, Arius officiated there. And in the ninth century the body of St. Mark was carried away."

"You mean by the Venetians?" I asked, for Father Mina had mentioned this matter before, and I also knew for myself that the famous Church of St. Mark in Venice was originally built in order to house the supposed relics of the Evangelist.

"Yes," the priest scowled. "Buono di Malamocco and Rustico di Torcello were their names, and our church has never forgotten them.

"But the Crusaders did us harm, too," he went on. "It was when they approached in A.D. 1218 (to use your era), that the Sultan Malik al-Kamil destroyed the church. Then at last all the ruins sank beneath the sea."

"And everything was lost forever?" I asked, feeling almost as sad as I imagined he felt.

"Not necessarily everything. Not necessarily forever," he replied.

"Perhaps," he went on to elucidate the last part of his comment, "you archeologists will someday explore there under the surface of the sea and find the ruins I have told you about."

The first part of his comment—"not necessarily everything"

—remained unelucidated. I was still wondering what it meant as we went back down the twisting stairs to the church below.

Once again in the little library room, Father Mina pulled down one more volume from the shelves.

I saw that this was a small book in Latin, and I read off the title: "*Acta sincera Sancti Petri Episcopi Alexandrini et Martyris*,[49] Genuine Acts of St. Peter, Bishop of Alexandria, and Martyr."

For a moment I was puzzled, for with the name of Peter I naturally thought first of the apostle and of Rome.

"This was our bishop here in Alexandria from A.D. 300 to 311, to speak in terms of the era which you use," explained Father Mina. "He was a brave man, and like many of our patriarchs, he died for his faith. In a time of persecution he was put in prison. The people, who loved him, tried to protect him, but he voluntarily gave himself from his prison into the hands of the soldiers to be executed, lest the soldiers fall upon the people and slay them.

"The soldiers"—and here Father Mina appeared to be deeply moved—"were so impressed by his action that they acceded to the one request he made. This was that he might, before dying, visit the burial place of St. Mark and receive a blessing from the bones of the Evangelist."

Now Father Mina was pointing to a line of the Latin text. "So," he continued, "they took him outside the east gate of the city, by the sea, to a place called Bucolia."

Here I read beneath the compact fingers of my friend: *in locum qui dicitur Bucolia.*

"Here there was a small memorial," Father Mina went on— and I saw that his forefinger was on the Latin word *memoria.* The word was often used, I knew, in early church history to designate a monument which commemorated a martyr, and even a Christian church building as a remembrance of a saint or a martyr.

"Also in proximity to this *memoria* was a small house inhabited by a virgin, dedicated to God"—the priest was pointing to the words *virgo Deo dicata*—"who lived there with her aged father. At the very moment that Peter rose from his devotions beside the tomb of St. Mark, this young woman was standing to pray, and she distinctly heard a voice which said: 'Peter was the first of the apostles; and now Peter is the last of the martyrs.' "

Although I had been slow to recall it, the striking saying attributed to the virgin reminded me that I had already heard this narrative which Father Mina was now reading to me out of the Latin text of the *Acts of St. Peter of Alexandria*. I had heard it as Father Mina's assistant was reading to me the translation of certain sections of the *History of the Patriarchs of the Coptic Church of Alexandria*. Although that work was in Arabic, I had already come to realize that it incorporated material which was found in a much earlier Greek *Acts of St. Mark*. Now I learned that it also contained information which was in this earlier Latin *Acts of St. Peter*. Even as I was reflecting afresh upon what a valuable collection of ancient tradition was preserved in the Arabic *History,* Father Mina was going on: "Then the sword of the soldiers descended."

Tears came into the eyes of the priest. But after a moment, he controlled his emotions and proceeded.

"As the apostle Peter was once crucified in Nero's Circus in Rome, and Paul was beheaded there beside the Tiber River, so here beside our sea our patriarch Peter suffered a like fate. As the virgin said, he became the last of the martyrs.

"Of course he was the 'last' only in the sense of being, at that moment, the most recent, and of course we have continued to have martyrs through all the centuries ever since. They are the glory of our church."

With a conscious effort, Father Mina recalled himself to the subject which he had set himself to explain to me on the basis of the *Genuine Acts of St. Peter, Bishop of Alexandria, and Martyr.*

"So, you see, we have evidence in this record that there was in existence when our bishop Peter died a well-known *me-*

moria of St. Mark. It may have been only a simple monument at his tomb; if not already at that time, then certainly not much later, it became a small church. The location was in no question at all; it was in the quarter anciently called Bucolia, outside the east gate of the city, and by the sea."

My mind worked rapidly. In my theological studies I had learned that the two great apostles of the earliest church, the apostle Peter and the apostle Paul, did in all probability experience martyrdom in Rome under Nero. Also there, around the beginning of the third century, a certain presbyter named Gaius had affirmed in published disputation with a leader in Asia that he, in Rome, could show at the Vatican and on the Ostian Way the trophies of those who had laid the foundations of the Roman church, i.e., the trophies of Peter and of Paul.[50]

In further investigation I had found that in Greek the word τρόπαιον, or "trophy," which Gaius used, meant the memorial of a victory that was raised on a field of battle, and it could therefore well mean a marker of some sort at the place of death, or at the grave, of a martyr of the Christian church. In this latter sense it was obviously the same as a *memoria,* and it was plainly in this latter sense that Gaius had used the term when he spoke of the "trophies" of Peter and of Paul at Rome. Also I had learned that there were actually archeological finds both at the Vatican and on the Ostian Way in Rome which tied in with early remembrance of Peter and of Paul at the two sites respectively, where now stand the Church of St. Peter in the Vatican and the Church of St. Paul outside the Walls.

Now, through the materials I had dug out for myself, and especially through the less accessible materials which Father Mina had brought to my attention and made available to me, I had found that there was a broadly parallel situation at Alexandria. There was an early and persistent tradition that Mark had preached and died here. There was evidence of a sort that I would call "archeological," in a sort of figurative use of the term, in the proof of the existence of a "memorial" at the grave of Mark which was a well-known monument at a well-known place at the beginning of the fourth century. It could have been called a "trophy" of Mark, just like the "trophies" of Peter and of Paul at Rome. Unfortunately, it could not be gotten at by "archeology" in the strict sense of the term because the site was now under the surface of the sea, and I, at any rate, was not equipped to do underwater exploration. Nevertheless, the record concerning the patriarch Peter constituted dependable proof that such a memorial existed and was accepted as authentic in his time and presumably from long before.

The primitive memorial and the original Church of St. Mark that was built over it were ruined and submerged beneath the sea. The Church of St. Mark in which Father Mina and I were conversing was a modern structure on a different geographical site. Yet it did not, I was now prepared to acknowledge, bear the name of St. Mark for any purely arbitrary reason. It was the heir of a long tradition which probably did, in some way or other, actually go all the way back to John Mark and to work he had done in this very city.

Was I too gullible? I had thanked Father Mina for his courtesy again, said farewell for the moment, and was once again seated at my customary small table in a back-street restaurant.

Was I too uncritical? Here I was, a product of famous American and German universities, a onetime student who had accepted without question the critical views of my professors, particularly of the one who had said that in effect we know nothing of Mark except what is in the few references that exist in the canonical New Testament, and of the other who had said that for all practical purposes we know nothing of the church in Egypt before A.D. 200. And here I was, on the verge of accepting "romantic inference," "apocryphal legend," and "ecclesiastical fantasy" as containing at least a nucleus of historical truth.

Was I too strongly under the influence of the man who by

purely accidental circumstance had become my friend—under the influence of Father Mina, the small, powerfully built priest, the priest with the compact fingers, the priest with the eyes which seemed to reflect such depths, the priest who spoke of his predecessor, John Mark, as if he knew him so well?

If I were too gullible, too uncritical, too heavily under a present personal influence, I must try to be dispassionate, to be objective—as my professors had taught and exemplified—to maintain an undecided mind, to wait for more evidence.

More evidence? Would that there were more evidence! Would that, when the primitive memorial and the original church had been facing destruction, someone had brought from them some long-preserved record that antedated all that I had been able to find, all that even Father Mina had shown me.

"There is more," Father Mina had said upon more than one occasion. Had I seen all that there was? Was there anywhere anything more, anything older, anything from the very beginning?

×

The shriek of a jet aircraft and the roar of a tremendous explosion came in close succession upon each other. The walls of the small restaurant swayed but did not collapse. All of us who were there waited, transfixed, for the next similar sounds, but none came.

The radio, however, was soon announcing that bombs were falling upon the airport at Cairo and upon the defense stations along the Suez Canal.

I had never forgotten my listening task in Alexandria, but I had also never picked up any information to tell me ahead of time that war would break out at this time. Now it had begun, and would not soon be ended.

But the bomb which fell in Alexandria was evidently released by accident by a plane whose intended destination was a target at Cairo or on the Canal. For the time being no more planes came over Alexandria, and no more bombs fell.

I ventured upon the street and, drawn by the magnetism of catastrophe, moved as many others were doing toward the place of the explosion.

It was the Church of St. Mark which had been struck directly. I was one of the first to arrive, and I pushed into the ruins, fear in my heart for my friend, for Father Mina.

Within, for the first time in my experience, the entrance to the subterranean crypt was open. It was now a gaping hole, and the door which I had so often looked at to wonder what was below was blown quite away.

I stumbled down the not entirely impassable steps. At the bottom my worst fears were confirmed. Father Mina lay sprawled there, dead. I could only hope his death had been swift. He must have descended for some reason to the lower regions before the bomb fell, and been caught there and overwhelmed by the shock of the explosion.

I bowed my head, and tears came to my eyes. This man had been my friend, and I felt a sense of great loss. He lay there now so still, and we could never again talk together as we had done so often. Yet as I gazed upon my friend in that one short, last moment, it seemed to me that I saw upon his face a look of inexpressible calm and joy, and I was comforted.

Then I saw it. In the short fingers of one hand he held a tightly rolled scroll. Although the circumstances were terrifying, my earlier training did not desert me. I recognized that it was a roll of papyrus, and on the exterior I made out the word MAP-KOY.

"Of Mark," it said. The letters looked to me very early in form, and papyrus was of course the predominantly used writing material at an early date. Was it an early record of Mark? Had Father Mina gone to get it out of a subterranean place of safe-keeping, in order to show it to me when I came the next time to the library of the church? Was this what he had meant when he had said more than once, "There is more"?

Perhaps all of this chain of thought amounted only to a colossal rationalization of my desire to take the scroll. But it was true that the city, under the shock of the bombing, was now in complete turmoil. It was true that the excited, the unaccountable, and the plunderers would momentarily be swarming through the ruins of the famous church.

I took the scroll, concealed it beneath my coat, and went away as rapidly as I could through the confusion of the streets.

The war was not soon over, and Alexandria, although it never bore the brunt of the main attacks, was in constant disturbance.

The disturbance was again my excuse—if such I must confess it to be—for taking the scroll with me when I departed. That departure was soon, for with the outbreak of the war whose beginning I had so conspicuously failed to predict, my government work was at an end.

×

Now, years later, having deciphered the entire scroll and learned from it all that I could, and having seen peace return, at least temporarily, to Egypt, I have been able to establish contact again with the church authorities in Egypt and to return the scroll safe and intact to the proper hands.

My temporary holding of the scroll could no doubt be questioned on legal grounds. Yet I can solemnly affirm my belief—and this now represents the judgment of time and not just the impulse of the moment on which I then had to act—that if I had not fortunately been in the position to take possession of the scroll and to carry it away temporarily to a safe place, it would, in the period of war turmoil in Alexandria, undoubtedly have been lost.

In fact, the church authorities in Alexandria were themselves so convinced of this, too, that they expressed to me not censure in any way but rather appreciation for service rendered, when at last I was able to bring the scroll back to them. This appreciation they made tangible by allowing me the right to make the publication which is here set forth.

Immensely interesting as were the contents of the scroll, there was one question which I was never able to resolve. As I have already explained, there was one Greek word on the exterior of the scroll, and it was the name of Mark in the genitive case, "of Mark." Presumably this was part of a title of the work, but if any other words stood originally with this one word to make a more complete title, I was never able to make out. Supposing that at least some such other word as "writing" was to be understood along with "of Mark," then the question is raised as to whether we have here a subjective genitive or an objective genitive.

If this is the "writing of Mark," in the sense of a subjective genitive, i.e., if Mark is the subject, then we could render, "Mark's writing," and assume authorship by Mark himself.

If this is the "writing of Mark" in the sense of an objective genitive, i.e., if Mark is the object, then we could render, "writing about Mark," and assume authorship of the document by someone other than Mark.

The text of the scroll may seem to favor the latter alternative, inasmuch as it is written in the third person, i.e., it speaks about Mark and says that he did thus and so, said thus and such, etc. On the other hand, it is not impossible that he would write a narrative about himself and deliberately choose to phrase it in the third person. But in that case another person must at least have finished out the record at the end.

Whether the document comes, then, from Mark himself, or from another person who was writing about him, may remain an open question. In the former case the document is naturally contemporary with Mark; even in the latter case I would hold that it probably is virtually contemporary too. I have already pointed out that the papyrus writing material and the characteristics of the handwriting are both consonant with an early date, and I would now say, more precisely, consonant with a date not more than a decade or two after the middle of the first century of the Christian era. That the document fits well in its contents into such a time will be seen, I believe, by those who peruse what follows in this book.

What follows in this book is, then, substantially what I found in the scroll, together with some items, needed to fill out the entire picture, which were derived from the researches into material which I found for myself and into material which Father Mina made accessible to me, as described in the earlier portion of this Prologue. That it was finally from the hands of Father Mina that I also received, as it were, the scroll itself increases the indebtedness which I can now no longer express to that noble priest himself, but which, with these words, I would at least like to put on public and permanent record. And if I express such appreciation to Father Mina, I feel that I am somehow, in the same breath, expressing appreciation to John Mark, the Evangelist of Alexandria.

Notes to Accompany the Prologue

For those who would like to investigate the sources to which I refer in the Prologue, I append here the following references. In the references these abbreviations are used:

GCS   *Die griechischen christlichen Schriftsteller der ersten drei Jahrhunderte, herausgegeben von der Kirchenväter-Commission der königl. preussischen Akademie der Wissenschaften.*

MPG   Jacques Paul Migne, *Patrologiae cursus completus. Series graeca.*

PO   *Patrologia Orientalis.*

1. Ernst Hammerschmidt, *Die koptische Gregoriosanaphora* (Berlin, 1957), p. 20.
2. *Ibid.*, p. 58.
3. Acts 12:12.
4. Acts 12:1-23; *Die Chronik des Hieronymus,* ed. Rudolf Helm, GCS Eusebius 7, 2d ed., p. 179; cf. Bo Reicke, *Neutestamentliche Zeitgeschichte* (2d ed., 1968), pp. 147, 149.
5. 1 Peter 5:13.
6. Eusebius *Church History* III.39, 15.
7. Colossians 4:10.
8. Acts 4:36.
9. Acts 11:27-30.
10. Josephus *Antiquities* XX.5, 2, §§100 f.; cf. G. H. C. Macgregor in *The Interpreter's Bible,* Vol. 9 (Nashville, 1954), p. 152.
11. Acts 12:25.
12. Acts 13:5.
13. B. T. Holmes, "Luke's Description of John Mark," *Journal of Biblical Literature* 54 (1935), 63-72.
14. Acts 13:13.
15. Acts 15:36-41.
16. Colossians 4:10; Philemon 24.
17. 2 Timothy 4:11.
18. Mark 14:51-52.
19. Herodotus II, 86, 95.
20. Luke 22:43.
21. Matthew 21:33; Mark 12:1.
22. Mark 6:40.
23. Matthew 13:32; Luke 13:19; Mark 4:32.
24. Mark 11:13.
25. Matthew 21:8; Mark 11:8.
26. Mark 4:1-9; 4:26-29; 4:30-32; 12:1-12.

27. Mark 4:26-29.
28. Edmund D. Jones, "Was Mark the Gardener of Gethsemane?" *The Expository Times* 33 (1921-22), 403-404.
29. Mark 16:5 f.
30. Eusebius *Church History* III.1; Socrates *Church History* I.19.
31. Epiphanius *Panarion haer.* XXIV.1, 1-2, GCS 25, p. 256.
32. Epiphanius *Panarion haer.* XXXI.2, 3, and 7, 1, GCS 25, pp. 384, 395.
33. Justin Martyr *Apology* I.29.
34. Eusebius *Church History* V.25.
35. "Fragments from the Lost Writings of Irenaeus," in *The Ante-Nicene Fathers,* Vol. I, p. 576, n. 5.
36. Eusebius *Church History* II.16 and 24.
37. Adolf Harnack, *Geschichte der altchristlichen Literatur bis Eusebius,* II, *Die Chronologie,* 1, *Die Chronologie der Literatur bis Irenäus nebst einleitenden Untersuchungen,* pp. 124 ff., 138 ff., 202 ff.
38. Eusebius *Church History* II.16.
39. Eusebius *Church History* II.24.
40. *Die Chronik des Hieronymus,* ed. Rudolf Helm, GCS Eusebius 7, 2d ed., pp. 179, 183.
41. Jerome *Lives of Illustrious Men* 8.
42. Epiphanius *Panarion haer.* LI.6, 10, GCS 31, p. 256.
43. Hippolytus *Refutation of All Heresies* VII.30.
44. "Kitab al-'Unvan, Histoire universelle écrite par Agapius (Mahboub) de Menbidj, éditée et traduite en Français par Alexandre Vasiliev," in PO 7 (1911), p. 482, fol. 11 v.; p. 494, fol. 17.
45. "Le Calendrier d'Abou' l-Barakât, Texte Arabe édité et traduit par Eugène Tisserant," in PO 10 (1915), 269.
46. *History of the Patriarchs of the Coptic Church of Alexandria,* Arabic text edited, translated, and annotated by B. Evetts, I, *Saint Mark to Theonas (300);* PO 1 (1907), 135.
47. In MPG 115, cols. 163-170.
48. Richard A. Lipsius, *Die Apokryphen Apostelgeschichten und Apostellegenden,* II.2, p. 345.
49. *Acta sincera S. Petri Alexandrini,* in MPG 18, cols. 461-462.
50. Eusebius *Church History* II.25.

X

Of Mark

1

In the Garden

Mark slept bare beneath a cloth of fine linen.

Although he was a Jew he had grown up in Cyrene, and had always been accustomed to Greek habits. There in all the five cities of the Pentapolis the Jewish settlers were surrounded by Greek colonists and Roman officials as well as by the black people of North Africa.

Mark often remembered the large estates of his father, Aristobulus, and his father's young brother, Joseph Barnabas. The men were Levites by family descent, and they maintained their Jewish faith by conscious choice. But by unconscious assimilation they had taken on most of the customs of the people by whom they were daily surrounded.

In Cyrene they were also not far from Egypt and, in one respect at least, Egyptian influence prevailed in their lives. With the complete concurrence of Barnabas, who himself remained unmarried, Aristobulus had married their sister. In terms of Egyptian practice, brother-sister marriages were so common that this union elicited no unfavorable comment. The sister was named Mary, and Mark was the offspring of Aristobulus and Mary.

Mark's full name was John Mark. John was a Hebrew name, Johanan when written out completely, which means "the Lord is gracious." When they gave this name to their child, Aristobulus and Mary felt that the name expressed their sentiments over the birth. Almost as a matter of course, however, they gave the small boy a second name, Marcus or Mark. This was a Latin word which means "a large hammer," and it was simply a very familiar name in the Roman world.

So John Mark's two names bridged the two worlds in which he grew up, the Jewish world and the non-Jewish world. Between the two names, he preferred Mark. Between the two worlds, he was more at home in the non-Jewish than in the Jewish.

So little was any irreconcilable opposition between the two worlds recognized in Cyrene, however, that it was only when he came to Jerusalem that Mark realized that, if a choice had to be made, he was more at home in the customs of paganism than in those of a strict Judaism.

The reason that Aristobulus, with his family, and Joseph Barnabas left Cyrene was that a disaster befell them there. In a period of temporary anarchy the Berbers swept in from the desert and plundered their estates. Fortunately much of their wealth was in portable form, and with this they fled, abandoning the estates to whatever might happen.

Barnabas went to Cyprus, where many Jews were settled. A man of impressive appearance, he continued to prosper there. Aristobulus, with Mary and John Mark, went to Jerusalem. There they were soon the victims of disaster again, for Aristobulus took a fever and died. The financial position of the family, however, was secure. Mary took a large house on the southwestern hill of the city. Perhaps with a nostalgic remembrance of the estate in Cyrene, she also obtained a plot of land across the Kidron Valley at the foot of the Mount of Olives. With care the olive trees that grew there so abundantly would provide a lasting source of income. Fortunately, John Mark was competent in agricultural matters from experience on the estate in Cyrene, and was now a young man of fully responsible age.

For himself, Mark felt most at home among other young Jews

in Jerusalem who had lived abroad. They called themselves Hellenists, maintained some proficiency in the Greek and Latin languages which they had spoken abroad, and continued the customs they had learned in the Greek and Roman environments in which they had lived.

Most of all, perhaps, the young Hellenists were set apart from their more orthodox fellow-countrymen by the physical exercises in which they engaged. They went daily to the open-air gymnasium called the Xystus, stripped off their clothes, and engaged in the most strenuous exertions and games. That they were wholly naked in these exercises was an affront to the orthodox, and the affront was not lessened by the fact that the Xystus was directly across the Tyropoeon Valley west of the Temple. For themselves, they quoted Herodotus, "Among some barbarous races it is considered disgraceful to appear naked," and—determined not to be barbarians—they went ahead with their Greek-style gymnastics.

That John Mark was particularly assiduous in physical exercise may have been due to the one physical handicap by which he was marked. While he was still only a small boy in Cyrene, all of North Africa had been smitten by a protracted drought, accompanied by the worst plague of locusts in the memory of any of the inhabitants. As food failed, starvation took the lives of many. In the household of Aristobulus, supplies lasted longer than in many homes, yet finally privation was acute there, too. Small John Mark suffered malnutrition for an extended time, and with it came a strange malformation. His fingers were stunted in their growth, and remained ever afterward abnormally short. It was perhaps to compensate for that deficiency that he exercised so strenuously in the Jerusalem gymnasium.

Save for the short fingers, John Mark was well built, relatively short perhaps, but compactly made. From his assiduous exercise, his chest was deep and his muscles firm. His forehead was high, the eyebrows well raised, the nose long, and the eyes a deep brown in color.

Believing that it contributed to his fitness for the naked gymnastics of the Hellenists, Mark made it a practice to sleep bare, and for a cover, except in the coldest weather, he used only a single cloth. That cloth, however, as befitted his favorable economic status, was of the finest linen.

This is how John Mark was sleeping that spring night in the watchtower in the garden.

✕

To be posted in the watchtower for the night was the second unusual task to which John Mark had been assigned that day.

"Neaniskos," his mother, Mary, had called to him toward the end of the morning.

Mary herself was scarcely as much of a Hellenist as her son. Nevertheless, almost unconsciously perhaps, she preserved in her speech not a little of the Greek which she had used so freely in Cyrene.

The word by which she called to Mark was the Greek word for "young man." She had used it, affectionately, for John Mark when he was but a little boy. Now he was very much a grown-up young man, but she still used the term endearingly, although also much by force of habit.

"Young man," she had said, "be kind to your mother, take yonder jar, go to the pool, and bring it full of water."

"It is a woman's task," he began to object, then desisted as he sensed a strange earnestness in the unusual request.

The connections which existed between his mother and the followers of Jesus might have been more obvious to John Mark if he had paid closer attention to matters at home and been less engrossed in his activities with the Hellenists, including the daily gymnastics at the Xystus.

In the northland there was a cousin of Mark's parents who was married to a fisherman named Simon. This kinship was so distant in degree, the geographical distance between the two families was so considerable, and Simon was ordinarily so occupied with his profitable business at the large lake in the north that Mark felt scarcely any acquaintance with him at all.

It was true that in the course of the past year Simon had appeared in Jerusalem on several occasions, and had come to visit Mary a time or two. Insofar as Mark gave any second thoughts to these visits, he only wondered vaguely if Simon were neglecting his business in the north.

What Mark did not know about were the long and earnest conversations which Mary had with Simon during these visits, and this was because the conversations took place after Mark had excused himself and hastened off to do gymnastics in the Xystus or to exercise his muscles in what some would have considered a more profitable way in agricultural activities on the family land at the foot of the Mount of Olives.

"Do you really believe that Jesus is the Messiah whom we have been expecting for so long?" Mary asked Simon, after she had learned that he had actually left his fishing business in the hands of his hired men, and gone off to follow Jesus wherever he went.

"Yes, Mary, I do." Simon was leaning forward, looking directly into the blue eyes of the woman who was a cousin of his own wife.

"You are the only one I can talk with freely here in Jerusalem. There are many enemies of Jesus here. The priests think he does not love the Temple. The scribes think he does not keep the Law. The Zealots think he is timid.

"But I tell you that I think that he is the Messiah. When the day comes he will make it known who he is.

"When I told him, one day, that I believed that he is the Messiah he told me that my name was Peter."

"You mean Rock?" Mary interrupted excitedly, for she recognized the Greek word immediately.

"Yes, Rock," said Simon, "and he said that his community would be built upon the Rock. Do you think he meant upon me, or upon everybody who would believe in him?"

"I do not know," said Mary, "but from all you have told me about him I do truly believe with you that he is the Messiah for whom we have always hoped."

When Simon, who was thus called Peter, came again in the early spring of the year and again talked long and privately with Mary, his face was deadly serious and his gray eyes were often shadowed with apprehension.

"I have asked Jesus not to come to Jerusalem again, for his enemies are stronger than ever, but he says that a prophet cannot die anywhere else. He is determined to be in the city at the Passover time. I fear greatly."

It was at that time that Simon and Mary made their plan. When Jesus and his men came, the Master would wish some solitary and natural place for prayer. For this he might use Mary's plot of land at the foot of the Mount of Olives.

He would also wish a place within the city to eat with his followers the Passover meal. Mary's large house would provide adequate accommodation for that. But the coming together of the group there should be managed in such a way as to attract as little attention as possible. Some would have to come in the daytime to make preparations. It would be better that Simon Peter should not be one of these. Even now he, as a leader among Jesus' men, might be marked, and his previous visits to the house of Mary might have been noted.

So when Jesus was nearing the city and desiring to arrange the meal, Simon would send a message with some lad to Mary to say "We are here." Then Mary would send her son to the Pool of Siloam to carry away a jar of water. By this act he would provide a recognizable sign—for otherwise only women performed this task—and some of Jesus' men, who had been mingling with the crowds at the pool, could follow him to the house. Finally, when all was ready, and under cover of darkness, Simon Peter could bring Jesus and the others.

In only one respect did the plans work out differently than expected. Mary expected to receive the cryptic message "We are here" from some nameless youth on the usual day of preparation of the Passover, that is, on the fourteenth day of the month Nisan. But the message came unexpectedly one day early. As was learned later, Jesus was under a strong presentiment of the end. He desired greatly to eat the official Passover with his followers, but he felt strongly that his enemies, whose hostility was now so unmistakable and whose power was so great, would make every effort to be rid of him before the great feast began. So he resolved to eat a sort of unofficial Passover and a last supper with his men on the evening before the evening of the great feast.

So the message "We are here" came a day early to Mary, but everything was so well planned that all went without difficulty anyway.

That was why, on that particular morning, Mary gave to John Mark the task which ordinarily a woman would have done, of fetching a jar of water from the Pool of Siloam. It was a task which John Mark only dimly sensed was of considerable importance to his mother. With only a moment's protest, he did what was asked. Although he did not know it, he made it possible for some followers of Jesus, and later for Jesus himself, to reach a safe place for what indeed turned out to be the last supper of their group.

The two men who followed John Mark from the Pool of Siloam to the house of Mary, his mother, did so at a discreet distance. Also, after identifying the house, they made no move to approach it for a considerable time—indeed, not until after Mark had departed for some of his usual activities. Then they came to the door, which was opened to them by Rhoda, the maid.

"The Teacher says, Where is my guest room where I am to eat with my disciples?" The words of the two men constituted a prearranged identification, and Rhoda admitted them immediately, and took them at once to a large upper room.

With the further assistance of Rhoda, who made several trips to the market for them, the two men labored for a considerable part of the day. The physical arrangements which they instituted in the upper room, using various belongings of the house of Mary, included a low table and reclining places adequate to accommodate a group of thirteen men. The meal for which they made ready would be, except for the lack of roasted lamb, as much like a Passover meal as possible.

When all was ready they went away, to return well after dark with their other companions and their leader.

In the interim after the two men went away and before the entire company came in the evening, John Mark returned to his home, only to be given the second of the two unusual tasks that he was requested to perform on that particular day.

"What?" asked Mark. "Has something happened to Ceres?"

The latter was their agricultural servant.

"Yes," answered Mary, "he returned from the land only a short while ago, and is burning with fever. I think he cannot go back tonight."

This fact was entirely true, and the assignment quite necessary, but even if things had not come about in this particular way, Mary would doubtless have found some other reason which would have made it necessary for her son to be absent from the house on that evening.

So John Mark slept that night in the watchtower which overlooked the olive trees in the family plot of land at the foot of the Mount of Olives.

But in the middle of the night his sleep was interrupted by a sharp and piercing cry. Awakening instantly, Mark wrapped the linen cloth that was his cover about his naked body and rushed down under the olive trees.

The light of an almost full moon in an unclouded sky illuminated a scene of confusion. Two groups of men confronted each other. In the forefront of the smaller group Mark recognized Simon. Beside him he saw a tall man with flowing hair. The latter was of commanding appearance, and evidently the leader of this group. At that very moment he was laying a restraining hand upon the shoulder of Simon, and saying to him, "Put up the sword, they perish by it who take it."

Simon was obviously in a state of great excitement, but slowly he let the sword slip from his hand and fall to the ground. Mark saw that it was stained with blood.

Opposite this smaller group was a larger group of men. One of them had obviously been the victim of Simon's sword. With an ear completely severed from the head, and streaming with blood, he writhed on the ground in pain. Although many of the others were armed with swords or clubs, they had evidently all been kept at least momentarily at bay by the sword which Simon must have wielded vigorously if not accurately. Now, as Simon's sword fell to the ground, they prepared to rush upon the smaller and otherwise unarmed group.

"Daily I have taught in the Temple, and you did not take me." It was the tall man who was plainly the leader of the smaller group who was speaking. Amidst a scene of tumult and violence, he was expressing himself calmly. "Do you now come by night and as if against a robber? Nevertheless, what is written must be fulfilled. So be it."

Before the words were finished, the onslaught of the larger group upon the smaller had begun. With Simon divested of his weapon and the others of the smaller group not armed at all, the unequal nature of a contest between the two groups was only too painfully evident. The tall man was quickly seized and bound with ropes, while his followers scattered and fled in all directions.

Mark, wrapped in his linen cloth, had drawn near. Now the sudden explosion of humanity, pursuers and pursued making a wild scene that expanded on all sides, enveloped Mark too. He was nearer the smaller group than the larger, and was naturally taken for one of the associates of the tall man who, so shortly before being made a captive, had spoken so calmly and with such an evident sense of predestination to those who had come to take him into custody.

A large man, bearing a club, flung his arms about Mark and wrestled him to the ground. The man did not realize, however, what kind of a gymnastically trained young man it was he had undertaken to capture. Mark, although felled beneath the man by the surprise and violence of the attack, was able to draw his legs up under the man's fat stomach and then kick him away. The man came back at him immediately, swinging his murderous club. This time Mark lightly sidestepped the man's heavy charge and, as he passed, swept the linen cloth from around his own body and flung it over the man's head. With the cloth he temporarily blinded the man and, by twisting it, began to strangle him.

By now, however, others of the larger group had noticed this particular fracas, and they began to stretch out their hands to seize Mark. Letting go the cloth in which his first assailant was still enwrapped, Mark twisted free from the clutching hands. His gymnastically trained and hardened body, now fully naked, was difficult to hold on to, and he slipped out of the clutches of each would-be captor and fled away into the darkness.

2

In the Tomb

"They almost caught me, too," said Mark as, on the next day, he related to his mother his nocturnal and dangerous experience at the Mount of Olives.

"I am so glad you were able to escape," said Mary. "And did you mean that Simon and all the others got away, too?"

"Yes, as far as I could tell," replied Mark. "But the tall man who was evidently the leader was bound and no doubt taken away."

"Sit down, if you have time," said Mary, and motioned her son to a place on the rug beside her. "I have not spoken to you of this before, because you are a very busy young man, and I thought you would not be interested. Also I wanted to keep you free of involvement if things went badly. But after what happened to you last night, I want to tell you what I know.

"Last night you recognized Simon. You know that he is a distant relative—to be exact, our cousin is his wife—and you know that, although his business is in the north, he has visited in our home a time or two in the past year.

"Although you have not been present to hear, he has had some long and earnest talks with me. He tells me that he has left his very good fishing business in the hands of his servants, and has attached himself to the company of the man called Jesus."

"That was the tall man I saw last night? The man Simon tried to defend with his own sword?" asked Mark.

"Yes, that must have been he," answered Mary. "I have never seen him, but Simon says that he is a tall man with flowing hair. He says also that people always notice him, and feel that he is very calm and very strong at the same time."

"That agrees exactly," responded Mark. "I only heard him say a few words, but he seemed to be entirely unafraid of his enemies. Also he seemed to feel that it was necessary for things to happen as they did. He said something about the fulfillment of what is written."

Mary leaned forward with eager interest. "Yes," she said, "he was referring to our Scriptures. He thought that what was happening had to happen because it was spoken of ahead of time by our prophets.

"Mark," Mary continued earnestly, "you know that in our Scriptures our prophets have said that someday the Messiah will come. He will be the Anointed of the Lord, and will deliver his people."

Mary paused, drew a deep breath, and then concluded simply: "I believe that Jesus is the Messiah."

"What does Simon think?" asked Mark, not yet greatly impressed.

"He thinks so too," Mary hastened to reply. "One day he told Jesus that that was what he thought. Jesus did not say Yes or No, but he did give Simon another name. He told him he would be called Peter and, as you know, that means Rock. Then he told him that he would build his community upon the Rock."

"I have been taught the Scriptures of our people," said Mark, as if he were thinking aloud, "and I have also been taught the philosophy of the Greeks. The Greeks spoke of a Golden Age in the past. Our prophets spoke of an age of peace and righteousness yet to come in the future. I only saw the man you call Jesus for a few moments last night. In that short time, however, I was so impressed by him that I do truly believe that any community he would build would be a community of peace and righteousness. Do you think it possible that he has actually come to begin the new age?"

"Yes," answered Mary. "Even though I have never seen Jesus myself, what Simon has told me has made me believe that he is the Messiah who will bring in the new age, the age of peace and righteousness, as you call it."

Mark continued on his own train of thought: "And if Jesus told Simon that he was a Rock and that he would build on him, it means that he is really placing a great deal of confidence in our distant relative."

"I suppose so," Mary agreed hesitantly, "but Simon himself seemed to feel that Jesus was speaking in a sort of indirect way. He seemed to think that Jesus might have been referring to something he had said, or to something he stood for."

Mary was puzzling over the idea. She laughed gently. She knew Simon better than Mark did, for hitherto Mark had scarcely known him at all. "He is an impetuous sort of Rock," she said, as if speaking only to herself.

Groping for a thought, Mark said: "Perhaps Jesus meant that Simon was the kind of person he could build his community on. Or perhaps he was thinking about what Simon said when he said he believed Jesus was the Messiah."

Mark shook his head in bewilderment over the very thoughts he had just been expressing. Then, as if he had just heard Mary's characterization of Simon, he burst out: "Anyway, you are right when you say that Simon is an impetuous sort of Rock. When I saw him last night he had just tried some rash swordplay, then the next thing I knew he was running off into the darkness."

Mark reflected a moment. "But after all, I cannot say anything about that. I ran too."

He smiled wryly as he thought how he had shed his linen cloth and fled naked, a slippery and elusive object. "I ran too," he repeated, "and I think I ran faster than Simon. I think he got away all right, however, but I do wonder where he has gone and whether anything has happened to him."

"I think Simon Peter can take care of himself," Mary said reassuringly. Then she added softly: "But what I wonder most of all is what happened to Jesus. You said that they tied him with ropes."

"Yes," said Mark, "that was the last that I saw. I thought he could have run before that if he had wanted to, but he did not even try. When the ropes were on his arms, I someway thought he was strong enough to break them if he wanted to, but he did not try that either. I guess they took him away, and I suppose he is in some prison today."

Mark suddenly remembered the date. It was the fourteenth day of the month of Nisan. The festival observances of orthodox Judaism were not of vast importance to him. He knew, however, that on this afternoon the Passover lambs had to be slain in the Temple courts. He looked at the slanting path of the sunlight on the floor, and thought, casually, that the slaughter would be going on even then. He knew also that when the sun went down and the next day began it would be the time for the Passover meal. When the roasted lamb was ready, each household would gather around its well-laden table, and the meal would be eaten. As it progressed there would be talk of the ancient Exodus from Egypt and of the hope for the Messiah to come. Finally, everything would be concluded with the singing of some Psalms.

Thinking, casually, through that sequence of Passover events, Mark tarried momentarily in his mind with the phrase he had formulated about the hope for the Messiah to come. His mother had just said that she believed that Jesus was the Messiah who had been so long hoped for. Mark had reported seeing the tall man, who was undoubtedly Jesus, being bound with ropes. He had expressed the thought that he was probably taken away and was probably even then languishing in some jail.

"The Messiah," Mark thought to himself, "the Messiah in jail. That is a contradiction in terms. Of course Jeremiah was incarcerated in a miry cistern, and other prophets were imprisoned and killed. But they were prophets. That would not happen to the Messiah. The Messiah would not let it happen to himself."

Breaking his silence, Mark only asked Mary: "Mother, why did you send me to the Pool of Siloam yesterday to carry home the jar of water?"

"Neaniskos," said Mary, reverting to the affectionate diminutive by which she often addressed her son, "I did not want to tell you at the time why it was. If anything went wrong I did not want you to bear any responsibility by knowing anything about the matter at all.

"You see"—and Mary seemed to go back in her mind over the chain of events which led her to ask the strong young man who was her son to carry a jar of water through the city, as ordinarily only a woman would do—"you see, Simon Peter came to me and said that Jesus wished to eat the Passover in the city with his men. He also said that Jesus now had many enemies in the city.

"In fact, Simon felt that he himself was probably already a marked man because of his association with Jesus. He thought that he should not come openly to my house anymore. So we devised the plan whereby you would unwittingly lead some of Jesus' men to our house to make preparations. Then after it was dark Simon and Jesus and the others would come too."

"But," Mark broke in, "that was yesterday, and the Passover is only today."

"Yes," agreed Mary, "so it was, and I was surprised too. You see, I was waiting for word from Simon Peter that some of them had reached the city and were ready to come to the appointed place and get the meal ready. Naturally I expected the word only sometime today. But it came yesterday. So I sent you off at once. Fortunately we were ready for them anytime."

"I suppose you gave them the large room upstairs," said Mark.

"Yes," answered Mary. "Two men worked there in the afternoon to make things ready, and Rhoda helped them. Then they went away, and all came back in the evening. I did not meet them, but Rhoda told me that they stayed until late—all, that is, except for one man who went away considerably earlier. At the end they sent a message of appreciation for the hospitality, sang some Psalms, and then went out into the night."

"I suppose that is when they came on out to where I was," said Mark.

"Yes," Mary replied. "I had no idea it would work out that way. It is true that I had told Simon earlier that Jesus could go out there to pray, if he wished, but I had no idea that he would be going there so late last night."

Mary leaned forward and put a hand on Mark's shoulder. "So the way it worked out, I involved you in it after all, did I not?"

Mark did not answer directly, for he was pursuing his own line of thought. Instead he asked, "But why do you think Jesus came a day early? He wanted to eat the Passover, but he came the day before the Passover. Passover is now, tonight."

"In the light of what has happened," Mary answered thoughtfully, "I can only think that Jesus had some presentiment of trouble, and wanted to eat with his men once again before it was too late. Now, if he is in jail, as you think, and if his men are all scattered, as you say they scattered last night, it *is* too late."

Mark wondered what this unhappy outcome of events would do to his mother's expressed belief that Jesus was the Messiah for whom her people had been waiting. Surely it would be difficult to maintain the belief now. And what about Simon Peter and the others? The way Simon was running the preceding night one might suppose that he had run on and on until he was once again back at his fishing boats in the north, back at the business he had left to follow a man who had ended up as a prisoner in a Jerusalem jail.

Along the line of these thoughts, John Mark might have gone further with the conversation which his mother had initiated, but just then a tremor ran through the house, causing pottery vessels to rock against each other and dust to shake down from the ceiling. It was only a momentary quaking of the earth, and all who lived in Jerusalem

were only too familiar with such events, which occurred, if not frequently, at least occasionally. Nevertheless, the brief interruption
provided a natural termination point in the talk between the two, and
it was evident that Mary proposed now to move on to her further
duties. These had to do with supervision of household activities, in
particular the supervision of preparations for their own Passover meal
of the coming evening.

"By the way," she remarked to her son as she prepared to depart,
"I have invited Simon of Cyrene and his family to be our guests for
our Passover meal tonight." This Simon had been a friend of Mary's
husband, Aristobulus, in Cyrene and, like Aristobulus and Mary, had
afterward moved to Jerusalem. He was married to a woman named
Esther, and they had two sons, Alexander and Rufus, both younger
than John Mark.

×

                The sun set, the evening came, and the roasted lamb
was ready to be served. But Simon of Cyrene and his family were not
yet present.

"He is not ordinarily late," said Mary. "Do you think anything
could have happened to him?"

"I do not know," Mark replied casually. Then he added: "Of
course, there are huge crowds in the city for the Passover. Perhaps
he has had trouble getting through the streets."

"I do not think he could be involved in any of the trouble you
were almost caught in last night." Mary was thinking aloud. "He does
not even know Simon Peter. Once I told him that a man with the same
name as his was married to a cousin of ours, but he took no interest
in the fact. I doubt if he has ever even heard of Jesus. No, I think he
is all right. But I do wish he would come. We cannot keep things ready
forever."

It was somewhat later when Rhoda, the maid, came to Mary to

say: "Simon of Cyrene is at the door, with his wife, Esther, and their sons, Alexander and Rufus."

Relief at the arrival of their belated guest and his family was soon mingled with renewed apprehension as Mary and John Mark noted the strange behavior of Simon of Cyrene.

Simon seemed dazed, unsteady, and deeply troubled. He took part in the meal, and in the various small ceremonies which accompanied it, mechanically and as if his thoughts were far away. Only with conscious effort did it seem that he managed from time to time to take some part in the conversation.

In privacy afterward, while Esther cared for the two boys in another room, Simon of Cyrene told Mary and John Mark what had happened. Even then his voice broke frequently, he trembled violently from time to time, and managed the narration only with great difficulty.

"Before the middle of the morning," Simon began, "I came into the street which leads from the Antonia fortress to the northwest gate in the city wall. You know how steeply the street climbs. There, toiling up the ascent, was a man, carrying a heavy beam.

"You know how the Romans make the people they are going to execute carry their own cross. This man was a prisoner. They were taking him out to crucify him. They had lashed him and beaten him, and his strength was far gone.

"Just as I got to the street and just as he got to where I was, he fell down right in front of me. For a moment I forgot all about the Romans. I bent down over the man, and I stretched out my hand to touch him.

"Then I could not forget about the Romans any longer.

" 'Say, you,' cried a Roman officer, 'are you a friend of this man? He thinks he is a king, and we are rounding up his friends too.'

" 'I never saw him before in all my life,' I declared," said Simon, "and that was true.

" 'Well, anyway,' said the Roman, 'we will give you something to do for him. Pick up the cross beam and carry it for him.'

"With that he gave me a shove, and I had to drag that heavy beam up across my shoulders.

"The man they said thought he was a king never said a word, but he looked at me and I have not been able to forget his look ever since. I would say that if I know anything, I know that he was innocent. His eyes were full of pain, but they were clear and they were unafraid. I would say he could have been a king if he had wanted to."

John Mark leaned forward with excitement. "Was he a tall man, a tall man with long hair?" he asked.

"Yes," replied Simon. "How did you know?"

"I was at our garden last night," Mark explained, "when a band of our people came with clubs and staves and captured a man like that. If they wanted to kill him they could not have done it, because only the Romans can execute anyone. Somehow they must have gotten the Romans to do it."

Mark thought a moment, then went on. "Yes, if the Roman officer said the man thought he was a king, that would be enough. The Romans cannot let anyone try to be a king."

Mark's mother had also been listening intently, but now she spoke quietly and with deep conviction. "It was Jesus."

Then she asked the question to which the answer was already evident. "Did they kill him?"

"Yes," answered Simon. "They nailed him up on the cross"— and Simon shuddered as he visualized the terrible scene—"and they executed two others along with him.

"I do not know who the two others were, for nobody said their names. I suppose they were supposed to be revolutionaries too— 'robbers,' the Romans call anybody like that.

"But the man for whom I carried the cross—there is no doubt about who he was. You know how the Romans sometimes put up a placard with the criminal's name and his crime when they execute him? Well, they put up 'Jesus, King of the Jews,' so that is who it was, all right."

Mary began to sob gently. "I believed that Jesus was the Messiah," she said through her crying. "I loved him though I never saw him. I hoped he would help us all. I believe he could have. And now they have killed him."

John Mark placed a consoling hand on his mother's shoulder, but could find no words to say.

"I stayed on through the day," Simon of Cyrene continued his account. "I wanted to go, because it was a terrible place to be, but I could not go away. I had helped Jesus, and he had looked at me, and I had to stay.

"I do not know if he had any other friends there or not, except there was a little group of women up close by him, and one young man with them for a while.

"It was not as long all together as I thought it would be, however. About the middle of the afternoon there was a quake of the earth, and Jesus' head fell forward, and I think he died right then."

"So his body is still out there, I suppose," said Mark. "The Romans leave bodies up until the birds eat them, you know."

"No," said Simon, "I helped Jesus on the way up there, and someone else came and helped at the end. I did not know who it was, but some people said it was a man named Joseph from the village of Arimathea, and he had some other man with him too.

"They came after Jesus was dead and they showed something to the soldiers, so I think they must have gotten permission from the Roman headquarters. They took down Jesus' body and carried it away somewhere off to the west of the skull hill where the execution was done."

John Mark recognized the name of the hill outside the northwest gate of Jerusalem where the Romans usually conducted their executions.

"I know where you mean," he said. "Just beyond the hill there is a place where there are a number of tombs. Those two men must have used some tomb that was just waiting to be occupied. But the Romans would have left the bodies to be eaten by the birds, and our people would have taken them down and put them all in the common pit of the criminals, so I am glad Jesus had friends to treat his body with more kindness.

"Did you see where they actually laid him?" Mark inquired as he concluded his observations.

"Yes," said Simon of Cyrene. "I was not as close as the women were. There were still two of them left, and they were right over at the place. But I could see that it was a tomb with a rolling stone to close it. I think it must have been the tomb of Joseph of Arimathea himself, because they said he was a rich man, and only a rich man can have a tomb with a real rolling stone for closure—you know, like the one at the family tomb of King Herod."

"So that is the end of the hopes of those who believed that Jesus was the Messiah," mused John Mark. Again he touched his mother's shoulder in a simple gesture of consolation. "I was about to believe it myself, but now we have come to the end, instead."

"I suppose so," agreed Mary, and her eyes were cast down with sorrow.

But then she looked up through her tears, and she asked: "Do you know what Simon Peter told me the last time he was talking with me? He told me that Jesus expected to die, but that he also said that he would be in the earth only as long as Jonah was in the belly of the whale, and that after three days he would rise again."

"I have no idea what that would mean," said John Mark, "and I guess Peter had no idea either, for as far as I know he has run away or is hiding out. I do not blame him, either. The Romans would be glad to capture anybody who had any connection with Jesus. If they kill a 'king,' they would be glad to kill his supporters, too."

"Do you feel that you are in danger, Simon?" Mary asked Simon of Cyrene.

"No," Simon replied. "The Romans made me carry that cross beam for Jesus, but they accepted what I told them, that I had never seen the man before. They do not know how I came to feel as the day went on."

"How do you feel about it all?" asked John Mark.

"I do not know any more to say than I have already," answered Simon. "I was willing to believe that Jesus was a king, and the Messiah would be our best king. But now Jesus is dead—" and Simon's voice trailed off into silence.

×

The next day was the Passover sabbath and, although John Mark did not take all of the observances too seriously, he was under obligation, like the rest of his people, to observe a day of quiet. It was also a day in which he thought much about what Simon of Cyrene had related and about what he himself had experienced.

Because his thoughts were still so active, he slept only lightly that night and was instantly awakened by the very slight tremor which was noticeable in the house in the early hours of the next morning. This was probably a very small after-quake from the somewhat more considerable earthquake which had been experienced on the afternoon of the day before the Passover. Ordinarily, no doubt, John Mark would have slept on undisturbed by so minor a movement, as the rest of his household was obviously sleeping on, undisturbed. But he was at once wide awake and, moreover, felt himself driven by an inner compulsion which he did not understand himself. He drew on a white linen robe and stole out into the dark streets. He knew the area to which Simon of Cyrene had referred as the place of the burial of Jesus, which lay just to the west of the hill outside the city wall where the Romans were accustomed to carrying out their crucifixions. He believed that he could find the tomb which was distinguished by its rolling-stone closure, as compared with the simpler graves otherwise found in the neighborhood. He slipped silently and swiftly through the empty streets of the city, and passed out through the side doorway of the northwestern city gate.

In a burial area otherwise occupied by relatively simple tombs, it was not difficult to find the tomb which Simon of Cyrene had described, the only one in the area with the rolling stone to close its entrance. The tomb had a small, square courtyard, cut into the hill. At the far side of the court was the entrance to the burial chamber. Here there was a channel in which a large circular stone, three-fourths as high as John Mark himself, could be rolled forward to close the entrance and rolled back to open it. Now the stone was partially rolled back. This, in itself, caused John Mark only slight surprise, for it occurred to him that the earth tremor which he had felt not too long before might have thus somewhat dislodged the stone. Indeed, under the circumstances, he felt that it would do no harm to push the stone yet a little farther aside, to admit to the interior of the tomb a little more of the very dim light of the yet very early morning. For this task his own strong muscles were adequate, although the rolling stone was heavy. Then John Mark went into the burial chamber.

Years afterward he could still hardly believe that it had happened to him. When he wrote down something about it, he spoke of himself in an almost anonymous way, save that he did use his mother's favorite expression for himself—*neaniskos,* "young man."

Within the burial chamber, at the back, John Mark found a single shelf cut into the rock wall. That was where the body would have been placed. But now there were only some linen cloths lying on the rock shelf. They were just like the linen cloth John Mark used to sleep under at night, but he knew that such were also used as wrappings for one who had entered into the sleep of death.

This must be the place where Jesus had been buried. But the body of Jesus was not here. The body had been placed here, according to the narrative by Simon of Cyrene, on the very eve of the sabbath, and during the sabbath, which was specially holy because it was the Passover sabbath, no one could have done anything. Now it was early on the morning of the first day of the week, and the city had scarcely begun to stir. Surely no one would have been here yet, as early as this. But the body which must have been here, and must have been wrapped in these very linen cloths, was gone.

John Mark sat down on one end of the rock shelf to ponder— the day before the sabbath, the sabbath day, and then this, the early morning of the first day of the week. He counted over the sequence of days in his mind, and suddenly realized that it was, using the method of counting which was customary among his people, "after three days." And his mother had said that Simon Peter had told her that Jesus had said that he would rise again after three days.

It had been that long, and the tomb was empty!

As John Mark pondered, he saw figures approaching. The oncoming sunrise was lightening the sky by now, and the persons—three women in all—were hastening along the path as if they knew precisely the place to which they were coming. They were carrying cloth and spices, and their errand was plain. They intended to perform, belatedly indeed after three days, but at the earliest possible moment because of the circumstances, the proper final ceremonies of the anointing of the body of the deceased. For such a solemn and requisite rite they could count upon being admitted to the tomb, if only they could find someone in charge who would roll back for them the stone which closed the tomb entrance.

The women came into the tomb courtyard, stopped momentarily in some surprise as they saw the entrance already open, then stepped on into the tomb chamber.

John Mark did not intend to frighten the women. Indeed, he hardly knew how the words came tumbling to his lips. "You are looking for Jesus who was crucified. He is not here. See the place. He is risen. Go and tell Peter."

Naturally the women were frightened. The unexpected circumstances, the apparition of the young man in the white robe in the dim light of the inner tomb, the tumultuous words which they could not take in as rapidly as they were spoken—all these things threw them into understandable confusion. They turned and ran.

3

In the Upper Room

John Mark knew that he had, unintentionally, frightened the women who had come upon him in a way that was as unexpected to them as it was to him. Whether they would go and find Peter or any other of the close followers of Jesus, and make known what was the situation at the tomb, he did not know. Whether, indeed, they could find Peter or any other of the men was none too sure. When John Mark had last seen any of them, they were running away from being captured themselves, and they probably considered that they were still in grave danger. Perhaps they had even left the city.

Nevertheless it seemed important to John Mark to make contact with them, if it could be done. Therefore he spent the balance of the day and well into the night wandering, as casually as he could, in the streets and in the environs of the city, seeking to pick up any clues, by things seen or from conversation overheard, as to where Simon Peter and the others might have gone.

When John Mark came home late that night, his mother met him at the door.

"They were here again," she said.

"Whom do you mean?" asked John Mark, with no intuition of what the answer would be.

"Peter, and the other men," Mary said. "The ones who came the other night to eat the Passover meal ahead of time with Jesus. The last meal," she added sadly, "he ever ate before he died."

"You mean they all came back again, and came here?" John Mark was still doubtful, for he had thought of them as probably widely scattered.

"Yes, they just seemed to want to all be together again in the very same place where they ate that last time with Jesus. I guess they thought this was the one safe place where they could still get together. I hope that is true. Anyway, we kept the doors safely locked." Mary looked out apprehensively into the dark street as she spoke.

"So they came in, one or two at a time, in the early evening. They brought some food, and I got out some things for them. After supper, they were there for a while, then again they slipped out, a few at a time."

Mary led John Mark on into the house and sat down, with the plain intention of continuing the conversation.

"I did not talk with the men when they left," she said. "But ahead of time, when he came, Simon Peter took me aside and told me a strange thing. He spoke about some women who had been friends of Jesus and had followed him, along with his company of men. So when the men fled from our garden, and when Peter himself went into hiding later in the day, these women still kept as close to where Jesus was as they could."

John Mark thought of how steadfast his mother had been when her husband, his father, had died. "I know," he said, "women are able to endure sorrow better than men, and they stand by and do anything there is to be done.

"Of course," he added, as an afterthought, "the women would have been less under suspicion than the men, and freer to move about the city."

"Yes," Mary went on, "that is what they did. They went all the way out of the city to the hill where Jesus was crucified, and they stood there during the whole terrible time until it was all over.

"When Simon Peter told me about this, he could hardly speak, because he felt so bad about not being there himself. But he told me who was there. There was Mary Magdalene—from the village of Magdala, upon the Sea of Galilee, you know. Jesus had healed her of a sickness that was as much in her mind as anything else, and she was very devoted to him. There was Mary the wife of Clopas and mother of James and Joses. Those men were two of Jesus' followers, and they called James the Younger, to separate him from another James in the group. There was Salome, the wife of Zebedee and mother of that other James and of John. You know, Peter has often spoken of James and John; they were fishermen up on Galilee along with him and his brother Andrew."

"Then there was nobody out there from Jesus' own family?" asked John Mark.

"Yes, there was"—and Mary went on with the explanation.

"Jesus' mother was there."

Mary's eyes filled with tears as she visualized the poignant scene. The mother's heart must have been pierced as with a sword, as she stood by and watched her son die.

"Was she all by herself?" asked John Mark, sympathetically.

"No," Mary replied. "You see, she and Salome are sisters, so they were together. In addition to that, one of Jesus' men was actually there. That was John, who is Salome's son and whom I have sometimes heard Peter speak about as a disciple whom Jesus loved specially. I do not know if Peter were jealous of that."

Mary had digressed for a moment with the expression of this question about the relation of Peter and John. At the same time it occurred to her that the identity of name between that beloved disciple and her own son meant that she ought to be careful, when talking with Simon Peter, to call her son John Mark, or Mark, lest Peter's thoughts be diverted to the other John, whom he might to some extent look upon as a rival.

John Mark, at the same time, was led to think of the identity of name between his mother and no less than three of the women of whom he had just heard as being present when Jesus was put to death.

"Mother, you have an honorable name," he said, as he touched her hand gently. "You are Mary, and standing by there when Jesus was put to death were three other Marys—Mary Magdalene, Mary the mother of James the Younger and Joses, and Mary the mother of Jesus himself."

"Yes," she replied, then added softly, "I wish I had known, then I would have been there too."

John Mark could not have wished such an ordeal for his mother, but he believed that she meant what she said. He also thought with special sympathy about the terrible experience that it must have been for the mother of Jesus.

"Did Jesus' mother stay all the way through to the end?" he asked.

"I think she would have," Mary replied, "but Peter was told that Jesus himself sent her away after a time, in the care of John, and that Salome, John's mother and her sister, went off with them too."

"So it was Mary Magdalene and the other Mary, Mary the mother of James the Younger and of Joses, who stayed to the last?" John Mark was piecing together in his own mind the items in the complex picture.

"Yes, and Peter told me," his mother went on, "that those two Marys not only stayed until Jesus expired, but that they also waited and watched until they saw two men—they found out that it was Joseph of Arimathea and Nicodemus—come and bury the body of Jesus in a nearby rock-hewn tomb. The tomb, they learned, belonged to Joseph, and was the only one in the area closed at the front entrance with a large rolling stone."

"Joseph must be a rich man," John Mark thought aloud. "That is the kind of a tomb that a wealthy man has. You know Herod's family tomb—" John Mark broke off in the middle of the sentence as he realized that he was speaking along the very same lines as Simon of Cyrene when the latter had been at their home for dinner on the night after he too had been, all unwittingly and unwantingly, a participant in the crucifixion events, and had given his report of what had happened.

Entirely independent witnesses had reported the same facts about where Jesus had been buried. John Mark had begun to wonder, after the strange excitement of his own early morning hours, if he had himself been confused and had gone into the wrong tomb, and if the words he had somehow felt impelled to utter at that time had been based upon that confusion. But no, the identification of the tomb of Jesus had been precisely as he had understood it. The execution place was all too horribly obvious. The one rolling-stone-closed tomb in the whole neighborhood was where he had been.

While he was thinking, his mother was going on with her account of what Peter had told her, and was coming to what she had intimated at the beginning of her report would be the strange climax of it.

"So, Peter told me, this very day those same women had found him and told him a strange fact. It was Mary Magdalene and Mary the mother of James the Younger and of Joses, who had seen the burial itself, and Salome, who had gone off early from the cross with her son John to care for the grief-stricken mother of Jesus—those three who, as soon as the sabbath was over, had purchased spices, and then this morning had gone early to the tomb. They were sure someone in charge there would roll back the stone and let them perform the customary last rites of anointing. But they found the stone rolled back already, and the tomb empty, and they ran away and were afraid."

Now John Mark knew the names of the women who had run at the sound of his voice that early morning, and he knew that they had reached Peter with their report that the tomb was empty. What he did not know was the one further item of information with which Mary now concluded her narrative.

"Peter also ran to the tomb when he got this report, and he found that John—who probably had word directly from his mother, Salome —was there just ahead of him. Peter and John both say the same thing, that the tomb was empty, and they wonder about it very much. That is what Peter told me when he came this evening, but I did not see him again before he went away in the night. Rhoda let the men out when they wanted to go."

John Mark was thinking hard. Indeed he felt that he had much thinking to do. The tomb of Jesus was empty. He knew that for himself. Three women knew it. Peter and John knew it. It was a fact. In the early morning when he had first encountered the fact, and when he had remembered the report that Jesus had said he would die and rise again, he had himself burst out, under some strange compulsion, with the words "He has risen!" But as the day had gone on, all kinds of other thoughts had come to his mind, and these he was still trying to sort out. Someday he would tell his mother about his own experience; for now it was all too confusing. John Mark let the conversation come to an end.

✕

In accordance with previously made plans, John Mark was away from Jerusalem for more than a week. When he returned he walked into the city by the street which passed the Pool of Siloam and led on up to the southwestern hill where his home was. John Mark paused by the Pool to rest, then noticed two men starting on up the street. One was recognizable by his powerful frame and rugged head as his own distant relative Simon Peter. The other was unknown to John Mark, but plainly a companion with Peter, presumably also, therefore, one of the men who had been associated with Jesus.

The surprising thing to John Mark was that these men were still in Jerusalem, and evidently not afraid to be seen walking about the streets. Apparently there had been no concerted effort to follow up the execution of Jesus by the rounding up of his men.

Halfway up the hill, John Mark overtook the two men. He greeted Peter, who seemed pleased to see him and introduced him to his companion, a man by the name of Thomas.

Trees and a rocky cavern in the hillside made a natural stopping place, and Peter seemed disposed to talk, so the three men sat there together for a time.

"I have been away, and am glad to see you," said John Mark

noncommitally, then added hopefully, "and to learn what has been going on in Jerusalem."

"John Mark," said Peter—and he seemed to take a deeper interest in the younger man than had ever been apparent before—"I wish to tell you how good your mother has been to us. You know that some of us were followers of Jesus of Nazareth and believed that he would be the Messiah of our people, and that your mother made a place for us all to eat together on the very last night before he was killed. Now she has continued to let us get together there, although she must have known that there is some risk involved. As you know, the palace of the high priest is up there on the hill, not too far away."

As he mentioned the residence of the high priest, an involuntary shudder shook the broad shoulders of Peter. As if under an inner compulsion to share the whole train of events with the younger man, with whom he had not previously been very well acquainted, Peter looked, with anguish in his face, at John Mark, and went on.

"That was where they took Jesus after they captured him that night in your garden at the foot of the Mount of Olives. That was where the members of the Council came together to question him. That was where I stood in the lower courtyard, by the fire, and said three times that I never knew him."

Again Peter's shoulders shook with emotion.

"Then I ran blindly down the hill to this very place, and wept and wept. Do you think he can ever forgive me?"

John Mark felt that Peter was asking the question of himself, almost oblivious for the moment that Thomas and he were still there with him. Also he noticed that Peter spoke as if Jesus were alive, somewhere else, not dead, and as if he might expect to meet him again someday and wondered what attitude the man would take toward him who had denied Jesus so grievously.

Peter returned to the thread of what he was telling John Mark.

"All that day I stayed in hiding, and the next day too, which was the sabbath, when no one could do anything anyway. Then on the first day of the week, before the day was too far advanced, some of the women who had been with us with Jesus came and found me and told me what had happened. The day Jesus was killed they stayed out there on that hill all day long, until, just barely before sunset, Joseph and Nicodemus came and buried his body. The two men put him in a rock tomb—I guess it belonged to Joseph himself—and closed it with a rolling stone—you know, one like at Herod's family tomb. After the sabbath was over, the women went back to anoint the body. The tomb was open. The body was gone. When they found me and told me, I ran all the way. It was so. John was there. He saw it too."

Up to this point, John Mark had heard part of the same story from his mother, so he knew that in mentioning John, the man with his own name, Peter was referring to the follower of Jesus whom Jesus was said to have loved especially and whom he had asked to take care of his own mother.

"Simon Peter," said John Mark very seriously, "I was there too, and I too know that it was so."

"You?" questioned Peter. "How could that be?"

"Simon of Cyrene," John Mark explained, "ate the Passover meal with us, and told us how Jesus was killed that day and where he was buried. After the sabbath was over, the next morning I woke up very early, and something made me go out to look at that tomb. It was open and empty, just as you said. While it was not yet very light, the women came and saw me and were frightened and ran away."

John Mark wondered if he should speak of one more thing, then decided that he would.

"After you came to our house to eat that last supper with Jesus, my mother told me something about how you were working with him instead of fishing, how you believed he was the Messiah of our people, and how he had lately told you that he would be killed and would rise again after three days.

"So, when I found that tomb empty, and remembered that Jesus was killed the day before the Passover and that it was then the day after the Passover, so it was what we would call 'after three days,' something made me call out to those women, 'He has risen!'"

"But I wonder," John Mark went on, "I wonder. At the time, it was almost as if something were making me say what I said. Now I have been away on this journey, and I have thought and I have thought. It seemed as if something wonderful might have happened, but now I wonder if some of your men just took the body away, or if some of the authorities did it?"

There was a certain compassion in the face of Simon Peter as he looked at John Mark.

"We also did not know what to believe. So John and I were able to get word to the others, and we all came back to your mother's home and to the upper room that night.

"All, that is," Peter made his reference to the others more precise, "except Judas, who had betrayed Jesus to his enemies and then killed himself, and Thomas, who was not there."

Peter looked with a friendly glance at his companion, who was still sitting with them quietly, but did not yet bring him into the conversation.

"All ten of us sat and talked and talked that evening. We did not know what to think. We knew that none of us had tampered with the tomb of Jesus. It was not likely that the authorities would have done so either. The Romans would not care. Our own priests would not break the sabbath. An earthquake could have moved the stone at the entrance. Some said they felt a small quake that morning. But how could the body have disappeared? The women even said that the grave cloths were still lying there.

"That was how we were talking. And the room was closed. And your mother had locked the house, so we would all be safe. Then all of a sudden Jesus was there with us. He looked the same as always, but when he put out his hands toward us and said, 'Peace,' the way he used to do, we saw that there were nail marks in his hands from where the Romans had nailed him to the cross."

A certain joy had come into Peter's face as he told of this event, but it was swiftly succeeded by a look of sadness as he spoke of the mark of the executioners' nails in the hands of the man for whom he had taken no brave stand when he was being tried.

"We were so amazed," Peter went on with his narrative, "that we did not know what to do or say. We just sat there, and looked, and did not know whether to believe what we were seeing or not. Then Jesus went away. He did not open the door, any more than he had opened it to come in. He just was not there anymore."

Peter turned to his companion. "Thomas did not believe it when we told him later about what had happened. He said he would have to see for himself."

"Yes," Thomas took up the narrative which Peter had begun. "Again on the first day of this week we came to your mother's house in the evening, and we went up to the upper room, and I was there, and it happened again. All of a sudden Jesus was there. Everything was closed and locked, and all of a sudden he was just there in the midst of us. It was the way it used to be, and yet it was different."

Thomas was a quiet, reserved, self-controlled man, but his hand trembled as he stretched it out to illustrate his next statement. "I put out my hand, and I touched him. I could feel the marks where he had been wounded with nails in his hands and a spear stroke in his side. Yet I could not really take hold of him, and after a little he was gone again, just the same as Peter said it happened the first time."

4

At the Pool of Siloam

After the conversation there on the slope of the southwestern hill at Jerusalem in which Simon Peter and Thomas told John Mark such amazing things, but in which Peter still seemed so heavily burdened with his own sorrow and shame, it was several weeks before Mark saw any of the men again who were known to have been followers of Jesus.

When Peter did come back again to his mother's house, John Mark saw at once that he was much changed. Peter and the other men who had been with Jesus were all from Galilee (with the exception, of course, of Judas, who was from the south but was now deceased), and they had gone back to the north. There at the lake Jesus had appeared to some of them again. On that occasion he asked Peter three times if he loved him, and as Peter said three times that he did, he somehow felt that he was canceling out the three times that he had said he did not know Jesus. This lifted Peter's heavy burden of guilt. Not only that, but Jesus also told Peter that he wanted him to feed his sheep; so Peter felt that he had work to do, although he did not yet quite understand what it would be. At any rate, he thought he should come back to Jerusalem. Here, on the Mount of Olives, Jesus appeared to some of them again, and told them that they were to go everywhere for him, but should first of all wait for the Holy Spirit.

So Simon Peter came back to see Mary, the mother of John Mark, and to ask if he could again bring his group together at her house. Mary agreed eagerly, for in the meantime she and Mark had had many long talks in which they shared all of their experiences, Mary by now being wholly convinced that Jesus was indeed the Messiah of their people, John Mark still remaining puzzled by all that he had experienced and heard.

It was well that Mary's house and grounds on the southwestern hill at Jerusalem were large and spacious. Peter and the men with him soon found themselves living there—where Mary found accommodations for all without apparent difficulty—and the other John brought Jesus' mother and several of the other women over from his home to Mary's house for the meetings that were held there. Not only that, but word of the amazing events that had taken place was gradually spreading, and other people were being attracted too.

Most of those who came together were well instructed in the ways of their ancestors and, at the appointed times, were present at the official ceremonies of their people in the Temple, the gleaming walls of which were impressively visible from Mary's house. Here also, at Mary's house, they pursued customs with which they had already been familiar, both in the Temple and in the synagogue, that is, they had readings from the Scriptures and prayers.

These meetings were, of course, not being authorized by any of the authorities of the Temple or of the synagogues, and it was not easy for an unauthorized group of common people to even get copies of the Scriptures. But in this respect the movement—if such it may be called —was assisted by an unexpected circumstance. Several priests were attracted, came regularly to the gatherings, and brought with them carefully copied rolls of Scripture books.

Generally speaking, the priests of the Temple had been opposed to Jesus. But these priests were ones who had already separated themselves from the Temple and its services. They had, in fact, previously been members of another movement, that of the people who were called Essenes.

The Essenes had read in the Scriptures a command about going out into the wilderness to prepare the way of the Lord, and they had undertaken to do exactly that, by forming a community on the barren hills above the Sea of Salt and devoting themselves assiduously to the study of Scripture and the practice of all the commandments. Since they did all of this in order to prepare the way of the Lord, it was evident that they were looking forward to some striking manifestation of divine activity in the hopefully near future. Accordingly, in their study of the Scripture, they sought to find, and to interpret as fulfilled or about to be fulfilled in their experience, the passages which referred to what God would do in the future and to the Messiah whom he would send.

It was understandable, therefore, that the priests who had been with the Essenes and were now among the slowly growing group of people who met at the house of Mary brought Scripture rolls with them. When these scrolls were unrolled, not only was the text of Scripture seen to be copied in very careful handwriting, but also passages with special Messianic reference were seen to be singled out with a special mark in the margin.

This mark was simply an × made by two quick diagonal strokes, and as such it was no doubt the easiest kind of a sign for a scribe or scholar to make in the margin of his scroll. But actually it had a deeper significance than that. It was also the last letter of the Hebrew alphabet. The priests, however, had to explain this. Most of the people present, although they commonly spoke Aramaic and sometimes Greek, also knew at least enough Hebrew to read in the Scriptures. But they were accustomed to the way Hebrew letters were written at that time and knew little of the very different shapes in which they were formed in much earlier times.

So the priests had to explain that this × mark was really an ancient form of the last letter of the Hebrew alphabet, the letter called Taw. That name for the letter simply meant "mark," and the original form of the letter was indeed a very elemental mark, a crossing of two lines, more or less at right angles and standing, sometimes, upright or, as here, sideways.

The priests also opened their scroll of the prophet Ezekiel and read a very interesting passage. Jerusalem, the prophet said, was filled with abominations and, on that account, would soon be visited by terrible destroyers who would smite all the wicked. But there were people in the city who were deeply sorrowful for all the sins of the city. The Lord wished them to be spared and to be saved in the midst of the destruction which would overwhelm everyone else. So ahead of the destroyers who were about to come, the Lord sent into the city a man clothed in linen, with a writing case at his side. He told him to go through the city and put a mark on the foreheads of the men who sigh and groan over all the abominations, and he told the destroyers not to touch the men who wore this mark.

The mark was, of course, the Taw, the last letter of the Hebrew alphabet, the name of which was "mark." That was why, the priests explained, the Essene scribes and scholars used this very same × to mark passages in the Scriptures which told about the future time in which the Lord would send his Messiah and the wicked would be destroyed and the righteous saved.

The priests showed what they meant by unrolling their scroll of the prophet Isaiah. In the margin of the column of writing to which they opened the scroll, there were two of the simple × marks, which the people now understood had the deeper and almost mysterious meaning that the priests had explained.

The first mark called attention to this passage, which one of the priests read out in full in his sonorous voice:

> Behold my servant, whom I uphold,
>   my chosen, in whom my soul delights;
> I have put my Spirit upon him,
>   he will bring forth justice to the nations.
> He will not cry or lift up his voice,
>   or make it heard in the street;

a bruised reed he will not break,
and a dimly burning wick he will not quench;
he will faithfully bring forth justice.
He will not fail or be discouraged
till he has established justice in the earth;
and the coastlands wait for his law.

One of the men in the group who had been associated with Jesus from almost as early a time as Peter and Andrew and James and John leaned forward with intense earnestness as he listened to the reading of this passage.

"That," he said, "is exactly what Jesus was like. You know how quiet he was, and how many sick people he made well, and how gentle he always was with them, especially if they were discouraged and about to give up all hope. But I wonder if he himself got discouraged at last and thought he had failed? Anyway, we know he did not fail, because the Lord raised him up. I believe he was the chosen one."

The priest went on reading at the next point where the × mark stood in the margin of the column before him:

I am the Lord, I have called you in righteousness,
I have taken you by the hand and kept you;
I have given you as a covenant to the people,
a light to the nations,
to open the eyes that are blind,
to bring out the prisoners from the dungeon,
from the prison those who sit in darkness.

Simon Peter was listening to the latter reading with special interest and attention.

"Is there any other place in the book of Isaiah where it also speaks about giving sight to the blind and setting prisoners free? I am trying to remember something that I once heard Jesus read, but it was not just like what you read now."

The priest spent some little time unrolling his scroll to a point

considerably farther along in its text, and at the same time rolling up
the part that he was passing over. Looking intently, he found what
he was searching for.

"Is this it?" he asked.

Then he began to read again:

> The Spirit of the Lord is upon me,
>> because he has anointed me
> to preach good news to the poor.
>> He has sent me to proclaim release to the captives
> and recovering of sight to the blind,
>> to set at liberty those who are oppressed,
> to proclaim the acceptable year of the Lord,
>> and the day of vengeance of our God.

"That is it," cried Peter, with some pleasure at his own acumen,
particularly inasmuch as he could hardly claim to be a profound
student of Scripture. But he did have a very sharp memory, on which
scenes and sayings tended to be imprinted.

"Several of us were one day with Jesus in Nazareth," Peter went
on to explain. "That was his home village, and the people there did
not think very highly of him, but anyway it was the sabbath day and
we were all in the synagogue. They had heard that he had been going
around the country teaching, so they invited him to read the Scripture
and say something about it.

"It was a sabbath day in autumn, and this was supposed to be
the reading for that particular day. So Jesus took the Isaiah scroll and
unrolled it just the same as you did, and found that passage and read
it.

"There was something different about it, however—" and Peter
searched his memory for an elusive point.

"Oh, yes," he said, as the point he was searching for came back
into the focus of his memory. "Jesus left out that last statement about
'the day of vengeance of our God.'

"I wish he had not, though," and Peter scowled fiercely as he recalled the scene. "Jesus said that the Scripture had been fulfilled that day, and he said some more things which made the people angry, and they drove him out of the synagogue and tried to throw him over a cliff at the edge of the town, but he just went away and did not try to strike back in any way."

"Yes," said another of the men, scowling with equal ferocity.

This man was James, son of Zebedee and Salome, and he was recalling something which happened on another occasion in connection with himself and his brother, John.

"I remember when we asked the people in some village in Samaria—it was not much of a place, and I have forgotten the name of it now—to give us lodging for the night, and they would not do it. John and I wanted Jesus to bring down fire from heaven on them, but he would not do it. Elijah did it," he grumbled, "and I do not see why Jesus could not have done it."

This was the way, then, that the presence of the several priests in the group which gathered in the upper room in the house of Mary made it possible for the reading and study of the Scriptures to take place at a depth and to an extent which might not otherwise have been likely in what was after all a rather heterogeneous assemblage of men and women.

Among the Scripture passages to which their concentration upon texts having to do with the last days and the time of the Messiah led them was one which was found in the book of the prophet Joel.

> And it shall come to pass afterward,
>   that I will pour out my spirit on all flesh;
> your sons and your daughters shall prophesy,
>   your old men shall dream dreams,
>   and your young men shall see visions.
> Even upon the menservants and maidservants
>   in those days, I will pour out my spirit.

One thing which this passage did was to bring joy and encouragement to Mary's serving girl, Rhoda, because she joined the group whenever her duties permitted, and she was glad to hear that even maidservants might hope to receive the Spirit when it was poured out in the last time.

More importantly, perhaps, the passage came to give direction to the prayers in which the group engaged. In part the prayers were led by the priests in the company, and what they uttered tended still to be expressed in rather formal and traditional phraseology. But more and more all of the people found themselves joining in saying aloud freely whatever came into their minds by way of petition and supplication, and more and more they found themselves asking for the pouring out of the Spirit, of which they heard in the passage in the book of the prophet Joel.

Simon Peter himself hardly knew what he ought to ask for in his prayers. It was very fresh in his mind that Jesus had asked him to feed his sheep, but he did not really know what that meant. He remembered, however, that on one occasion when he had told Jesus that he believed that he was the Messiah, Jesus had told him that flesh and blood had not revealed it to him, but the Father in heaven. Peter hoped, therefore, that something might yet come to him that would show him what he ought to do, and so he too, more and more, in his prayers asked for the Spirit to come.

×

Although John Mark kept himself aloof from the meetings which he knew were taking place in his mother's house, he did occasionally encounter his distant relative Simon Peter.

"Peter," said Mark, on one such occasion, "you once told my mother that Jesus used to say that he would have to be killed, but that he would rise 'after three days.' How could he ever have known about things like that?"

Simon Peter was better equipped to give an answer to such a question after the meetings in which he had been engaging, where the whole group had been searching in the Scripture rolls for what was said about the Messiah and about the end of days. Drawing upon his memory, freshly stocked from the studies of the group, Peter recited from a Psalm and from the prophet Hosea:

> For thou wilt not abandon my soul to Hades,
> nor let thy Holy One see corruption.
> Thou hast made known to me the ways of life;
> thou wilt make me full of gladness with thy presence.

> After two days he will revive us;
> on the third day he will raise us up,
> that we may live before him.

"I believe," Peter went on, "that Jesus studied these passages, and that he knew that he was the Messiah, and that he believed that these promises would be fulfilled in him."

Once again, Mark spoke to Peter about his own experience in finding that the tomb where Jesus had been buried was empty, and how the thought that Jesus had risen had swept over him, yet how in the days which followed other possible explanations of how the tomb could have come to be empty had come into his mind and caused him to doubt.

As if he read even the details of the thoughts in the mind of John Mark, Simon Peter said: "We who were the followers of Jesus did not remove his body. We did not even know where he was buried, because, when he was captured and condemned, we all ran away."

As he spoke of this defection of Jesus' closest followers, in which he had shared, Peter's face was sorrowful, but he was no longer torn with the uncontrollable remorse which he had previously exhibited.

"Only when the women came and told us on the morning of the first day of the week did John and I know about the tomb and that it had been found empty. Then we ran and found that it was so. Then Jesus himself appeared to us, so we know that he was raised from the dead.

"We have told many people about this," Peter pressed on to his clinching argument, "and if the enemies of Jesus wanted to prove that it is not so, and if they stole his body away, all they would have to do would be to bring forth the body, but they have never done it. And"—he added quietly—"they never will."

On another occasion when John Mark talked with Simon Peter, he expressed the other kind of puzzlement which had perplexed his mind.

"When I went to school in Cyrene," he said, "we had to study the writings of Plato. Plato wrote down the teachings he had heard from Socrates. Here is what Socrates taught. I had to draw the diagram as an exercise at school."

At this point Mark brought forth from a fold in his robe a small sheet of papyrus. On it was a compact diagram:

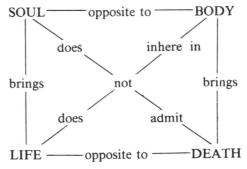

Peter looked at what Mark showed him with less than complete comprehension, partly because the subject matter was unfamiliar and partly because the language was Greek, the fine points of which he understood less well than Aramaic. John Mark explained in Aramaic.

"Socrates taught that opposites do not admit each other. The soul gives life to the body, but without the soul the body has to die. So the body is what he called mortal, and has to die, but the soul is exactly opposite, and is immortal.

"When we were studying this, we had to learn by heart one sentence from Socrates. I can still recall it. It went like this: 'When, therefore, death approaches a man, the mortal part of him may be supposed to die, but the immortal portion departs safe and uncorrupted, having withdrawn itself from death.' "

Simon Peter just shook his head in puzzlement, but John Mark pressed on. "So that is what I always believed. When a man dies it is just his body that dies, but his soul is imperishable, and will really exist in another world."

Mark paused momentarily to try to make sure that he was setting forth his thoughts logically.

"So I can believe that Jesus was a great and good man, and that when his enemies put him to death, his soul could not perish but was set free to go and dwell among what the Greeks call the immortals. But why was his tomb empty, and why did you and the others say that you saw him? I do not think you can see an immortal soul."

Peter shook his head stubbornly. "I do not know about all of that," he said, "but I know that we saw him. Thomas saw him. You heard Thomas say that he did. He touched him. No one is going to fool Thomas. He knows it was no bodiless spirit; it was Jesus."

Mark was impressed, as he had always been, with the great sincerity of Simon Peter. He thought again about the Scripture passages that Peter had quoted: "Thou wilt not . . . let thy Holy One see corruption. . . . On the third day he will raise us up."

Those Scripture passages sounded different to Mark from what he had been quoting from Socrates and Plato. What if the body were not contrary to the soul? What if a person could die and be raised up a whole person? You could include in that the idea of Socrates and of Plato about an immortal soul, but you could not reduce that to just the persistence of an invisible, intangible soul, a bodiless spirit. What if God had raised up Jesus to show that Jesus really was his Messiah, and to show even now how death would be overcome?

It was along those lines that John Mark was thinking, as again a conversation with Simon Peter came to an end.

✕

Seven weeks had gone by since the Passover when Jesus died. John Mark might not have kept such careful track of the time, but his people did because there was another feast to be observed. During the Passover observances there was a ceremony on the day after the sabbath in which a sheaf of first-ripe barley was offered to consecrate the spring barley harvest season, and seven complete weeks, or fifty days, after that there was a further festival which was therefore called the Feast of Weeks or, by those who spoke Greek, the Pentecost or fiftieth-day feast.

On that day John Mark came back from the garden at the Mount of Olives to the house of his mother at about the middle of the morning. He was accustomed to the fact that, especially on the first day of the week, there would be gathered at the house the company of men and women who joined with Peter in Scripture reading and prayer. Now, however, and at a surprisingly early hour of the day, there was a much larger crowd of people present. Something unusual had attracted them, and Mark saw at once that something different from the usual gatherings was taking place.

Simon Peter and some of the other men had come out from the upper room of the house of Mary onto the flat roof, and Peter, from that vantage point, was addressing the people who filled the spacious grounds of Mary's estate.

"We are not drunken," Peter was saying, and it was evident that some unusual disturbance had taken place. "After all"—and there was something of Peter's old fisherman humor in his voice—"it is only the third hour of the day."

A stir of appreciation for this witticism ran through the crowd.

"You know that the Scripture promises that in the end time the Spirit will be poured out upon men. It is that which has come to pass."

It was an amazing statement for Peter to make, but Mark remembered how changed and calm Peter had been after he came back down from Galilee the last time, and now he could not but observe that Peter was changed still more, and that he was now somehow speaking as if filled with power and authority. Mark remembered that Peter had told him that the group meeting at his mother's house had been praying for the Spirit to come, because that was what the Scriptures promised, and now he felt that Peter was simply reporting what had actually happened.

But Peter was continuing. He told how God had sent Jesus as his Messiah, and how lawless men had killed him. He told how God had raised him up.

All this John Mark knew about. Parts of it he had discussed earnestly with Peter. But what came in the climax of the address was new to him. Yet he recognized the sense of power and authority with which Peter was speaking, and it made a deep impression on him.

"You must believe that Jesus is the Messiah, and you must be baptized in his name. Even if you helped to kill him"—and it seemed as if Peter were including everybody, most of all himself, in the responsibility—"you will be forgiven. And," he concluded, "you will receive the gift of the Spirit."

This time John Mark did not remain aloof. When Peter's address was over, and long lines of people moved down Jerusalem's southwestern hill to the Pool of Siloam, Mark was among them. At the vast double tanks, fed by the fresh waters of the Gihon spring, Peter and the men with him stood under the marble colonnades and gave their instructions, and the men and the women who accepted what they said laid off their robes and descended into the waters. They stood there while Peter and the men with him spoke over them the name of Jesus the Messiah, and then they immersed themselves, and came up dripping, but somehow exalted.

John Mark did likewise, and the tumult of conflicting thoughts that had been in his mind for weeks was quieted. He, too, was a believer. As he walked away when it was all over, he went past Peter. Peter laid a hand momentarily on his shoulder.

5

On the Mount of Olives

After the baptisms on the Pentecost day, even the spacious house of Mary, the mother of John Mark, on the southwestern hill of Jerusalem, no longer provided sufficient room for the coming together of all of the believers. As the most nearly adequate single place, the main meetings were still held there, but, in addition, smaller groups met at the houses of other persons who were willing to make a place available.

Peter, with John Mark now often as his companion, went about among the several gatherings. Jesus had told Peter to feed his lambs, and Peter was now trying to do that. Some of the small groups were so enthusiastic that they met every day; all, at any rate, found themselves irresistibly drawn to come together on the first day of the week.

The first day of the week was the first day after the sabbath and, on the sabbath, most of the people felt themselves bound to continue to be present at the services of their people in the courts of the Temple, as they had been accustomed to doing. But on the following day they could come together freely in the new gatherings.

It was also on the first day of the week that the women had found the empty tomb, and it was on the evening of that day, and on the evening of the same day a week later, that Jesus had first appeared, risen, to the small group of his followers gathered together in the upper room at the house of Mary. So, on this day, they often hoped that Jesus might come to them again.

When even a small group was together in some home, they would ordinarily enjoy a simple meal together. When Peter was present, he would take the opportunity to recall the last supper he and the men had eaten with Jesus in the upper room at the house of Mary on the last evening before Jesus was captured and killed. The whole scene would come back to his mind so vividly that he would act out what Jesus had done on that occasion.

Peter would take up the loaf of bread that was on the table, say a short prayer of thanksgiving over it, break it, and hand it to the others, saying: "When Jesus ate with us the last time, he took bread, and blessed it, and broke it, and gave it to us, and said that it was his body. After he was killed, we realized that he meant that his body was going to be broken, the way that loaf of bread was broken. John also reminded us that he had sometimes said that he himself was the bread of life, of which if a man would eat, he would not be hungry."

In the course of the meal Peter would also pick up a cup and express thanks for the fruit of the vine, then tell all to drink, because Jesus had done likewise and had said that the cup was his blood of the covenant, poured out for many.

Under the influence of his companionship with Peter and his participation in the meetings of the believers, John Mark was taking more interest in the study of the Scriptures of his people. Whenever Peter spoke about the bread, Mark would think about how the people on their ancient Exodus from Egypt had found manna to eat in the wilderness of Sinai. When Peter spoke about the covenant blood, poured out for many, Mark would think about the covenant that God was said to have made with the people at Mount Sinai, and about the new covenant which Jeremiah had said the Lord would make with the house of Israel and the house of Judah in the coming days. He would also think about the servant of the Lord, whom Isaiah described, who poured out his soul to death and bore the sin of many.

Finally, at the close of the supper, Peter would lead the whole group in saying together a very short prayer which he had taught them. It was in Aramaic, which was the language most of them spoke most of the time. The words were *Marana tha,* and they were in the imperative of prayer, meaning "Our Lord, come!"

When John Mark asked Simon Peter privately about this prayer, it was not because he did not understand the Aramaic. This was, in fact, the world language of his people, and he had grown up in Cyrene speaking it, as well as the Greek language which was spoken by most of the populace. What John Mark sought, rather, was understanding of the prayer itself. As often, Peter referred to the Scriptures of their people.

"You know," he said, "that the prophets often spoke about the day of the Lord which is to come. They said that it will be a day of darkness and of judgment. They said that after his messenger prepares the way, the Lord will come suddenly to his temple. When we came to believe that Jesus was the Messiah, we saw that John who had baptized him must have been the messenger who was preparing the way, and when we went into the Temple with Jesus in those last days and saw him drive out the money changers, we thought that he was beginning the judgment.

"After the judgment, comes the kingdom," Peter went on. "So we thought also that we would soon sit on thrones with him in that kingdom. But it did not happen, for they killed him. But God raised him up, so we know he is the Messiah even though he died. So we know he will come, and he will establish the kingdom, and we pray for it to happen soon."

Peter had spoken with intense earnestness, and he added aloud, in all earnestness, the prayer he had been explaining, *Marana tha,* "Our Lord, come!"

"How soon do you think it will be?" asked Mark.

"I do not know," replied Peter, "but he once told us that some standing there would not taste death before they saw the kingdom come."

A sudden thought struck John Mark. "Perhaps when you saw

him again, after he died, and after God raised him, perhaps that was it. That was when he came again."

Peter pondered the suggestion. "Yes," he agreed, "that is part of it. But there is more; he will come again, and everyone will see his kingdom."

"I hope so," said John Mark quietly.

But other ideas were presented also. On one occasion, in a meeting of the larger group, two others of the men who had been with Jesus gave from their memories things which Jesus had said. One—this was Matthew speaking—said that he remembered Jesus had said that where two or three were gathered together in his name, he was there, and that he himself always thought about that saying when he joined in the supper prayer, *Marana tha.* The other—this was the John who had run ahead of Peter to the empty tomb—said that he remembered that Jesus had said, not long before the time of his death, that he would come again and receive them to himself, and John thought now that that meant that even if he himself should die, Jesus, who was risen, would come for him.

As he listened to these ideas, too, John Mark could only say again to himself, quietly, "I hope it may be so."

✕

John Mark was well aware of the fact that it was a characteristic ability of his people, no doubt developed over a long period of time, to retain a sharp remembrance of what they had seen and heard. Thus he was not surprised, even as considerable time went on, at the precise statements which Peter and some of the others still gave of things they had heard Jesus say or things they had seen him do. Of course, he noticed also, sayings and narratives of a generally similar import were often phrased differently by different reporters, and he had to think that different observers saw and heard and remembered even the same things sometimes differently.

John Mark often thought about how, as he had learned in school in Cyrene, Plato had written out the teachings of Socrates, and, as he had learned among his own people, Baruch had taken down the oracles of Jeremiah and had recorded events in the life of the prophet, such as when he had worn the yoke of Babylonian captivity and when he had been imprisoned in the miry cistern. Mark wondered why some of the men who had been with Jesus, and who were from time to time recalling and reporting, with such apparently vivid memories, things which they had heard him say or seen him do, did not write down some of it all. When Mark spoke to Peter about it, Peter only said that Jesus had told him to feed his sheep, and that was what he was trying to do.

But Peter continued to speak in the meetings of the believers, and in incidental conversations, of events in which he had participated with Jesus, and of sayings which he had heard him utter. Also, Peter was now traveling more widely in the country, and occasionally, in his absence, he would ask Mark to be present in some gathering or to perform some task. On such occasions, if there were conversation, as there almost always was, about the life and death and rising again of Jesus, John Mark would feel some confidence in speaking forth about the events at the end for, after all, by the strange combination of circumstances which he never ceased to remember with amazement, he had himself been present at some of the things that had happened.

Otherwise, however, for any contributions that he could make to discussions, John Mark drew as best he could upon his remembrance of what he had heard Simon Peter tell or, sometimes, of what he had heard said by the other men who had been with Jesus.

Finally, to aid his memory, John Mark began to make written notes for himself. Now his room began to recover some of the appearance of his corner of the house in Cyrene, when he had been in school there. He had sheets of papyrus, and pen and ink. With these he wrote down, in neat Aramaic characters, brief records of what he had heard.

Often Peter would narrate a brief happening which ended with some pointed saying of Jesus. Mark's notes came to contain many of these.

Sometimes Peter would relate a longer sequence of events, such as those of a memorable day at Capernaum. This was a sabbath day, and Jesus and Peter and some of the other men attended the synagogue service in the morning. Jesus was asked to speak, and his attitude of immediate authority, contrasting with the usual appeal to precedent by the rabbis, made a great impression. Also a demonized man challenged him, and he healed the man, which caused an even greater stir. At home, afterward, in Peter's house near the lake, Jesus also healed Peter's mother-in-law of a fever. By evening, when the enforced non-activity of the sabbath was over, many sick people were brought to the house. The next morning, however, instead of capitalizing on his success there, Jesus went out very early to a lonely place to pray, then went on to other towns, saying that he had to tell about God's kingdom in the other places too. All of this narrative, accordingly, went into Mark's written records.

Again, Peter's voice would darken with sorrow for what he had to tell. But, although his own role was one of failure, he would speak forthrightly and honestly, and withal calmly, as one long since forgiven and no longer distracted by fruitless remorse, and this atmosphere would someway make itself felt in what Mark put down. Of such sort was the narrative in which Peter told of how he stood in the courtyard of the palace of the high priest and said thrice, at a maid's challenge, that he had never known Jesus, but also heard the high priest ask Jesus if he were the Christ and heard Jesus say, "I am; and you will see the Son of man coming with the clouds of heaven."

Yet again what Peter told would attain special effectiveness because it would happen to be related on the very spot where the event had originally taken place. This was how it was, one day, when John Mark started out to accompany Simon Peter on a short journey up and over the Mount of Olives. A little way short of the top they sat down to rest under the shade of an overhang of rock, and looked back and down upon the city of Jerusalem. Directly opposite and below them was the great gleaming Temple; farther away, on the southwestern hill, was the house of Mary and, not too far away from it, the palace of the high priest; and to the northwest, outside the city wall, was the hill which the Romans used for executions, and the garden area in which was the still-empty tomb of Jesus, never yet used in any further way by its owner.

"We sat at this very place," Peter began, "James and John and Andrew and I. We had been there in the Temple, and Jesus had said that the stones of it, great as they are, will all be thrown down. I think he meant that the Zealots were driving us toward war with Rome— as they still are—and that this would mean the destruction of everything."

"But it has not happened yet," said Mark, with some hopefulness.

"No," replied Peter, "and we asked Jesus when it was going to happen, because we wanted to know too. We thought it would mean the end of the world."

It appeared as if Peter were going to take time, once again, to tell John Mark at some length about what he remembered, and Mark was prepared to listen with keen interest. The requirement of proceeding on their journey, however, led Peter to make only a brief statement, with a promise that on another occasion he would tell Mark more fully about the matter.

"Jesus said that there would be war, indeed, but that this would be only the beginning of the sufferings that would precede the end of the world. Finally, however, the Son of man will come in the clouds —that is what he told the high priest, too—and he will send out his angels and they will gather the elect from the ends of the earth."

"But is there any way to know when the time is drawing near?" Mark pressed back to the original question.

"No," said Peter soberly, "Jesus told us that no one knows the day or the hour except the Father only. So he told us always to watch."

John Mark thought that Simon Peter had finished, but Peter was still thinking, and he went on with one more statement.

"Jesus did tell us about signs that would come before the end, and there is one which I remember particularly, because I have read about it in the Scriptures too. In the book of Daniel it speaks about the coming of an Anointed One, who will also be cut off. I believe that Jesus was the Anointed One, and he was cut off when he was killed. After that the Shiqquts Shomem, the Desolating Abomination, will be set up, and only after that will it be the end. Jesus said that too."

6

The Abomination of Desolation

When Peter spoke the Hebrew words from the book of Daniel he virtually spat them out of his mouth—Shiqquts Shomem, Desolating Abomination—and Mark shuddered involuntarily as he heard them, for their very sound was ugly. Later Mark found the same passage in a Greek copy of the same book, for to him Greek was a more familiar language than Hebrew. In Greek, the words had an ugly sound too—*bdelygma eremoseos*, Abomination of Desolation—and Mark shuddered again in spite of himself.

When would it come, this unspeakable horror which had to be fulfilled before the end of the world and the final establishment of the kingdom for which all of the people hoped? Those who, like Peter and John Mark, believed that the promised Anointed One, the Messiah, had already come in the person of Jesus, and that this had been proved to be so by his being raised from the dead, could only suppose that the further unrolling of events, and the appearing of the horrible Abomination, would be soon.

It was not many years until a shudder of horror ran through the whole land, and the conviction that the setting up of the Abomination was at hand seized almost everybody. At Caesarea a ship, come directly from Rome, entered the harbor, and a bearded passenger disembarked as inconspicuously and quickly as possible, and slipped through the streets of the city to the northern quarter, where he entered the synagogue. Gathering the leaders of the synagogue, he looked at them with eyes full of tears, and spoke with trembling voice.

"Our Temple is lost," he said. "The madman has ordered a colossal statue to be set up within the inner sanctuary. It is to be dedicated to himself as the new Zeus made manifest."

Those who listened knew that the messenger was speaking of the Roman emperor Gaius Caligula, then in his third year of reign. Tiberius, his predecessor, who had ruled the world in the days when Jesus was doing his work, had perished under unusual circumstances, and this man, son of Germanicus and grandson of Drusus, brother of Tiberius, was not free of suspicion, indeed, was plainly said by some to have been the murderer. Nevertheless, the empire generally accepted him as its new master without complaint. Both his father and grandfather had been famous generals, and stories were told of his own exploits in the army camps where, even as a child, he wore the half-boot of the soldiers, the *caliga* from which he got the nickname Caligula, "Little Boots," which stayed with him all his life. Also, at the outset of his reign, he bestowed unusual benefactions upon the people of Rome, and gained their appreciation.

Even in Jerusalem, at first, the people looked hopefully toward the new era of his reign, and sacrifices were offered in the Temple on his behalf. Also Prince Agrippa, grandson of Herod the Great, was living in Rome and was treated favorably by Gaius. In fact the two men were friends—if the honorable word friendship could ever be properly applied to the changeable relationship of Gaius to anybody. The friendship, if it is to be so called, may have begun on no more solid ground than that both Agrippa and Gaius relished elaborate banquets, to which they invited one another. But it was considerably advanced when the two men were riding in a chariot together one day and the name of Tiberius, then still on the throne, was mentioned.

Agrippa said, "I hope that the day will soon arrive when this old man will pass off the scene and appoint you ruler of the world."

All would have been well except that the driver of the chariot, a freedman of Agrippa, heard the words too and, upon a later occasion, purchased his own deliverance from punishment for stealing by saying that he had a secret message for Tiberius, and conveying the incautious remark to him.

Tiberius then had Agrippa put in prison and laden with a heavy iron chain. But as soon as Gaius was on the throne, which Agrippa had flatteringly wished for him, the new emperor not only brought his friend forth but also, in place of his iron chain, gave him a golden one of equal weight, and along therewith bestowed upon him certain territories in the northeastern part of his homeland for a small kingdom.

While the beginning of the reign of Gaius Caligula seemed to augur well, then, for the people of Rome and also for the people of Israel, at least to the extent that a prince of their land was in the imperial favor, it was not long until the nature of a creature of monstrous cruelty and vice began to show itself. Disguised in a wig and a long robe, Gaius reveled at night in gluttony and adultery; he lived in habitual incest with all his sisters; at his banquets, no guest was safe from seeing his own wife suddenly dragged away by Gaius to his own private quarters. The persons he caused to be killed, on all manner of charges, both genuine and spurious, were innumerable; the refinements of torture with which their deaths were accomplished were such as only a fiend could devise.

Because his power was full and absolute, any pretense of the sharing of authority having been swept away early in his reign, anyone who withstood Gaius in any way did so at the greatest peril. The authority he exercised was in fact, he claimed, not only worldly but divine. Julius Caesar and Augustus had, of course, been declared divine after their deaths, and Augustus, having most plainly saved the world from chaos, had even been looked upon from the provinces with worshipful adoration during his lifetime. With Tiberius, ever possessed by a deep melancholy, such thoughts had had no place. But Gaius, now, said flatly that he was a god, indeed nothing less than the very highest god, Zeus, finally seen in bodily form in himself.

The physical appearance of Gaius, of course, did little to help such a claim along. He was actually sound neither of body nor of mind. He was very tall and very pale. His body was huge, but his neck and legs were very thin. His eyes and temples were sunken, his forehead broad and grim, his face forbidding and ugly, and his hair thin and entirely gone on the top of his head, although his body was hairy. He was tormented with sleeplessness, troubled with fainting fits, and actually very easily frightened by even commonplace occurrences.

To hide this unprepossessing self and less inadequately simulate the god he claimed to be, Gaius wore robes covered with precious stones, exhibited himself with a golden beard, put on his head a radiate sun crown, and held in his hand a thunderbolt, a trident, or a caduceus, which were emblems of the gods.

It was also obvious that a god, such as he, should have images of himself set up in many places. Since a sculptured likeness rendered with any fidelity to his own physique would have been only ludicrous, he had the most beautiful statues of the gods brought from Greece— among them nothing less than the Zeus of Olympia, the magnificent work, in ivory and gold, of Phidias—took the heads off these statues, and put his own in their place. Other statues were made afresh, sometimes of solid gold, but in these care was exercised to modify the less pleasing features of the man they represented, and to provide an impression of dignity and power.

For these images there also had to be temples, so the statues were either installed in existing shrines, or new sanctuaries were built. In one special temple dedicated exclusively to his godhead, the solid gold life-sized statue of Gaius was dressed every day in clothing such as the emperor wore, and daily sacrifices of flamingoes, peacocks, and the like were offered.

There were many people in Rome and even throughout the empire who were ready, for obvious reasons, to go along with the pretensions of Gaius to divinity. In Rome some of the richest citizens bid high for the honor of serving as priests in his cult. From Syria, his governor, Lucius Vitellius, came back at the end of his term of office and adored the emperor by flinging himself on the ground before him —nor would he ever appear before him except with head veiled as if in the presence of glory.

It was, however, in the very region from which Lucius Vitellius had just returned that the greatest resistance could be expected to the divine claims which Gaius was so openly making. In Syria itself such pretensions were, of course, not new. Two hundred years before, King Antiochus had arrogated to himself the title Epiphanes, which meant the "manifest" god, and the people generally had accepted it, although some irreverent ones said it might better have been *epimanes,* "raving mad."

But, administratively, Syria oversaw the affairs of the land of Israel to the south, although the emperor was also represented there directly by his own procurator, and in Israel there was no easy tolerance for the divine claims of palpably human men. This Antiochus Epiphanes had learned to his sorrow. His own statue as Zeus-Antiochus, put up in the Temple in Jerusalem, was assailed in the Scriptures of the people as the "desolating abomination," his armies were driven from a score of battlefields, and his holdings in the land of Israel were lost.

Now Gaius Caligula was also thinking about the land of the Jews. If he could have been called a student of anything it was only oratory, and certainly not history or literature, nor was he inclined to learn any lessons from what had happened in the past or been written in books. He did, however, know about Antiochus Epiphanes, and he also knew that the innermost sanctuary of the Temple in Jerusalem was said to have remained empty ever since the expulsion of what Antiochus had placed there, even as it had always been devoid of any image before that time.

It angered Gaius to think of a single place within his wide empire where his own divine glory was not obviously radiating. He pondered a plan.

×

At about the same time that the ship docked at Caesarea from which the bearded man went to the synagogue to say "Our Temple is lost," another ship from Rome came into the harbor farther north at Ptolemaïs. From this ship a messenger also disembarked, and proceeded on his way. He, too, went with circumspection, avoiding careless contacts and unnecessary conversation. Such circumspection he might have deemed less important if he had known that the contents of the sealed communication which he carried from the emperor had already leaked out through some unknown channel at court, become known to a few in the Jewish community at Rome, and been communicated only shortly before in the synagogue at Caesarea. This messenger was an imperial courier with a letter from Gaius Caligula, and he went over the mountains to Antioch to deliver the missive to Petronius, who was then occupying the position of governor of Syria, held formerly by the sycophantic Lucius Vitellius.

The letter from Gaius, which Petronius unrolled and read in the privacy of his own chamber, commanded that the governor should see to the making, by the best artists, of a colossal statue, gold covered, of the emperor, and the placing of the same in the sanctuary of the Temple in Jerusalem. On the trip into the land of Israel, to install and dedicate the statue, Petronius should take two of the four legions under his command, not to add dignity to the dedication but to be able to destroy anyone who tried to prevent it—as Gaius tacitly acknowledged some might well try to do.

Although he was appointed by the same emperor as his predecessor and equally obligated to obedience, Petronius was not of the same obsequious, fawning sort as Lucius Vitellius. He was, in general, disposed to take a friendly attitude toward the people under his rule and, with respect to the Jews, he had taken some trouble to make inquiry into their customs and to gain instruction in their teachings. He now decided to call the Jewish leaders together, to try to make the emperor's demand seem reasonable, and hoped to obtain from these influential men acquiescence in what he would have to do.

The meeting with the Jewish leaders was at Ptolemaïs, where the imperial courier had first come ashore to bring the command of Gaius Caligula. It was not, however, only a coterie of elite leaders of the Jews who presented themselves before Petronius in this place, but masses of the people, men, women, and children, running into the tens of thousands of persons. Ever since the message had come to the synagogue at Caesarea of what was afoot, the ominous tidings had been circulating everywhere among the people and arousing the gravest of apprehensions. When Petronius called the leaders to consultation, there could be no doubt that the time had come when the governor would make some kind of official proclamation of the intended action, and thus, by spontaneous action, people streamed to the place from all over the land.

Petronius set forth the imperial command, explained his own duty to carry it out, and made what he hoped would sound like only a casual reference to the two legions of soldiers who would accompany him when he came to install and dedicate the image.

Then the Jewish leaders, standing before him, began to tear their garments, pluck hair from their beards and heads, and solemnly protest that the action would constitute a blasphemy in which they could in no wise concur. The multitudes of the people also set up a great lamentation, casting dust upon themselves, weeping copiously, and professing it better that the Romans should kill them all—men, women, and children alike—than that the Temple should be defiled as was proposed.

These protestations, which were conducted both at Ptolemaïs and also at Tiberias, whither Petronius went next, were so vehement and so prolonged that the governor was appalled and his naturally kindly nature deeply touched. Furthermore, the magnitude of the crowds and the duration of the demonstrations meant that vast numbers of people were absent from their homes and their lands for a long time, and the midwinter planting of grain, for which the time was already much overdue, was being neglected. For food and for taxes, this could have dire consequences.

Petronius was, of course, in a strait between obedience to the emperor, to whom he was obligated, on the one hand, and his feelings for the people, on the other hand, as well as his apprehension of the turmoil in which the land would be enveloped when the fateful image was brought there.

There was, however, one aspect of the matter of the image which provided a slight easement of the difficulty in which Petronius was placed. In this case Gaius Caligula had not sent an image that was already made to be put up in the Temple, but had instructed Petronius to see to the making of such an image, and Petronius had commissioned artists at Sidon for the task. But a statue of colossal size, covered with gold, and executed with the care appropriate to an image of the emperor himself, not to say of the great Zeus, would take time to prepare.

It occurred to Petronius, therefore, that he would write to the artists and urge them to be in no haste, but to take as much time as necessary to bring their work to the highest standard of excellence, remembering that perfunctory effort generally brought short lived results, and that to execute a great matter with pains and knowledge always requires a long time. Also in due time he would write to Gaius Caligula, report that he had made the initial announcement of the project to the Jewish leaders and people, but that the urgencies of the late planting season and then of the harvest season, which would inevitably follow, would make it inopportune to consummate the endeavor for some time yet.

To the people Petronius did not dare to disclose the full extent of the delaying tactics that he had in mind, but he did manage at last to persuade them to return for the time being to their fields, where their work was so overdue, and thus he extricated himself from the immediate pressures by which they had surrounded him.

✕

Wailing did not cease in the land. Students of the Scriptures turned again and again to the book of Daniel, and read of the Desolating Abomination. Surely this ultimate horror was now at hand. Some of them read on in the book of Daniel to what the seer also said about the end, which would only come after the Desolating Abomination was set up and was also cast down. In that longer view they found some hope.

The conviction that the Abomination of Desolation was at hand was shared fully by Peter and John Mark and the others associated with them, and was held all the more strongly because they knew that Jesus himself had spoken of the climactic sacrilege which was to come. The hope for some triumphant consummation of all things in the end time beyond the Abomination, which was the more or less vague Messianic expectation of many of the people, was also held with the greater strength by these men because of their belief that Jesus was the Messiah who had already come and, being risen from the dead, would surely, after the worst had happened, come again.

If there was hope in the midst of terror, this was it. Jesus had said that the Abomination of Desolation, of which Scripture spoke, would be set up; he also said to wait and watch for the coming of the Son of man. It was written on the sheets of papyrus on which John Mark had put down the many things that he had heard from Simon Peter.

It came to John Mark that he must bring together all that he had collected, and anything else that he could gather from any of the others besides Peter, and write it out for all to read. It was the only good news there was in the grim time, the only light in the darkness. Jesus was the Messiah, he had spoken of woe to come, he had been killed himself, but he was not dead; he was alive, and he would come again and everything would be made bright and new and good.

So it was that in that agonizing springtime, which was at the beginning of the fourth year of Gaius Caligula—the "Little Boots" who had attained the proportions of a demon—the stubby, strong fingers of John Mark clutched his pen, and he wrote column after column of Aramaic record.

When at last he was finished, and a whole roll of papyrus was filled, Mark looked back at one passage he had written with special interest.

> But when you see the abomination of desolation set up where it ought not to be (let the reader understand) . . .

That was how Jesus had said it, according to what Simon Peter had told him. As Mark understood it, Jesus had meant that whoever read in the Scriptures and found the reference by Daniel to this thing of terrible sacrilege should understand that Daniel was really referring to something that was yet going to come to pass. But now it gave Mark a sense of quiet satisfaction to think that the reader would also be reading in the record he himself had written.

7

Agrippa and Caligula

The usual ceremonies to mark the beginning of a new year of reign went off smoothly for Gaius Caligula at Rome. The senate obediently voted him again for the fourth time the annual rank of consul and the dignity of the tribunician authority. There was no reason to think that his own officialdom anywhere in the world would be less than instant in acquiescence to his every wish.

But the first frustration was already at hand in a regnal year which itself would never be completed. The letter from his governor in Syria was awaited every day, and never came. This was the letter which should surely have been in hand before this, and which should surely report that his great golden statue was now standing in the Temple in Jerusalem and being worshiped by thousands—even if other tens of thousands who resisted the project had been slaughtered by the legions.

When at last the letter did come, it threw the god-king of the world into a towering rage. Petronius had the audacity to say that the project was not only as yet incomplete, but was even moving slowly. The artists were giving great care to all delicate details, that the statue might not fall short of the magnificence which it should represent. That, thought Gaius, could be true and even necessary, considering that the subject matter was indeed splendid. But the people had raised objections, and Petronius had had to pacify them temporarily to get them back to their agricultural work, lest famine ensue and taxes be uncollectible. And that, thought Gaius, was intolerable. When should a Roman governor ever take account of the objections of the populace to anything?

The marks of this rage were still evident in the bloodshot eyes and frowning forehead of Gaius when his friend Agrippa came in to pay to him his usual respects. Since Gaius seemed to look at him most searchingly, Agrippa wondered if he had done something to offend the emperor. Of the whole matter of the statue for the Jerusalem Temple he had not yet heard anything. Soon Gaius made known the cause of his agitation.

"Your excellent people," Gaius said to Agrippa, "who alone of all men do not acknowledge Gaius as a god, appear by their recalcitrance determined to bring upon themselves a great disaster."

"What is that, my lord?" asked Agrippa, himself now gravely alarmed, for in spite of his usual appearance of interest only in high living, he was actually quite deeply attached to his people and their customs, and was also hopeful that he himself, grandson of the great Herod, would eventually play a role in their rule which would go far beyond the small kingdom in the northeast which, through his friendship with Gaius, he already possessed.

"I have ordered a statue of Zeus," replied Gaius—refraining for the moment from mentioning that Zeus was to appear in the likeness of Gaius himself—"set up in the Temple in Jerusalem, and your people have come forth in great numbers to obstruct the enterprise."

Gaius was about to add further details when Agrippa showed every evidence of the deepest physical distress. He turned every kind of color in a moment, from the redness of blood to the paleness of death. He began to tremble and shudder convulsively, and was on the point of falling to the floor, when his attendants caught him and, being ordered by Gaius to take him home, carried him out on a stretcher.

For that day and most of the next, Agrippa lay in a coma. After he finally came to himself and took nourishment, his first request was for writing materials. He took a tablet and began to compose a letter to the emperor.

"My opportunity, my master," he wrote, "of interceding with you face to face has been lost through fear and reverence, fear which overwhelmed me in the presence of the menace, reverence by which I was struck dumb in the presence of your sublime greatness. But in my own handwriting I will declare to you the petition which, instead of the suppliant's olive branch, I beg leave to present."

After this ingratiating beginning, Agrippa went on to rehearse salient and favorable points in the history of the relationships of Rome and his own people.

"Did not Augustus, your great-grandfather, upon hearing by report the story of the Temple, and that it had in it no work of man's hands, no visible effigy of an invisible being, marvel and pay it honor? Did he not order that the daily whole burnt offerings to the Most High God be continued and even charged to his own purse?

"Did not your maternal grandfather, Marcus Agrippa, being in Judea when Herod my grandfather was king of the country, come up from the coast to the capital, visit the Temple, and make many dedicatory gifts to it?

"Did not your other grandfather, Tiberius Caesar, also respect the laws and customs of our people? Did he not rebuke his governor, Pilate, when the latter put up in Herod's palace in the holy city some shields coated with gold? Although the shields were put up in his honor and inscribed with his name, Tiberius commanded that they be taken down and taken away to Caesarea on the coast.

"How much more now would it be in contradiction to the laws and customs to which our people are bound if a human likeness were to be put up within the sanctuary? From the days of our ancestors, it has been deemed to be the gravest offense against our religion to paint or mold any likeness of the invisible deity. If such were to be erected in our Temple I verily believe that our whole nation would bring itself to death rather than to submit. I believe the men would slaughter their whole families, women and children alike, and finally immolate themselves upon the corpses of their kin."

After much more of the same sort, Agrippa came to his request. For himself he asked nothing. Gaius had already granted him a kingdom, the greatest gift of fortune that a man can possess. Even this he would willingly surrender, if only the ancestral institutions of his people be not disturbed. His only request was that Gaius abandon all further thought of erecting the statue in Jerusalem.

"For otherwise," Agrippa argued in conclusion, "I will seem to be a traitor to my people, or I will appear to be no longer considered your friend. There is no other alternative, and what greater ill could befall me than these? If I keep my place among your companions, I shall be accused of treachery to my own nation. If you are indeed hostile to me, then do not imprison me as Tiberius did; rather bid me take myself out of the way forthwith. For of what value would life itself be to me, whose one hope of salvation lies in your goodwill?"

Thus Agrippa wrote, and as Gaius read the lengthy letter he was himself to some extent touched and moved. Agrippa had asked nothing for himself. Agrippa was his friend. The Jews might prove troublesome beyond the worth of the whole matter. They might even alienate Petronius, whom they had already evidently to some extent intimidated.

Under the temporary pressure of these emotions and thoughts, Gaius dispatched a communication to Petronius.

"If you have already set up my statue, let it stand," Gaius wrote, "but if not, do not trouble yourself further but dismiss the legions and proceed with the other matters for which I originally sent you out. For I no longer require the erection of the statue, showing favor to Agrippa in this, a man whom I hold in too high esteem to gainsay his request and his bidding."

Perhaps, thought Gaius, the statue was already in its place. If so, he was under no obligation to take it down. Agrippa had only asked him to give up all *further* thought of erecting the statue. That sacrifice, in deference to the request of his friend, he was now making.

The sophistry of his instruction was an index of the undependableness and changeableness of the mind of Gaius. By the time an answer came back from Petronius that the statue was not in place, Gaius was in a mood to take up his project again and to requite Petronius for his dilatoriness in the first place.

The unfinished statue could remain in Sidon, unfinished, to allay suspicion. Another statue, of equal splendor, could be made in Rome, where its intended destination would be kept secret. The latter he would then take with him, on a projected coastwise journey to Egypt, and would himself, with appropriate forces alongside, take up to Jerusalem and see into place.

As for Petronius, whose prompt action at the beginning might have forestalled all the difficulties, and whose outright complicity with the Jews Gaius was now beginning to suspect, he was dispatched a final directive.

"Since you have held the gifts that the Jews have bestowed upon you in higher regard than my orders, and have presumed to minister in everything to their pleasure in violation of my orders, I bid you act as your own judge and consider what course it is your duty to take, since you have brought my displeasure upon yourself. For I assure you that you shall be cited as an example by all men now and hereafter, to point the moral that an emperor's commands are never to be flouted."

The instruction to Petronius to commit suicide went out on a ship which was weather-bound by winter seas for three months. Within that time the conspirators, whose activity such a reign as that of Gaius inevitably produces, did their work. Having been on the throne three years and ten months, Gaius Caligula was assassinated.

The ship which carried news of the assassination to Syria had a fortunate passage, and Petronius received this news twenty-seven days before he received the command for his self-immolation, and thus was set free before he knew he was condemned. As for two colossal statues of Zeus in the guise of Gaius, they could remain unfinished, one in Sidon and one in Rome.

8

The Builders of the Wall

The threat of a desolating sacrilege was lifted from over
the heads of the Jewish nation, but a new shadow fell swiftly over that
growing group among them who believed that their Messiah had
already come, and would, after tribulations, come again.

Once again in Rome, as one emperor died and another came to
the throne, the Jewish prince Agrippa was in a position to encourage
the assumption of power by the new ruler, and to benefit by the same.
The new ruler was Claudius and, in youth, Claudius and Agrippa had
been in school together. When Gaius died, there was the possibility
of strife between the senate and the army, but Agrippa managed to
see the right people and speak the right words to obtain near
unanimity in support of Claudius. With Claudius on the throne,
Agrippa received from him, in gratitude, in addition to the small
kingdom he already possessed, the whole kingdom which had once
belonged to his grandfather. Thus, like Herod the Great, his grandson
now ruled all the land of Israel, and back of him were the authority
and the favor of Rome.

Having arrived in Jerusalem, which was now his own capital,
Agrippa offered sacrifices of thanksgiving, for although brought up in
Rome and in earlier life addicted to the pleasures of the world capital,
he was now resolved to manifest a strong devotion to the traditions

of his people, and to be scrupulous in the observance of all the prescribed rites and ceremonies. He also brought to the Temple, and hung up over the freewill-offering chests, the golden chain which had been presented to him by Gaius Caligula, equal in weight to the one of iron with which his royal hands had once been bound. Thus he symbolized, and gave thanks to the one God of heaven for, the signal deliverance by which his once-fallen fortunes had risen now to such resplendent eminence.

The image of great piety that Agrippa projected had its practical purposes. It would, he was sure, commend him to the Pharisees, and they, he knew, being noted for their strict accuracy in the interpretation of the law and their rigorous adherence to it, were the most influential leaders of the people. In his estimate of the situation, Agrippa was entirely correct, and the relations which developed between him and the Pharisees were mutually beneficial. Agrippa's royal favor allowed the Pharisees to extend their influence and enhance their power; he, in turn, was greatly strengthened in his position by their support.

With their strict interpretations, it was commonly said that the Pharisees were putting up a "fence around the law," and a common epithet for them was "builders of the wall." Depending upon the point of view, such words could be complimentary, meaning that the Pharisees were protecting the law, or critical, meaning that they were excluding anything but their own ideas.

Agrippa also aspired to be the builder of a wall. On the north side of Jerusalem, so many houses had been built that the city now extended far outside its northernmost wall of defense. The king, therefore, laid out the line of a new wall which would enclose the new areas, and began to build. This new wall extended far around outside the hill where the Romans had at one time carried out their executions and outside the garden area where the tomb of Joseph of Arimathea still lay empty.

There were problems, however, about both the wall of Agrippa and the wall of the Pharisees. Agrippa's wall was only partially built when it came to the attention of Claudius at Rome. The latter was still disposed to be friendly to Agrippa and to his people, but he was also a practical administrator of his large empire, and he did not intend to overlook some activity which might, in the future, make it more readily possible for a subject people to resist his authority. Accordingly he instructed Agrippa to desist from the building of the new wall, and it remained, for the time being, unfinished and at only a fraction of the height which it was intended to reach.

As for the wall of the Pharisees around the law, the work of Jesus had long since seemed to them like an outright attack on the system which they were endeavoring to defend. Jesus had certainly conducted himself in a way that did not always agree with the requirements and the implications of the law. He had broken the rule of sabbath rest by healing sick people on the sabbath whose cases could as well have waited for a later day, and he had allowed his followers to do work on the same day. He had not been careful about the ablutions that the law required, and he had not practiced the fasts by which anyone who professed any kind of leadership in the religious realm should have additionally commended himself. He had spoken in a way that sounded as if he thought his own pronouncement were superior to what Moses had said. He had invaded the Temple, he had spoken of its destruction, and he had uttered blasphemy in associating himself with God.

All of that, of course, had long since been taken care of. Jesus had been executed. But the execution of the leader did not end the movement. The followers of Jesus had continued to meet, they had gained new adherents, and they were now, for all practical purposes, constituting a new sect.

The sect was, in the simple fact of its existence, obnoxious, for there were already too many sects among the people. It was, however, difficult to deal with, both theologically and politically.

The reason that it was somewhat difficult theologically for the Pharisees to deal with the sect of the followers of Jesus was that, superficially considered, they both appeared to support the same doctrines. They both believed in the Messiah. The Pharisees often read from psalms, which were attributed to Solomon but which actually some of their own members had composed only about a hundred years before, in which there was an earnest prayer for the coming of the Anointed One.

> Behold, O Lord, and raise up unto them their king, the son of David,
>> At the time in which thou seest, O God, that he may reign over Israel, thy servant.
> And gird him with strength, that he may shatter unrighteous rulers,
>> And that he may purge Jerusalem from nations that trample her down to destruction.
> And he shall gather together a holy people, whom he shall lead in righteousness,
>> And he shall judge the tribes of the people that have been sanctified by the Lord his God.
> And there shall be no unrighteousness in his days in their midst,
>> For all shall be holy and their king the Anointed of the Lord.

But the problem consisted in the fact that the followers of Jesus said that he was the Anointed of the Lord, and the Pharisees had long since decided that he had been a danger to all that they believed in, so they could not at all consent to believing that he was after all the Messiah for whom they were looking.

Theologically, also, both the Pharisees and the sect of the followers of Jesus believed in the resurrection. If one had been speaking about the priestly party of the Sadducees, this would not have been true. The Sadducees believed at the most in a shadowy after-existence in a dark underworld place called Sheol, and many of them went so far as to say flatly that souls simply perish together with bodies. But the Pharisees taught that every soul is imperishable, and they looked forward to a resurrection and a future world. The souls of the wicked would indeed suffer eternal punishment, but the souls of the righteous would pass into another body and enjoy a good reward. This was, of course, only going to take place in the last times, and that was a long, long while off.

Since Jesus himself had defended the idea of the resurrection over against the skepticism of the Sadducees, the Pharisees might have been expected to welcome his teaching in this respect, and to feel a kinship with his followers, at least in regard to this doctrine. The problem was, however, that the followers of Jesus would not stop saying that Jesus was raised from the dead already, and that they had seen him and talked with him. Such a thing as that, however, obviously could not take place until the end of time, so it certainly could not have taken place already. Also the followers of Jesus kept pointing to his empty tomb, and the Pharisees could not deny that it was empty and that no one had ever been able to find the body of Jesus anywhere else, so they were considerably embarrassed in the argument at this point.

Politically, the difficulty under which the Pharisees had labored for a long time in taking decisive action against any groups of which they disapproved consisted in the fact that as a group they themselves, although widely influential among the masses of the people, were not particularly in favor with the ruling powers. Once upon a time, indeed, they had enjoyed a better position. When Queen Alexandra was ruling, more than a hundred years before, they were in high favor. At that time the queen's brother, Simon ben Shatah, was their own famous lawyer, and he practically controlled the government. Under those circumstances it was easy for the Pharisees to wipe out opposition and to exterminate dangerous movements. In fact, Simon ben Shatah was so powerful and, it might be added, so violent that, whereas previous Pharisaic custom had allowed but a single execution on a given day, he killed no less than eighty witches on a single day.

After that, however, the Pharisees lost their favored position, as far as political relationships were concerned, and it was necessary for them to exercise their influence and attempt to gain their ends in more indirect ways. So when they undertook to get Jesus put out of the way, they had to cooperate with the Sadducees, whom they so often opposed, and all of them together had to devise a very clever approach to the Roman procurator to get this official to do what they wanted.

But now, once again, the Pharisees were in a favorable political situation. Claudius in Rome was well disposed to Jews everywhere. And Agrippa, their own king, was ruling in Jerusalem and was zealous for all the customs of the law, and he and the Pharisees worked hand in hand on most matters.

9

Agrippa and Simon the Pious

It was now in the second year of Claudius and in the second year in which Agrippa was ruling over the whole territory of his grandfather. Along with possession of all the lands of Herod the Great, Agrippa also enjoyed the use of his grandfather's sumptuous palaces and strong fortresses. Some of the buildings, in fact, combined the chief features of palace and fortress in one structure. This was true of the palace on the western hill in Jerusalem, and also of the fortress at the northwestern corner of the Temple area.

In the palace on the western hill were immense banqueting halls, and bedchambers for a hundred guests. The interior fittings were varied and splendid. Incrustations of rare stones were on the walls, and the beams overhead were of carved cedarwood. All around were circular cloisters, with columns of marble. Open courts of green grass and groves of various kinds of trees were intersected by long walks, which were bordered by deep canals. In numerous pools rose statuary of bronze, out of which water was constantly discharged, and many tame pigeons fluttered in the air. But with all the sumptuousness of this palace, it was at the same time a fortress, being surrounded on the vulnerable sides to the north and west by the high walls of the city, and protected on the north by three lofty and massive towers. Although it belonged now to his grandson, Agrippa, the palace was still commonly called Herod's palace, for it was Herod the Great who had built it and fitted it out in all its magnificence.

In reverse fashion, the building at the northwest corner of the Temple area made first of all the impression of a powerful fortress, which it was, and then was seen, within, to be also a sumptuous palace. This building stood on a foundation of natural rock, which was scarped to make unclimbable cliffs on the sides, and it rose above the rock with sheer walls and high towers. On the east and the west there were great gateways which were closed with huge wooden doors. On the south side there was an iron gate and seven steps which led down to the level of the outer court of the Temple, thus providing direct connection with the area which it was a primary purpose of the fortress to dominate and to control. Within the fortress were soldiers' barracks and a vast paved courtyard, the great stone blocks of which were already deeply rutted by the wheels of chariots. But in the upper levels of the fortress were, again, splendid apartments. The name of the massive pile was Antonia, for when Herod the Great rebuilt it, his best friend was Mark Antony, and he bestowed upon him the compliment of giving his name to the most powerful structure in Jerusalem.

Herod's palace was the place where, now, the plot was made, and the Antonia the place where the execution and the imprisonment were carried out.

Simon the Pious walked slowly up the western hill toward the palace of Herod, where he was to be the dinner guest of King Agrippa. The steepness of the hill dictated the slowness of his pace, but he would have gone with what he considered unhurried dignity in any case, for it would not be seemly for a leading Pharisaic lawyer to do otherwise. As he went, the tassels at the lower corners of his long robe swept the street with a sort of imperious movement. His face was grave, which also he would have considered proper under any circumstances; but now there was a further reason for it, for he was much concerned over the unexpected continuance and even surprising spread of the sect of the followers of Jesus, a sect the very existence of which constituted, he believed, a seriously divisive influence among his people.

As Simon the Pious was admitted to the palace grounds, the tame pigeons flapped lazily out of his way. He strode toward one of the fountains, picked up a pottery bowl which was placed there for the purpose, filled it with water, and poured it carefully over one hand, making sure that the water covered the hand as far as the wrist. This he did, too, for the other hand, then repeated the entire ceremony once again, so that both hands had received ablution with a first water and a second water. Then he was ready to be ushered into the banquet hall.

"Simon he-Hasid," his name was called out in stentorian tones as he was brought in, and there was a stir of approval among the other guests already assembled, as they recognized the presence of the prominent leader of the Pharisees. His place was that of honor, beside Agrippa himself, and he greeted the king with proper ceremony but without any touch of subservience. His gaze also swept over the heavily laden tables of the banquet, and a slight smile of approval crossed his face as he observed that the only bread provided was unleavened, which was in strict accord with the regulations for the seven days following the Passover.

In the course of the evening Simon the Pious steered the conversation with Agrippa adroitly. He made known the approval which was general among the Pharisees for the reign of a king so obviously devoted to strict observance of the customs of the people. He alluded to the dangers which were latent in the tendencies, observable in several directions, toward the proliferation of sectarian movements. One of these in particular, he confessed, caused him great anxiety. This was the movement of the followers of Jesus. It was true these people said Jesus had told them that he did not intend to destroy the law but to fulfill it; nevertheless, they had learned from him a certain laxity about the prescribed rules. In addition, they were getting many adherents from among people who had come back from living in pagan lands, such as Cyprus and Cyrene, Greek-speaking Jews, who were all too open to the customs of the Hellenistic world.

"Oh, yes," said Agrippa. "I remember about Jesus. In Rome I saw the report which Pontius Pilate sent to Tiberius about him. He said that the priests said Jesus wanted to be a king, so he had to execute him, although he doubted if he were really very dangerous."

"Do you know why Pontius Pilate acted the way he did?" Simon the Pious narrowed his eyes, and looked directly at Agrippa. He was about to recall several historical happenings which constituted a series in which he was determined the king would play the next decisive role.

To introduce the series, Simon the Pious asked another question. "Do you remember Sejanus?"

Agrippa remembered him all too well. "Ah, yes," he replied, "Lucius Aelius Sejanus—he was prefect in Rome under Tiberius, and he wrapped the emperor around his little finger. He was zealous to destroy our nation and, if he had lived, he might have succeeded."

"That is right," nodded Simon the Pious. "And you know that was when Pontius Pilate came out to govern us. Pilate hated us, too, and with Sejanus back of him in Rome, he did anything with us he wanted to. He robbed the Temple, desecrated this holy city, and slaughtered our people. He was inflexible, merciless, and obstinate. In those days, if we had asked him to do anything for us, he would have done exactly the opposite, just to spite us.

"But do you remember what happened to Sejanus?"

"I certainly do," said Agrippa. "It made a very great impression upon us in Rome. For a long time Tiberius had persisted in calling Sejanus his friend and co-worker, but it was common knowledge that Sejanus wanted to be emperor himself. Finally Tiberius learned that the lingering illness and death of his only son, Drusus, years before, had been from slow poison administered by Sejanus, and that Sejanus was now plotting to kill him and Gaius both. So—it was in the fall, at the beginning of his eighteenth year—Tiberius had Sejanus struck down."

Agrippa and Simon the Pious were now almost vying with each

other in recalling details of past happenings which had vitally affected the fortunes of their people, and this was exactly what Simon wanted. He himself went on: "The fall of Sejanus was certainly welcomed here. With his baleful influence out of the way, we dared to hope that Tiberius would treat us in a kindlier way, and that is what came to pass."

Agrippa nodded affirmatively. "I know that after Sejanus was out of the way, Tiberius sent out a letter to his procurators in every place and told them to speak comfortably to the members of our nation in the different cities, and to assure them that penal measures applied only to the guilty. He also told the procurators to disturb none of our established customs, but even to regard them as a trust committed to their care, because our people are naturally peaceable, and our institutions are an influence promoting orderly conduct."

"Yes," Simon the Pious agreed, "we noticed a great difference in the behavior of Pontius Pilate after that. He no longer tried to affront our leaders at every turn, but actually seemed to be considerate of them and their opinions. He no longer slaughtered our people the way he had done before, either. In the old days he once fell upon some Galileans who made a small disturbance in the Temple so swiftly that their blood ran down with the blood of the sacrifices they had just offered. Later, after Sejanus was no longer backing him up and urging him on, he kept our famous Barabbas, who had committed murder in an insurrection, in prison for a long time, as if he could not decide what to do with him.

"That was when our priests decided that they could get Pilate to get rid of Jesus. It must have been a year and a half after the fall of Sejanus, and they had been watching Pilate's behavior carefully. They had been watching Jesus, too, and it looked as if his movement were going to cause more and more trouble if it were not stopped. It was Passover time; it was time to cleanse the land of the leaven of ferment." As he spoke, Simon the Pious looked again at the unleavened bread on the king's table, and let Agrippa see his gentle smile of approval.

"So they arrested Jesus," Simon went on with his narrative, "and they heard words of blasphemy from his own lips, and they took him to Pilate, because he was the only one who could carry out a sentence of death. And Pilate—the new and different Pilate, as one might say —responded in the way our priests thought he would. He was no longer eager to shed blood and he made the trial quite long, but he was also no longer going to offend our leaders if he could help it, and when they showed him that Jesus wanted to be a king, he knew that he had to pronounce him guilty of crime against Rome, and have him killed. That agrees with, and explains, Pilate's report, which you saw, does it not?"

"Yes," said Agrippa, and supposed that Simon the Pious had finished his excursion into some history that was of interest to both of them. But Agrippa's dinner extended through many courses and, after a time, Simon the Pious managed to introduce the subject of the followers of Jesus again.

"Unleavened bread is good for the soul," said Simon the Pious, as he reached for another piece of the bread on the king's table. Then he went on, reflectively: "But a little leaven works its way into a vast lump of dough until, if one is not careful, the whole is leavened. As we were saying, Pilate put Jesus to death because our priests knew that this was for the good of our nation, but the followers of Jesus have not ceased to work and to cause trouble."

"Have you not been able to get anybody to do anything about it?" asked Agrippa.

"For a time we were able to do something about it ourselves," replied Simon the Pious, as he seized the opportunity to carry forward the narrative he was trying to present to the king.

"I am sure you knew Lucius Vitellius in Rome?" he went on.

"You mean the man whom Tiberius sent out to be governor of Syria and to try to hold off the Parthians?" responded Agrippa. "Yes, of course. He was notorious in the city for his passion for a freed-woman, whose very saliva he used to mix with honey and rub on his throat every day. And when Gaius was emperor, he was the first to fall down and worship him. But I understand Vitellius was friendly to our people. Perhaps," Agrippa added as an afterthought, "it was because he did not want any enemies at his back while he faced the Parthians."

"That may have been it," agreed Simon the Pious. "Anyway, as you say, he was our friend. By that time Pontius Pilate had made some more blunders, especially when he massacred some Samaritans who gathered at Mount Gerizim to look for the sacred vessels they thought Moses had hidden there, and Vitellius put an end to his ten-year rule and sent him off to Rome."

"Yes, I know," said Agrippa. "By the time Pilate got to Rome, Tiberius was dead, and Gaius was on the throne, and Gaius told him to kill himself, so Pilate became his own murderer and executioner."

"Vitellius, of course, did not have the power to appoint a procurator," Simon the Pious went on, "which only the emperor could do, but he sent his friend Marcellus down to administer our land. Marcellus lived at Caesarea, and we thought of him as the acting procurator, but he mostly let us do our own way about everything.

"Vitellius himself even came to Jerusalem at Passover time"—again Simon the Pious glanced at the unleavened bread on the king's table, to emphasize that this very time was a season when great things had come to pass for the welfare of their people—"and made an offering in the Temple. After that he told us that he had gotten permission from Tiberius for the vestments and ornaments of the high priest to be returned to the Temple. You know that from the time of the first procurators on, the Romans had been keeping those things in the Antonia, and only allowing the high priest to have them on special occasions. Now the high priest had his own things again, and that meant that he was once again really in charge of our nation."

The face of Simon the Pious glowed as he recalled that high time. Then a look of gravity and even of sternness returned to his face.

"That was when we were able to do something about the followers of Jesus," Simon continued. "There were many Hellenists among them by then and, with their free ideas, they were a great danger to our customs. So the high priest brought one of their leaders—his name was Stephen—before our council, and he made a long and very seditious speech. He said that if we had really studied and observed the law, we would have seen that Jesus had been sent to do away with the Temple and the customs of Moses. Instead, he said, we had murdered a righteous man, just the same as we had always killed the prophets. He even said that he could see the Son of man in heaven, at the right hand of the Most High, and I think he meant that was Jesus.

"Anyway, at that time, the high priest and our council knew that Marcellus would not interfere, and Vitellius was off in the East trying to deal with the Parthians, and they could go ahead and execute a man who was so dangerous to the interests of our people. So they stoned Stephen for his blasphemy."

Simon the Pious nodded his head in affirmative approval of the careful adherence to the law represented in the action he had just narrated.

"And," he added, "many of the followers of Jesus were scattered."

"That was good," said Agrippa. "I hope it took care of the matter."

"That is the problem," said Simon the Pious. "It did not. Our favorable situation under Marcellus only lasted about a year. Then Gaius Caligula sent Marullus as his procurator, and we were under a stern rule, and he alone could carry out any death sentence. Lacking that power, we could not do anything effective against the followers of Jesus. It is true that many of the Hellenists among them were scattered, but many of the people of our own land still belonged to the movement, and their leaders were still right here."

Simon the Pious had conducted the conversation precisely to the point he had intended, the point at which it only remained to be seen if a king with all the power that Agrippa had, and with all the zealous interest in the integrity and the customs of the people that Agrippa had thus far manifested, would now take the action to which the course of events, so carefully rehearsed, obviously pointed.

Agrippa responded with the apparent casualness to which he had schooled himself in his participation in political affairs.

"Who are the leaders of whom you speak?" he asked.

"Peter and James and John," answered Simon the Pious. Although he was speaking now not of the Hellenists such as the Greek-named Stephen among the followers of Jesus, but of the men of the land, Simon the Pious also called the first of the leaders he mentioned by his Greek name, Peter, rather than by his Hebrew name, Simon, for the obvious reason that his own name was the same.

"The three of them," he continued with a brief explanation, "were fishermen in Galilee, they were close associates of Jesus, and they are now called the pillars of the group."

"Pillars—" said Agrippa, half to himself, "they are what hold up a house; without them it cannot stand."

A look of satisfaction passed across the face of Simon the Pious, but he tried to hide it, and waited silently.

"Where do they live, these leaders?" Agrippa tried to make the inquiry still sound casual.

"The house of Mary, the mother of John Mark, on the southwestern hill, is the main meeting place of the group," Simon the Pious began his answer.

Agrippa broke in: "Is that the John you said was one of the pillars?"

"No," Simon the Pious answered. "John Mark is one of the Hellenists; he used to live in Cyrene. He did not go away—yet." Simon drew out the last word, to emphasize that he was still thinking of how many of the Hellenists had been scattered, and of how good it would be if more of them might be driven out too. Then he returned to the even more important theme of the original pillars of the movement, and to the question of their place of residence.

"They meet at the house of Mary, and I think Peter stays there part of the time, but he also travels about a great deal. James and John are brothers, and they have a small house in the lower city. Their father was Zebedee, but he is dead. Their mother is Salome, and she lives with them. The mother of Jesus, named Mary, is Salome's sister, and Jesus asked John to take care of his mother, so she lives there too. James is the older of the two men and, I would say, the more forceful. John is the younger and gentler and, I would say, rather harmless. Also he does a good deal to help his mother take care of her sister."

Agrippa smiled slightly as he noted the accurate knowledge which Simon the Pious had gathered concerning the leaders of the movement that he considered so inimical to the best interests of the people. Agrippa felt that he was correct in the original thought which had led him to invite Simon the Pious to his banquet. The Pharisees worked very carefully at whatever they did, they were a strong force in the land, and their support would be worth whatever he could do to gain it in the greatest measure possible and to retain it continuously. What they wanted at the present juncture was perfectly plain, and fully within his own capabilities and authority to accomplish.

Agrippa handed Simon the Pious another piece of unleavened bread. It was indeed the season when it was especially the divine will that Israel should be delivered from every insidious and dangerous element.

10

The Prison

James the son of Zebedee stirred uneasily in his sleep. A very vivid picture was taking form in his dreams. When he awakened in the morning it was still clearly in his mind. He and his brother John had gone up to Jesus and asked him if they might sit at his right hand and left, in his glory. Jesus looked at them intently and asked if they could drink his cup and be baptized with his baptism. They said they could. Then Jesus said that only the Father could say who would sit at his right hand and left, but he could say that they would indeed drink his cup and be baptized with his baptism.

In the light of the early morning, as his mind adjusted to the reality of his surroundings, James realized that the dream was a nocturnal remembrance of an event that had happened when John and he were going across the countryside in the small band of the closest followers of Jesus. In fact, as he began to recall the details, it was when they were all following Jesus up the road toward Jerusalem. They had thought that Jesus might be going to finally establish in the holy city the kingdom he had often spoken about, so they asked their question about places of honor beside him, a question which they had no sooner uttered than they had regretted.

But about the cup and about the baptism, he had often afterward thought. After Jesus was killed, it was perfectly plain that that was what he had been speaking about. The cup was suffering, the baptism was overwhelming disaster. So Jesus had meant that John and he would share in his own suffering and disaster. James often thought about that.

Undoubtedly that was why he had had the dream. The event, often recalled in waking hours, had formed itself in his mind even as he slept. And yet it had been vividly real. It had seemed as if Jesus were right there again, looking into his eyes and saying the words with all emphasis.

The experience was so real that it stayed with James all the way to the place and moment of his execution. Soldiers of Agrippa stormed into his house, dragged him from his bed, and roughly hustled him off to the Antonia. There, in the course of the morning, Agrippa held the semblance of a trial, and condemned James to die as a fomenter of disturbance among the people.

James, in the one speech of defense that he was permitted to make, said that Jesus, whom he believed to be the Messiah and savior of the people, had also been killed as a disturber of the peace, and he himself was quite willing to die in the same way. Indeed, Jesus had told him, he said, that he would drink his cup and be baptized with his baptism.

At this simple testimony, one of the soldiers who had brought James to the judgment place was so moved that he declared that he too believed that Jesus was the Messiah, and asked James to forgive him for what he had done.

James considered this for a little, and then said, "Shalom, peace be with you," and kissed him.

Accordingly, both men were executed.

The sword was sharp and the blow was sure. But even as the blade descended, the lips of James were forming the words, "The cup that I drink you will drink; and with the baptism with which I am baptized, you will be baptized."

✕

In the afternoon Peter and John Mark were among the band of sorrowful followers of Jesus who carried the body of James to its last resting place. One of the believers had a small plot of land on the upper slope of the Mount of Olives, across from the Temple, and James was buried there.

As his companions grieved aloud, Peter stepped forward and said, "It was here that Jesus paused that day when he came to Jerusalem, and wept over the city. Now, at this same place, we too are weeping. But he told us that those who mourn will be comforted, and those who weep will laugh. He said that those who confess him before men, he will confess before the Father in heaven. Our brother James has acknowledged him faithfully here; Jesus will acknowledge him there. In this we rejoice, though now for a little while we have to suffer trials."

To mark the grave of James, they placed an unshaped stone, and cut into it his name and a simple upright cross mark.

John Mark looked at the sign thoughtfully. It was really the Hebrew letter Taw, and he remembered how in the book of Ezekiel the angel marked the righteous in Jerusalem with this sign on their foreheads that they might be spared in the time of destruction. He remembered also how the Essene priests had placed the same mark beside other passages in the books of the prophets which also told about deliverance in the future. So, thought Mark, the Taw was the sign of salvation.

As the Taw sign was marked in the margins of the books of the prophets opposite passages which spoke of future deliverance, it was usually written in a sideways form like an ✕. These passages were often read in the meetings of the followers of Jesus, because they believed that he was the Messiah who had already begun the time of deliverance. Because of his early life in Cyrene, John Mark thought as much in terms of the Greek language as of the Semitic, and this was true of many others in the community who were known as

Hellenists. To all of them the ✕ mark looked not only like the Hebrew letter Taw but also like the Greek letter Chi, and that was the initial letter of the Greek word *Christos,* which was the translation of the Hebrew *Messiah,* the Anointed One. So John Mark and many of the Hellenists had come to think of the Taw mark as being not only the mark of future salvation but also the sign of the name of the Messiah.

But the Hebrew Taw mark was written not only in the sideways position, ✕, where it looked like a Greek Chi; it was written equally well in an upright position, with one stroke vertical and the other horizontal, + , and it was in this form that it so happened that the sign was now cut into the stone at the grave of James. In this form the followers of Jesus had begun to think of the sign in yet another connection. After all, the Romans had put Jesus to death by their horrible method of crucifixion, and that meant that they had nailed him up on an instrument which was in the shape of a cross. That, too, was what this sign stood for!

All of these meanings ran through the mind of John Mark as he stood silently before the stone at the grave of James. The sign of salvation, the sign of the Messiah, the sign of his cross, was there. As Jesus had said he would, James had drunk his cup and been baptized with his baptism. Now the martyr rested beneath his sign, the sign which also promised deliverance. John Mark felt a certain sense of calm and content even in the time of tragedy.

✕

The fact that Simon Peter had returned to Jerusalem just in time to be present at the burial of James did not escape the notice of the many observers who made it their business to report all kinds of news to the court of Agrippa. From the same sources also Agrippa learned how widespread was the pleasure which the general populace exhibited over the execution of James. A feeling that decisive action against a potentially dangerous movement was at last being taken seemed to be the prevailing sentiment. He had been right in following the suggestion so delicately presented to him by the Pharisees through Simon the Pious and taking that decisive action.

Decisive action was good, and now Peter, probably the most important leader of the movement of the followers of Jesus, was on hand. So thought Agrippa.

It was again in the early morning when the soldiers of Agrippa made the arrest. John Mark and Mary, his mother, watched with sorrow and fear as Simon Peter was led away. Peter himself remembered that Jesus had told him that when he was old others would carry him where he did not wish to go, and wondered if he were already old enough for that prophecy to be on the point of fulfillment in his death.

At the Antonia fortress Peter was flung into a stone prison cell, high up in the highest tower of the fortress. But in this case he was not speedily brought out, hastily tried, and promptly executed, as had been the case with James. It was in the last of the days of Unleavened Bread, and Agrippa was occupied with various ceremonies. Also he felt that his action in trying and executing Peter might attract wider and more favorable attention if it were carried out just after the feast was over. Therefore, for the present, he left Peter in the prison.

In the prison, Peter's cell was about four paces square, and Peter took the four steps in each direction many times every day. High overhead, a single slit between the stones allowed a slight amount of light to enter the cell, enough to tell when it was daytime and when it was nighttime. The cell was closed with a heavy stone door, and this was pushed open only when Peter's meager prison fare was thrust before him, or when soldiers came in to maintain a watch over him.

Four quaternions of soldiers were assigned to the four watches of the night, each squad being on duty for three hours. In each period, two soldiers chained themselves to Peter within the cell, while two others watched outside.

Thus Peter was safely incarcerated, and while he slept on the hard stones at night and paced the cell by day, the feast drew on toward its close.

11

The Gospel in Greek

On the last night before the end of the feast period, Peter slept fitfully in his cell. The guards had sought to torment him by letting him catch fragments of their conversation, in which they spoke of the rumors that on the next day Agrippa would conduct Peter's trial and accomplish his execution.

At the same time in the house of Mary, the mother of John Mark, many of the followers of Jesus were gathered together and were praying for Peter, as they had done almost unceasingly ever since his incarceration began.

The earthquake which resulted in the freeing of Peter struck in the early hours of the night. A rumbling sound seemed to emanate from the bowels of the earth, and the highest tower of the Antonia, in which Peter's cell was located, swayed dangerously.

In a dereliction of duty for which they were summarily put to death on the following day, the soldiers who were guarding Peter disencumbered themselves of their chains and their responsibilities, and rushed down and out into the comparative safety of the broad courtyard of the Antonia.

Peter, finding himself suddenly free to go, drew on his sandals, wrapped himself in his mantle, and went forth. For the moment everything was in complete turmoil in the fortress—doors and gates were standing open, and personnel were running back and forth. Peter passed by unnoticed at points where ordinarily any passerby would have been challenged by sentries, exited at the iron gate on the front side of the fortress, and descended the seven steps to the level of the outer Temple court below.

From there, Peter knew his way very well, and he went swiftly through the streets of the city to the southwestern hill and to the house of Mary, the mother of John Mark.

By reason of the dangerous times, the door was barred securely from within, and Simon Peter stood without, knocking eagerly. Rhoda, the maid, came to the door, and called from within to ask who was there. When Peter answered she was so amazed and overjoyed to hear his voice that she ran to tell the others, and left Peter still standing outside, still knocking.

Inside, even the faithful friends who had been praying so earnestly for Peter's release could not at first believe that he was really there, and they told Rhoda that she was mad. But she insisted that he was there, and Peter continued knocking outside, so they opened the door and he came in.

Raising his hand in a gesture which quieted the excited talk that had broken out as they saw him, Peter gave a brief account of his experience in captivity and of his wonderful deliverance. Also he asked that word of the events be given to James the brother of Jesus, and thus he intimated that this man, now a believer and well known in their midst, might henceforward be looked upon as their leader. As for himself, it was obvious that he had to try to complete his escape by departing from the city and passing beyond the territories of Agrippa.

"Where will you go?" they asked him.

"To another place," he replied. The complete vagueness of the answer was a necessary precaution not only for himself but also for the company. If they were questioned, as they undoubtedly would be, they could reply in all honesty that they did not know where Simon Peter had gone.

"I will go with you," said John Mark to Peter, and a look of pleasure brightened the face of Peter.

When Stephen had been stoned and many of the other Hellenists had scattered, a half dozen years before, John Mark had stayed on in Jerusalem. He was at that time hardly prominent enough among the followers of Jesus to attract any attention, and he was beginning to be interested in collecting the reminiscences of those who had known Jesus personally, particularly the remembrances of Peter, which, under the impact of the threat of the Abomination of Desolation, he had finally put together in a written document.

Now, however, both the new persecution and the sense of companionship that had developed between himself and Peter, who had indeed baptized him, led to his swift decision to accompany Peter, if the latter would be pleased to have him. That Peter would be pleased, John Mark had now learned at once from the look on Peter's face.

For a journey of unknown destination and unknown duration, John Mark quickly gathered a few belongings, including a copy of his manuscript about Jesus. He bade farewell to his mother and to his friends—including a girl named Sarah, who looked at him with admiring eyes—and stepped out with Peter into the darkness of the night.

The Orontes River sparkled and danced in the bright light of the Syrian sun.

Peter and John Mark had extricated themselves from the city and the lands where Agrippa and the Pharisees were so vigorously undertaking to suppress anything foreign to the ancient customs of the people, as they judged the movement of the followers of Jesus to be.

With the scattering of many persons at the time of the martyrdom of Stephen, and with the departure of John Mark now, most of the Hellenists were gone. With the death of James the brother of John and with the flight of Peter, two of the most prominent leaders were out of the way. As he left, Peter had indicated that James the brother of Jesus should assume the leadership of the community. This man had also seen Jesus risen from the dead, and had become a believer. But he was still steeped in the customs of his people and, under the pressure of the national feelings which Agrippa and the Pharisees were promoting so assiduously, he now even accentuated his adherence to ancestral practices, without considering that this in any way compromised his conviction that Jesus, his own brother, was indeed the long-expected Messiah of the people. So devoted was he, in fact, to such practices as fasting and prayer that he became known as James the Just, and his knees were as hard as those of a camel from so often falling upon them in his intercessions.

Under such leadership it could be expected that the community of the believers in Jesus might drop back somewhat out of excessive public attention and be spared, at least for a time, such attacks as those that had resulted in the death of James the brother of John, and in the departure of Peter and John Mark.

Also, although Peter and Mark could not know it at the time, Agrippa himself was to die suddenly of a horrible disease within two years' time, and be replaced again by procurators, direct from Rome, who would restrict, at least for a time, the excesses of Jewish national feeling. It was, accordingly, a propitious time for Peter and John Mark to betake themselves to other places, and to leave the community of believers in Jerusalem to develop in its own way.

Two large cities lay upon the main routes of travel to the north, and outside of the realm of Agrippa, namely, Damascus and Antioch, and in both, because of the work of those who had been scattered even earlier from Jerusalem, there were small communities of believers in Jesus.

The first of these, Damascus, was the nearer but, although it was safely outside of the political jurisdiction of Agrippa, precisely because of its nearness, it could readily be reached by emissaries from the religious authorities in Jerusalem. Peter and John Mark, therefore, bypassed Damascus and went on to Antioch.

"The river is beautiful," said John Mark, as the two men watched the waters swirling past their feet. They had entered Antioch by the East Gate, proceeded along a handsome colonnaded main street, and turned to the right on another colonnaded street which ran to the Orontes, opposite the tip of the island on which, surrounded by two channels of the river, was one of the four main quarters of the city.

"Yes," Peter replied darkly, "but the waters are laden with the vices of a great city, and they flow on as if to flood the world." It was plain that Peter felt less at home in this very large city than did Mark to whom, from his earlier life in Cyrene, at least the atmosphere of the wider Hellenistic world was more familiar.

Past the two men, as they stood at the end of the bridge which led across the river to the island, poured a constant stream of humanity—Syrians, Greeks, Macedonians, and, at least occasionally and recognizably, Jews.

Finally Peter accosted a man, coming off the bridge, who was quite unmistakably a fellow countryman. The salutation of Peter was in Aramaic, but the other man responded in Greek, and John Mark, with greater familiarity in that language than Peter, quickly entered the conversation. The upshot of the matter was that their new acquaintance invited Peter and John Mark to go with him to seek quarters in the settlement where he lived.

Together they went back to the main colonnaded street, and paused momentarily in the shadow of a statue of the emperor Tiberius.

"Did he build this street?" asked John Mark, indicating the figure of the emperor.

"No," replied the man, "the street was the work of Antiochus Epimanes."

Having made sure that no one was immediately at hand to overhear him, the man had snarled out the last word, *epimanes,* thereby availing himself of the familiar jest whereby Antiochus was called "mad," rather than *epiphanes,* or "manifest," as the king had wished to be saluted in recognition of his claimed divinity.

"But up there," and the man gestured toward the lofty mountain that overlooked the city from the east, "is the wall that Tiberius built on that side of the city."

They turned down the great street of the "mad" Antiochus, and walked on toward the Daphne Gate, near the river, at the southwestern corner of the city.

Gesturing toward another street, also handsomely colonnaded, the man said: "And that was built by our own Herod the Great." Again there was something of a snarl in his voice as he said "the Great," to express his divided opinion of the famous king who had indeed rebuilt the Jewish Temple in Jerusalem, but had, with equal readiness, built the temples of pagan gods.

"I think," said John Mark, "that our people have been favorably treated here in this great city."

"Yes," said the man, "except that while Caligula reigned, those who hated us could do as they pleased, and many of us were slain. But that did not last very long, and again we are free to follow our own laws. There are still many of us here; some live in the city, some are settled on the plain to the east, and many live where we are going now, not far from Daphne."

They were passing, as he spoke, beneath the Daphne Gate.

"The goddess of the laurel tree, into which she was changed when Apollo was pursuing her," said John Mark, who remembered the name of Daphne well from the days when he lived amidst the Greeks of Cyrene.

"Yes, and in Daphne," said the man, referring now to the district which bore the name of the goddess, "you will see many trees of the goddess, and many fountains and waters—and much evildoing, too."

Somewhat less than an hour's walk outside the gate, and somewhat short of the evidently notorious district of Daphne itself, they came to the large settlement of their own people. Here Peter and John Mark found simple quarters, and the man showed them the way to the synagogue where, he said, services would be held that evening, for with sunset the sabbath would begin.

X

The synagogue service was crowded not only with Jews but also with Gentiles. Not far away the dissolute of Antioch pursued Daphne in the person of the courtesans who glided through the laurel groves, but here high-minded pagans joined with the people of the law in listening seriously to the exposition of the way of separateness and holiness.

Peter, to whom Antioch had at first seemed oppressive, took heart as he saw the many people at the synagogue service. Then his heart sank again as he realized that the service of the synagogue was, except for certain liturgical formulas in Hebrew, conducted in Greek. As he had some reason to expect would be the case, he was recognized as a visitor from the homeland, and invited to speak. Although his command of the language was slight, he began as bravely as he could in Greek. Soon, however, he fell back into his natural Aramaic. Then John Mark took his place beside him and rendered the message into the other language.

Peter spoke first of some passages in the Scriptures which foretold the coming of the Messiah and the new age, then said that he wanted to tell them about Jesus who, he believed, was the Messiah. He himself had been with Jesus for several years, he explained. He had heard Jesus tell his followers that the kingdom was in the midst of them; he had seen Jesus do such mighty works as to heal the hopelessly sick. Finally men had put Jesus to death, but God had raised him from the dead. Peter himself had not only gone to his empty tomb, but had also seen Jesus again, alive. God had, therefore, assuredly made him both Master and Messiah, this Jesus who was crucified.

As John Mark finished rendering into Greek what Peter had said —". . . both Lord and Christ, this Jesus who was crucified"—there was a stir throughout the synagogue, but no overt expression of hostility. In general it seemed that the Jews, who formed the main body of the congregation, received Peter's declaration with reserve, but the Gentiles, who were on the periphery, heard it with special interest. In particular John Mark noticed one young man in the back whose face took on an appearance of intense excitement as he heard the statement that Jesus had been raised from the dead. Afterward, many gathered around Peter and John Mark. Some wanted to ask further about Jesus, a few said that they were already believers in Jesus and would be gathering in the home of one of their number on the morrow to break bread together. To this gathering they invited Peter and John Mark.

In the home gathering it was again a surprise and an encouragement to Peter to see how many were present, now predominantly Gentiles, but also some of his own people. The visitors were asked to say what they would.

This time John Mark brought out the record that he had written about Jesus and read some of it to the people, making a rough translation of the Aramaic into Greek as he spoke. Then he also rendered into Greek the address which Peter proceeded to deliver.

Because they were gathered together in a home, Mark had thought it appropriate to present from his record a portion about Jesus at home at Capernaum when a paralyzed man was brought before him, being even let down through the roof because of the crowd, and was healed. Peter also, in his address, had again referred to the mighty works which Jesus had done, even healing the crippled and the sick.

John Mark knew that in Jerusalem and some other places Peter himself had healed some lame and sick persons, but such an event he had never seen with his own eyes. Now he did.

There was a woman in the group whose posture had attracted the notice of John Mark. She had been seated, but deeply bowed forward, and Mark had casually supposed that she was manifesting a special devoutness in her prayers. She had, indeed, been praying most devoutly, but now, as she tried to rise and move forward, it was evident that her bent posture was a matter of a horribly crippling and deforming curvature of her back.

With difficulty she managed to move herself forward, in front of Simon Peter, her lips moving in a soundless continuation of her prayers. Peter stretched out his hands, laid them upon the woman's head, and said, using now Greek as John Mark had done: "In the name of the Lord Jesus Christ, be healed."

The woman, whose bent back had for so long constrained her to look only at the ground, began to lift her head and to straighten her form. She began to speak, softly and wonderingly at first, then more loudly and rapidly, ending with a cry of praise: "I hear the wind blowing. . . . I feel fire burning in my back. . . . I am being healed . . . the pain is gone. . . . I am well . . . praise be to the Lord Jesus Christ."

×

Bad as was the reputation of the district of Daphne by reason of what was done in some of its more secluded glens, it was undeniably a beautiful region of trees and waters, with not a few fine residences in one area.

It was here, in one of the large pools of sparkling water, that Simon Peter, with John Mark to assist him, conducted baptisms, in the name of Jesus Christ, of those who were accepting his message and enrolling themselves in the company of believers. There were many of them now, for the presence in Antioch of a man who had actually been among the companions of Jesus, the forceful way Peter spoke, and the happening of miracle, all attracted a wide measure of attention.

Also, that which John Mark was able to set forth in a simple and straightforward way from his carefully compiled record of what Jesus had done and said was of much effect. In many cases people asked Mark if they might read his document directly, but when they saw that it was in Aramaic and realized that he had just been giving them the gist of it in his own free rendering into Greek, they knew that they could not get much benefit from it directly. Therefore it became desirable that an actual Greek translation of Mark's document should be made.

This was a task for which John Mark himself had, at that time, little leisure to devote himself, being heavily occupied with his activities in close association with Simon Peter. There was a newly baptized member of the community, however, who had lived for a time at Jerusalem, had learned Aramaic there, and was eager to undertake the making of the translation.

Two factors, in particular, influenced the results which the translator produced. For one thing, he realized that Mark's document contained many accounts that he had collected from eyewitnesses as they related them in Aramaic and many sayings of Jesus which had also been given originally in the same language, and accordingly he desired and felt under a sort of sacred obligation to keep these materials as nearly as possible in their original form, even though when he made a quite literal translation it did not result in the most highly polished and correct Greek. For another thing, he was not really as well versed in the Aramaic, which he had learned, as in the Greek, which was his own native tongue, and accordingly he sometimes made a translation which was not quite correct or which, being conventionally correct, yet missed some subtle point which was contained in the Aramaic.

At a few points the translator was so impressed by the fact that he was writing out the very words that Jesus had said that he simply spelled the Aramaic in Greek characters, then explained for his Greek readers what the Aramaic words meant. In this way he recorded that when Jesus spoke to the small daughter of a synagogue ruler named Jairus, who was believed to be dead, he said, *Talitha cumi,* which means "Little girl, arise"; when he healed a deaf-mute, he said, *Ephphatha,* that is, "Be opened"; and when he prayed to God in the Garden of Gethsemane, he said, *Abba,* "Father."

Literal adherence to the Aramaic and, in some cases, consequent loss of some shades of meaning, appeared elsewhere. In Aramaic, for example, many successive clauses were characteristically connected by repeating one simple conjunction, *waw,* over and over again. Although this conjunction could actually have many different shades of meaning, such as while, when, but, for, although, since, because, and so on, it was most simply considered as the equivalent of the Greek "and." Falling into this way of rendering the *waw,* the translator now wrote out in Greek the passage which told about how, on one occasion, the relatives of Jesus came seeking him and asking for him, in this way:

> And his mother and his brothers came.
> And standing outside they sent to him and called him.
> And a crowd was sitting about him.
> And they said to him, "Your mother and your brothers are outside . . ."

Actually, in the original Aramaic the third *waw* was probably intended to have the meaning of "because," to explain that Jesus' mother and brothers stood outside and sent word to him, instead of coming in, *because* the crowd was settled about him.

Again, where Mark's document told about the healing of a little daughter of a Syrophoenician woman, it said that the woman went home and found the child on her bed. This was expressed by the passive participle of an Aramaic verb which literally meant "thrown," but was commonly used with the meaning of "lying." This the translator rendered literally with the Greek word for "throw," so that the sentence said to a reader who did not understand the derived meaning in the original that the Syrophoenician woman went home and found the child thrown upon the bed.

In some cases, also, there was ambiguity in the Aramaic text, and it was possible on that ground to make mistakes in translating. In one passage, for example, the translator looked at the small Aramaic particle *di,* which was both a relative pronoun and a conjunction. He took it as a conjunction meaning "in order that," and made the passage read to the effect that Jesus spoke to outsiders in parables *in order that* they might see indeed, but not perceive, and hear indeed, but not understand. Actually the true rendering of the particle should have been as a relative pronoun, so that the statement was that Jesus spoke in parables to outsiders *who* saw indeed, but did not perceive, and heard indeed, but did not understand.

Beyond that, it was possible to make an outright mistake in reading the Aramaic. This was especially possible because Aramaic, like Hebrew, was written with consonants only, and it was necessary for the reader to supply the vowels himself when he pronounced the word. While he could generally recognize correctly what was intended, he might on occasion supply the wrong vowels and read the wrong word. In addition to that, some of the consonants even looked much alike, and could be mistaken if not looked at very carefully.

It was problems of this sort which led the translator of Mark's Aramaic document to write one sentence which was particularly due to cause readers much puzzlement as time went on. This was the statement that "the Pharisees and all the Jews do not eat without washing their hands with the fist."

How a man could wash his hands with his fist was naturally puzzling, so Greek readers tried to think what was wrong with the sentence. The Greek word for "fist" was *pygma,* and it occurred to some of them that this might have been a mistake for the quite similar word *pykna,* which means "frequently." With that word the sentence would have said that "the Pharisees and all the Jews do not eat without washing their hands frequently." Even in that form, however, the sentence was not entirely clear.

What actually happened was that the translator made an outright mistake. He confused the two very similar letters *daleth* or "d" and *resh* or "r," and thought he saw *ligmod,* "with the fist," whereas in reality the word was *ligmar,* "at all," and the translation should have been, "the Pharisees and all the Jews do not eat at all without washing their hands."

When the translator was finally through with his work, and John Mark read his document in its new Greek form, he did not fail to notice points of the sort which have just been enumerated, but to him they chiefly conveyed the feeling that the underlying original Aramaic was still showing through the translated Greek, and for that he was glad, so he left them as they were. Now his compendium of the main facts about Jesus, and of typical teachings of his, was available in both of the languages, Aramaic and Greek, which were so widely used in the whole world in which his own people were dispersed and in which the Greeks dwelt, to both of whom it seemed increasingly evident the message about the Christ was destined to be carried.

12

The House of Theophilus

The young man who was in the synagogue service where Simon Peter and John Mark first spoke in Antioch, and whose countenance lighted up with such intense interest as he heard that Jesus had been raised from the dead, became known personally to Peter and Mark in due course of time. He appeared at many of the meetings in which Peter told more about Jesus and Mark presented materials from his compendium.

For a long time the young man seemed shy and pensive, kept in the background, and slipped out quietly. But at last he made himself known.

"I am Clement, and I come from Rome," he said, speaking in excellent Greek, although presumably he was at home first of all in Latin.

"You have come a long way to be here in Antioch," said Peter.

"Yes, and it is a long story, too, but if I may I would like to tell you about it."

As a result of this initial approach, a time was set, and Peter and John Mark talked at length with Clement.

"My home is on the Via Labicana in Rome, not far from the Forum," said Clement.

"It must be an exciting place to live," said John Mark, "a place where something is happening every day." Mark remembered the Roman cities of Cyrene, where the forum also was the center of much activity.

Clement nodded his head in acknowledgment of Mark's comment, but went ahead on his own line of thought.

"My father was Faustus, and he was of the family of the emperor Tiberius. My mother was Mattidia, and my older brothers were twins, Faustinus and Faustinianus.

"The circumstances of my childhood were not unfavorable until, in my eighth year, my mother went away."

"She deserted you?" interjected Peter.

"No," replied Clement, "it came about in this way, my father later told me. My mother had on one occasion a dream in which she was shown that unless, along with her twin sons, she immediately left the city of Rome for a period of ten years, she would, together with the twin boys, die a fearful death.

"My father loved his family, so he at once provided my mother and my brothers with all essentials and sent them off by ship to Athens, where Faustinus and Faustinianus would have the opportunity of a good education. Myself alone he kept at home to be a comfort to him."

"It was a sad breaking asunder of your family, indeed," said Mark.

"Saddest was this," continued Clement. "From time to time in the next several years my father sent messengers to Athens with money for my mother and brothers. The first messengers did not return. The last ones came back with the report that they could find no trace of our family, that there were rumors of shipwreck at the time of their voyage, and that in all probability they had never even reached Athens.

"In desperate sorrow my father placed me—then twelve years of age—under the care of tutors in Rome, and set out to seek our lost family.

"That was twenty years ago," Clement concluded, "and I never saw him again. I grew up an orphan, and I wander in the world disconsolate."

"What did you study in the schools in Rome?" asked John Mark, thinking to relieve the sad memories which had just been exhibited with some hopefully more pleasant reminiscences.

"Philosophy," replied Clement briefly. Then he went on: "As it gradually became evident to me that my entire family, mother, brothers, and father too, had in all probability perished, and that I would never see them again, I occupied myself more and more with the thought of death and with the problem of immortality."

A look of compassion was on the face of Peter as he gazed at Clement, speaking so sadly and earnestly, and John Mark listened intently, wondering what had been taught in the schools at Rome.

"I deeply desired," Clement continued, "to find out what had happened to my family if they had, indeed, departed from this life, and whether I might believe that they did still exist, or whether I must admit that they had passed into oblivion.

"For myself also I wondered whether, after departing this life, I would be no more, and no one would remember me, seeing that time, which knows no limits, brings everything, even everything, into nothingness. Would I then be without being, or acquaintance with those who are, neither knowing nor being known?

"Such were my thoughts, and as I pondered these and similar questions, I became pale and wasted away. If at any time I sought to drive away these thoughts, as being of little use, the waves of anxiety rose all the higher upon me."

John Mark was not unsympathetic with the physical afflictions which were the concomitants of the mental distress of the youthful Clement, but he pressed the question in which he was most interested.

"What did the philosophers say?"

"They said now one thing, and now another," Clement replied. "Doctrines were asserted, and again they were controverted. Contests were waged, and the arts of syllogisms and the subtleties of conclusions were discussed. At one time it was said that the soul is immortal, at another time that it is mortal. When the view prevailed that it is immortal, I was thankful; when, on the other hand, it was said that it is mortal, I went away sorrowful.

"Worst of all, I could not settle upon either opinion as convincing. I had the impression that the respective theories were regarded as false or correct not in accordance with the nature and truth of the arguments, but in accordance with the talents of the persons who set them forth. As soon, therefore, as I realized that opinions could gain ground, not through the weight of facts, but simply through the personality of their champions, my confusion concerning these questions increased still more. I groaned in the bottom of my heart, for I was not able to come to a firm decision, and I was also not able to put away from myself such thoughts altogether."

As the conversation drew toward a close, Peter and John Mark assured Clement that they would try to make known to him more fully the facts about how Jesus was put to death, and then raised from the dead, so that Clement might share with them the strong belief that they had that there is indeed life after death.

But another conviction had been forming in Peter's mind as he listened to the sad recital of Clement. Now, as they parted, he uttered it: "Clement, I believe that your family is still alive, and you will soon see them again."

"But their forms are dim in my memory by now, and they would have changed much from when I saw them last. How then would I even recognize them?" Clement asked disconsolately.

✕

The small ship which carried passengers to the offshore island of Aradus had Simon Peter, John Mark, and Clement on board. In addition to their work in Antioch, Peter and Mark were making journeys out into the countryside and up and down the coast. At the same time Clement had become so attached to them—although he was not yet persuaded of either Peter's assurance that he would see his family again or of the doctrine of the resurrection—that he had asked to go about with them.

"You would confer upon me a great favor if you would allow me to perform the functions of a servant, and go about with you," Clement had said to Peter.

"Do you intend that you would take care of many splendid tunics, and all my changes of rings and sandals, and prepare pleasant dainties, as if for effeminate men?" Peter chided gently, then went on in more serious vein.

"Do you not know that I use only bread and olives, and rarely herbs cooked in the pot, and that this is my only coat and cloak which I wear? I, too, was brought up as an orphan, with Andrew my brother, and although I have a wife, she could not come with me when Mark and I fled here from Agrippa the king, and she lives still at the Galilean lake and cares for her aging mother. So we are accustomed to our own care, and to the hardships of our present journeys."

Having said as much, Peter changed his manner and invited Clement to go with Mark and him, not as a servant, but simply as a welcome companion.

The island of Aradus was three days' journey down the coast from Antioch, and offshore some thirty stadia, and its inhabitants were fishermen and commercial voyagers. Having finished their work of speaking the word in a number of the coastal cities, Simon Peter and John Mark were ready to rest briefly, and Clement had suggested the visit to the island as a brief time of relaxation. There were reputed to be, on the island, two pillars of vine-wood of such very great circumference as to be notable, and also several of the works of Phidias, and these should be of interest to see.

At the dock on the island, however, Peter decided it was not worth while to go to see the sights, and remained behind while Mark and Clement went off. It was not long until Peter noticed a woman who sat outside before the doors and begged constantly for her livelihood.

"Dear woman," said Peter, "what lack have you that you beg for support, rather than working with your hands for your livelihood?"

"Alas," said she, "my hands are withered and have no strength in them. Had I only the courage of a man, and were there a precipice above the waves, I should have long since cast myself down and made an end of my life."

In the conversation which ensued, Peter's compassionate interest drew forth from the poor woman her story. She was nobly born, and had become the wife of a man related to those in high authority. In due time she became the mother of twin sons, and later of another son. But her husband's brother became infatuated with her, and she was in a grievous predicament. She wished neither to defile herself by succumbing to his advances, nor to expose him to her husband and thus to set brother against brother, and reasoned that it was best for her to leave the city for some time, until the passion of the evil man should subside. She would take her twin children with her, but leave the other son with his father as a comfort.

To accomplish this end, without divulging the true state of affairs, she fabricated a dream, in which she was instructed to depart forthwith from the city with her twin children, lest a miserable death befall the entire family.

The false dream so alarmed her husband that he sent the wife and two sons off by ship to Athens. But the ship was driven by furious winds, went to pieces in the night, and was wrecked. She alone was tossed upon a rock, and later rescued, while all the others on board presumably perished. So it was that she was at once bereft even of her twin sons, gradually from sheer sorrow deprived of strength in her hands, and at last reduced to maintaining her life by beggary.

While the woman was still speaking, John Mark and Clement returned, but Peter, who was growing more and more excited, asked them to proceed to the ship and wait for him there. Then he pressed the woman to tell him her family, her city, and the names of her children. But she, detecting his agitation, became suspicious that something was amiss, and answered falsely that she was an Ephesian and her husband a Sicilian, and she also changed the names of her three children.

Supposing that she spoke the truth, Peter's countenance fell, and he said: "Alas! O woman, I thought that this day was to bring you great joy, suspecting that you were a certain person of whom I was thinking, and whose affairs I have heard of and know of accurately."

Hearing of a great joy which she might be about to miss, the woman changed her tone and adjured Peter, saying, "Tell me, I entreat of you, of the matter of which you are informed, that I may know if there is among women any one more wretched than myself."

Still not knowing that the woman had spoken falsely and still feeling deep pity for her, Peter began to tell her the truth: "There is a certain young man in attendance upon me, thirsting after the discourses on religion, a Roman citizen, who told me how that, having a father and mother and twin brothers, he has lost sight of them all. 'For,' says he, 'my mother, as my father related to me, having seen a vision, left the city of Rome for a time with her twin children, lest she should perish by an evil fate, and having gone away with them, she cannot be found. And her husband, my father, having gone in search of her, also can no longer be found.' "

While Peter said these words, the woman listened attentively, then swooned away as if in a stupor. Peter caught her and, when she had regained consciousness, exhorted her to confess what was the matter with her. She, lifting her face toward Peter with an expression of rapture, cried, "Where is this youth?"

Peter, now comprehending the whole matter, said, "Tell me first the truth; otherwise you cannot see him."

Then she earnestly said, "I am that young man's mother."

Peter demanded, "What is his name?"

And she said, "Clement."

Then Peter said, "It is the same, and he was one of the two who spoke to me a little while ago, whom I asked to wait for me on the ship."

✕

It was a touching reunion which followed on board the small ship. Remarkably enough, even this was not the end of the matter. Peter had expressed to Clement the strong conviction that he would again see his family and, obviously, the rediscovery of the mother did not constitute a complete fulfillment of this prediction, assuming that it was the entire family which was meant. In the succeeding months the balance of the prediction came true. Under different circumstances but ones not less surprising than the circumstances which surrounded the finding of the mother, the twin brothers and the father were discovered—for all had, in fact, survived their respective vicissitudes—and thus the whole family was reunited.

Naturally enough, in view of the fact that it was really through Peter that they had all found one another after so long a time, the whole family of Clement became, at least for the time being, associated with the circle of which Peter and John Mark were the center in Antioch. They participated in the gatherings, listening to the discourses and readings, and studying earnestly the teachings that were presented.

From his early training in the schools in Rome, Clement in particular was philosophically inclined, and had ability in expressing himself in writing. The natural world had always been of much interest to him, and he had read in Latin the writings of many students of natural history. Through his new associations he learned of the Jewish Scriptures, was delighted to find that they were available in Greek translation, and began to read widely in them, often coming to John Mark for help on matters that he did not understand. Most of all he rejoiced to read in Mark's compendium concerning what Jesus had done and taught, and to listen to Peter in his public discourses on the same subject.

Although he was a Gentile and had been raised in Roman paganism and polytheism, it was not difficult for Clement to accept belief in the one God, as taught in the Scriptures and declared by Simon Peter and John Mark. To him this belief seemed to accord well with his own observations of the unity and harmony of all things in the universe.

One day Clement brought to John Mark a number of paragraphs he had written on this theme, and Mark nodded approvingly and appreciatively as he read the almost poetically phrased composition.

"The heavens revolving under the government of God are subject to him in peace. Day and night run the course appointed by him, in no wise hindering each other. The sun and the moon, with the companies of the stars, roll on in harmony according to his command, within their prescribed limits, and without any deviation. The fruitful earth, according to his will, brings forth food in abundance, at the proper seasons, for man and beast and all the living beings upon it, never hesitating, nor changing any of the ordinances that he has fixed. The unsearchable places of the abysses, and the unfathomable realms of the lower world, are controlled by the same ordinances. The vast immeasurable sea, gathered together by his working into its allotted places, never passes beyond the bounds placed around it, but does as he has commanded."

At this point in his small essay on the peace and harmony of the universe as evidence of the work of the one God, Clement showed his acquaintance with the Greek version of the Scriptures which he had been reading under the tutelage of John Mark. He enforced the point he was just making with a quotation, as he remembered it, from the book of Job concerning the sea. "Thus far shall you come, and no farther, and here shall your proud waves be stayed."

Then Clement went on: "The ocean, impassable to man, and the worlds beyond it, are regulated by the same enactments of the Lord. The seasons of spring, summer, autumn, and winter peacefully give place to one another. The winds in their several stations fulfill, at the proper time, their service without hindrance. The ever-flowing springs, created for enjoyment and health, supply, without fail, sustenance for the life of men. The smallest of animals meet together in concord and peace. All these things did the great Creator and Lord of the universe appoint to exist in peace and concord, and to all things does he do good."

As for the thought of death and the problem of immortality which had weighed so heavily upon the pensive mind of the youthful Clement, there was now an increasing tendency for him to accept as entirely true the testimony of Simon Peter that he had seen Jesus again, alive, after his death, and to believe that this was, in fact, the first tangible proof with which he had ever become acquainted that there was indeed a resurrection and a life beyond the grave.

Characteristically, Clement combined this thought also with what he observed in the natural world. In another small essay which he wrote one day, Clement expressed himself almost as if he were already a full believer, which he indeed almost was, although he had not yet officially presented himself for baptism.

"Let us consider," he wrote, "how the Lord continually proves to us that there will be a future life, as he has also shown us by raising Jesus from the dead. Let us contemplate the resurrection which is at all times taking place. Day and night declare to us a resurrection. The night sinks to sleep, and the day arises; the day departs, and the night comes on. Let us behold the fruits of the earth, how the sowing of grain takes place. The sower goes out and casts each of the seeds into the ground, and it falls on the ground, dry and bare, and is gradually dissolved. Then out of its dissolution the mighty power of the providence of the Lord raises it up again, and from one seed many arise and bring forth fruit."

Surprisingly enough, it was an element in what was really Clement's pagan background, combined with an interpretation from the Jewish Scriptures, that provided what seemed to Clement like a final sign attesting to him the reality of the resurrection, and that gave to him therewith the final impetus which led to his decision to be baptized and to cast his lot with those who believed in Jesus. The sign was encountered in the house of Theophilus.

✕

On one particular day in Antioch it seemed as if the
Spirit moved in the midst of the community of the believers in Jesus
with as evident a power as on that memorable Pentecost day in
Jerusalem years before. Especially the healing power, which had been
manifest through Peter's words and touch on not a few occasions
previously, was felt mightily. So many people were coming to listen
to what Peter had to say, and to bring into his presence those who
were distressed with many kinds of sicknesses, that Peter went up on
a height in Daphne. There he ordered all the multitude of sick people
to be ranged before him, and addressed them all with these words:

"As you see me to be a man like to yourselves, do not suppose
that you can recover your health from me, but only through him who
has shown to those who believe in him a perfect medicine for body
and soul. Therefore let all this people be witnesses to your declaration
that with your whole heart you believe in the Lord Jesus Christ, that
they may know that they themselves also may be saved by him."

Upon being so addressed, the whole multitude of the sick cried
out with one voice that he was the one God whom Peter preached,
and that they did truly call upon Jesus Christ that they might be
saved. Thereupon many of the sick felt an indescribable power flowing
through their bodies, and the paralytics, being cured, began to run to
Peter's feet, the blind to shout on the recovery of their sight, the lame
to give thanks on regaining the power of walking, the sick to rejoice
in restored health, and some even, who were barely alive, being already without consciousness or the power of speech, were raised up,
and ones of whom it was said that they were possessed by demons
were set free. Among these was Mattidia, the mother of Clement,
whose hands, withered for so long, were, to her great joy, fully restored.

So powerful was the manifestation of the Spirit on that day that
a great many persons, both among the sick who were healed and
among those who witnessed what had happened and could not doubt

it because they had seen it with their own eyes, declared that they believed in the Lord Jesus Christ and desired to be baptized. These now included Mattidia and Faustus, the mother and father of Clement, and Faustinus and Faustinianus, his twin brothers. But Clement himself yet hesitated.

So great an addition of numbers was made in this way to the community of the believers that one of those newly baptized, a certain Theophilus, who had a large house in a pleasant section of Daphne, opened it as a place for the preaching of Peter and the assembling of the multitude who came together every day to hear the word, being utterly persuaded of the healthful doctrine which was vouched for by the efficacy of the cures.

The house of Theophilus was set in spacious grounds, laid out in the style of a Roman villa, and contained many rooms and courtyards. The most notable feature was the use of mosaic pavements and floors in many of the courts and rooms.

The pride of the villa was the mosaic of the phoenix, which occupied the entire area of the largest courtyard. This enormous mosaic pavement was obviously the work of very skilled craftsmen, who had patiently fitted together an almost endless number of tiny pieces of colored glass and stone, so that the entire pattern made upon the observer the impression of a great and carefully wrought tapestry.

Around the four sides of the vast rectangle was a broad border. In the border the recurring design was that of two rams, fine horned heads lifted proudly, facing each other across a beautiful plant. Inside this border the main field of the mosaic exhibited a floral pattern, containing more than 7,500 roses. In the center of the whole area was the representation for which all the rest of the work, exquisite as it was in its own right, provided a handsome frame. Here, executed in proportion to the vastness of the entire mosaic, was a mountain of rocks and, standing proudly on the summit thereof and more than the height of a man in size, a phoenix.

This great bird was shown in profile, standing erect on its two tall legs, and raising its body and head up as if about to take off in flight. The double curve of the long neck was graceful, and the lift of the head was proud. Notably catching the attention of the viewer was the brilliant eye, encircled with black, in the side of the head of the phoenix. Around the head was a halo in mauve gray, out through which streamed five rays of light, one proceeding vertically. The colors of the bird were green with brown and gray in the shadows, yellow and white in the highlights. The rocks of the mountain were green, dark brown, and maroon. All together this representation, set in the immense tapestry of flowers, produced an impression of both beauty and majesty, and was well fitted to remind the person who viewed it of the glorious theme which, to many thinkers, the phoenix symbolized.

Because the courtyard with the mosaic of the phoenix was the largest enclosed area in the house of Theophilus, it was the place where the chair was placed from which Simon Peter spoke to the people when the largest numbers of his listeners came together.

Immediately, the first time he was present in one of these gatherings, Clement took note of the phoenix, standing there so proudly on his mountain of rocks, and evinced great interest in it. He gradually recalled from the literature with which his earlier schooling had made him familiar various references in various writers to this wonderful bird.

A verse in Hesiod, memorized in schooldays, came back to mind, and Clement said it over to himself.

A chattering crow lives out nine generations of aged men, but a stag's life is four times a crow's, and a raven's life makes three stags old, while the phoenix outlives nine ravens.

Clement tried to multiply out in his mind the various numbers of years suggested by the verse, to arrive at some idea of the prodigious longevity ascribed to the fabulous bird, but gave up the attempt. Then he remembered that some said the total was 1,461

years, the same as a Sothic cycle—the time from the appearing of the
Sothis star at sunrise to its appearing then again, as calculated by the
Egyptian astronomers.

Herodotus, however, had returned from Egypt to report that
the bird came there once every five hundred years, as the people
of Heliopolis had told him. The home of the phoenix, according to
Herodotus and others, was in Arabia. There, they said, it lived to
this enormous age, then made itself a nest of twigs of spice trees.
On this it died, by setting the nest on fire and burning itself alive.
But then it came forth again from the very ashes in the freshness
of renewed youth, and flew off to Egypt to deposit what remained
of the spicy receptacle of its death and rebirth on the altar of the
sun at Heliopolis.

While Clement was reminded of these accounts by the sight
of the phoenix mosaic, and set about assessing them to see if they
might provide him with yet another avenue of illustration for the
conception of the afterlife which he was endeavoring so earnestly
to build up, it was quite different with Simon Peter. Peter had
only a vague idea of the conceptions associated with the phoenix,
but he felt instinctively that this was a representation of paganism,
with which he should not have anything to do. Indebted as he was
to Theophilus for the hospitality of his large house, and for its excellence as a meeting place for the community of the believers, he
at first made only indirect inquiries of Theophilus as to the nature
of the mosaic.

"I purchased the villa from a Roman official," said Theophilus
in answer to what Peter asked. "I think he believed that the phoenix
was an appropriate symbol of the recurrence of the years and of the
renewal and everlastingness of the empire."

Before Peter made an issue with Theophilus of his own scruples
concerning this pagan symbol, John Mark, noting the growing problem, talked with Peter about it.

"Do you remember," Mark asked Peter, "how you told us about
the vision that you had at Caesarea, where you saw a great sheet let

down from heaven, in which were all kinds of animals and reptiles and birds of the air, and you heard a voice that said, 'What God has cleansed, you must not call common'? Do you suppose one of the birds of the air was a phoenix?"

While Peter was still thinking about the implications of Mark's question, Mark went on: "While I was in Cyrene I read the poetry of Ezekiel of Alexandria. He told about the departure of our people from Egypt, and he said that when they reached Elim, where there were twelve springs of water and seventy palm trees, they were met by a wonderful bird, of a sort which none of them had ever seen before. It looked something like an eagle. Its legs were red, its breast was purple, and around its neck was something like saffron wool. Its head was held up proudly, its eyes were piercing, and its voice most impressive. In short it seemed like the king of all birds, and must have been a phoenix. The fact that this wonderful bird appeared to them gave the people much courage to go on across the wilderness."

At this point John Mark found that he was becoming interested on his own account in the remarkable bird, the representation of which, in different colors, was so vividly before him there in the mosaic in the house of Theophilus.

As his custom was, he sought diligently in his copy of the Greek translation of the Scriptures. Finally, with considerable excitement, he came upon a verse in a Psalm which said: "The righteous man shall flourish as a *phoenix.*"

It was true that in Greek the one and the same word, *phoenix,* was both the name of the fabulous bird in which Mark was presently interested and also the ordinary word for a palm tree. Accordingly, the passage was really ambiguous, and the second portion of the verse, which was parallel with the first part, went on, "as the cedar in Lebanon he shall be increased," making it probable that the whole verse really said:

> The righteous man shall flourish as a palm tree,
> as the cedar in Lebanon he shall be increased.

Still the word in Greek was *phoenix,* and you could think, every time you read it, that it was speaking of the wonderful bird, for that was its name too.

The righteous man shall flourish as a phoenix.

When John Mark showed this passage to Simon Peter, Peter was not greatly impressed by it, but at least desisted from raising any further questions with Theophilus about the suitability of the mosaic as a decoration in the courtyard which was so generously being made available as a place for Peter to speak and for the believers to gather.

With Clement, however, it was otherwise. He had already arrived at the thought that some of the sequences in the natural world, such as night and day, suggested the sequence of death and life. Then the remarkable mosaic in the house of Theophilus had recalled the story of the wonderful bird, whose reported experience was a veritable symbol of death and resurrection. Now John Mark showed him the passage in the Scriptures which, taking the words most literally, declared that the righteous man should flourish like the phoenix. Surely that meant that though the righteous man should die, he would also be raised up again. But that was exactly what Simon Peter said had happened already to Jesus.

Clement felt a great surge of conviction welling up within him. At the earliest opportunity he took his stand on a corner of the phoenix mosaic, in front of Peter, declared that he believed in Jesus Christ, and was thereafter baptized.

In another small essay, Clement wrote: "Let us consider that wonderful sign of the resurrection which takes place in Eastern lands, that is, in Arabia and the countries round about. There is a certain bird which is called a phoenix. This is the only one of its kind, and lives five hundred years. And when the time of its dissolution in death is at hand, it builds itself a nest of frankincense and myrrh and other spices, into which, when the time is fulfilled, it enters. Then it sets fire to this nest, and dies in the flames, yet comes forth from its own ashes into a new life. After this, it takes up what is left of its nest and, bearing the same, passes from the land of Arabia into Egypt, to the city called Heliopolis. And, in open day, flying in the sight of all men, it places what it carries on the altar of the sun; then, having done this, it hastens back to its former abode. The priests then inspect the registers of dates, and find that it has returned exactly as the five-hundredth year was completed.

"Do we then consider it a great and wonderful thing that the Creator of the universe will raise up again those that have piously served him in the assurance of a good faith, when even through a bird he shows us the mightiness of his promise? For the Scripture says, 'The righteous man shall flourish as a phoenix.'

"Having then this hope, let our souls be bound to him who is faithful in his promises and righteous in his judgments."

13

Simon Magus

It was not long after Clement and his family were reunited and all were baptized that they decided to return to their home in Rome, and took their departure. They had spoken so often and so much of the great capital city of the world that Simon Peter and John Mark felt an increasing desire to go there, too. In the meantime Simon Peter's mother-in-law had died at Capernaum in Galilee, and Peter's wife had come on to join him. Now the three, Peter and his wife and John Mark, took passage to Rome and, before the second year of Claudius was over, arrived at the imperial city.

They landed at the seaport of Ostia, proceeded into the heart of the city, and turned aside from the Forum to the Via Labicana, where they found the house of Clement, and were made welcome. There, much had already happened. Almost immediately after getting back to the city, Clement's father had died and, shortly thereafter, Clement's twin brothers had decided to go to Spain. Clement and his mother, Mattidia, therefore, occupied their large house alone.

Also, Clement and his mother, having returned to Rome as baptized believers in Jesus, had already made contact with at least a small number of other persons in the city who were believers too. These were, in the first instance, several Jews and several proselytes to Judaism who had been in Jerusalem on the notable Pentecost day a number of years earlier when Peter and his companions had spoken so effectively about Jesus, and when so large a number of persons had been baptized. These several Jews and proselytes had been among those then baptized and, having returned to Rome, had brought there the same message that they had heard from Peter, and had persuaded to belief a number of additional persons, both several more Jews and several Gentiles.

When these heard that Simon Peter was now present in the home of Clement, they gathered there with much eagerness to hear him, and Clement and his mother made their home available for gatherings of the believers, just as Theophilus had done with his house in Antioch.

Those who came were also much interested in Mark's compendium of the main facts about Jesus, and of his typical teachings. As their numbers increased, there were many who were most at home in the Latin language. It was not long, therefore, until it seemed that it would be useful for Mark's document to be put into Latin, and several persons worked together to do this.

The translators were interested and pleased on finding that in its Greek form the document already contained a number of Latin words. This showed them that the influence of their language had spread widely in the whole world that was ruled by Rome.

Thus they read that when a paralyzed man was lowered through a roof into the presence of Jesus, he was lying on a *grabatus,* or pallet; when Herodias asked for the head of John the Baptist, the king sent a *speculator,* or executioner, to perform the task of decapitation; and when Jesus was put to death, the officer who stood there facing him was a *centurio,* or centurion. All of these words, and others, were there in Mark's document, plainly Latin words, but written in Greek form, and all the translators had to do was to write them directly over into Latin.

×

Mark's document on what Jesus had said and done was now in all three languages, the original Aramaic and also Greek and Latin. How fortunate this was, was especially borne home to him when he went down into the catacombs at Rome.

A Jewish man and his wife who had come to hear Peter at the house of Clement, and had been baptized by Peter in the Tiber River, suffered the death of their little daughter, and Peter and John Mark went with them and a small company of friends to the place of burial.

An inconspicuous entranceway in the hillside outside the city admitted to a steeply descending stairway. Once within the doorway the little company would have been in total darkness, save that several persons carried oil lamps. By this flickering illumination they found their way deep underground where long corridors branched off in several directions.

John Mark marveled at the labor that had been expended by the Jewish community in Rome for what must have been many years to prepare such a subterranean cemetery. He saw that the excavation was in earth of a volcanic sort, which could be cut cleanly and which stood firmly. On the walls he noticed occasionally the drawing of a pick and shovel, and recognized that some patient digger of the catacomb had left his sign behind him.

On either side, in rows one above the other and extending far along the sides of the corridors, were burial niches, neatly closed with bricks or slabs of stone. Almost always on these closures were simple inscriptions, and it was here that John Mark noticed that his people living in Rome had written only occasionally in Hebrew or Aramaic, most often in Greek, but not seldom in Latin.

"Annia, wife of Bar-Calabria," Mark read in Aramaic.

"Here lies Judas, a priest"—this was in Greek.

"Deuteros, sweet scribe, well meriting praise"—this was in Latin.

Although the predominance of Greek and Latin over Hebrew and Aramaic in the inscriptions showed how fully the Jewish community was at home in its Roman environment, there was no doubt about its adherence to the ancestral faith of Israel, for this was shown by the signs which often accompanied the inscriptions, these being symbols of the Jewish faith, most often the seven-armed lampstand, like the great lampstand in the Jerusalem Temple, and the palm branch, which was carried in the Feast of Tabernacles.

At last the small band of people, of which Peter and Mark were a part, paused before a small open niche in the wall. Therein the body of the little girl, carefully wrapped in linen, was gently placed by the parents.

As the company stood in silence, Peter began to speak. He recited some words from the customary burial service of his people, then went on in his own words.

"The God of our fathers has also raised up Jesus from the dead and given him glory, so that our faith and hope are in him. Through his resurrection we have been born anew to a living hope, and we rejoice in an inheritance which is imperishable, undefiled, and unfading. Without having seen him you love him; though you do not now see him you believe in him; though you now no longer will see your little daughter you know she is safe with him."

To John Mark it seemed that Peter had spoken with special exaltation and eloquence, yet he saw that tears were still flowing from the eyes of the bereaved parents. A sudden thought came to him, and he brought out his own document, quickly found a particular passage, and read it to them.

"And they were bringing children to him, that he might touch them; and the disciples rebuked them. But when Jesus saw it he was indignant, and said to them, 'Let the children come to me, do not hinder them; for to such belongs the kingdom of God. Truly, I say to you, whoever does not receive the kingdom of God like a child shall not enter it.' And he took them in his arms and blessed them, laying his hands upon them."

As Mark finished reading, the father quietly repeated after him, "And he took them in his arms and blessed them . . . ," and, for the first time, a certain look of calm spread over the faces of both parents.

Most of the others now went away, but Peter and Mark remained with the parents while another man cut into the piece of stone with which the grave niche was to be closed this inscription:

Here lies a child, Marcella.
She lived four years.
May your sleep be in peace.

Beneath the inscription was a seven-armed lampstand and a palm branch. As he looked at the work, another thought came to John Mark. He remembered the day when he and Peter had stood before the grave of James the son of Zebedee on the slope of the Mount of Olives, and had seen the Jerusalem believers cut into his stone marker the sign of the Taw, the cross mark which signified the name of the Messiah and promised salvation in his name.

Mark showed the man who was cutting the inscription how to add this sign, and it was done. Finally the closure slab of the simple grave was in place, and they all turned to leave. The last thing upon which the light of their lamps fell was the sign of the cross.

✕

An inscription of a different sort caught the attention of Simon Peter and John Mark a few days later. Where the Tiber River made a large curve as it flowed through the city, there was an island in the middle of the stream, and the island was reached by a bridge from either bank of the river. The island was named for Tiberius, and was filled with shrines and statuary. Peter and John were walking across the island when Peter stopped short in front of a statue and pointed to the words which were carved on its base.

Simoni Deo Sancto
To Simon the Holy God

"No, not here, not Simon again!" cried Peter. But much as he wished he could banish what he saw by denying it, there was no mistaking the likeness carved there in stone.

Peter's mind flew back to a day in a city of Samaria a number of years before. He and John the son of Zebedee had gone there, following upon work done by one of the other members of the Jerusalem community of believers. This man was Philip, and he was one of the Hellenists who were scattered from Jerusalem when Stephen was martyred. In the land of Samaria he had been very successful in telling the message about Jesus and in healing the sick in his name, and many people had become believers.

One of those who said he believed Philip's message and was baptized was a man named Simon. He was a native of the city of Gitto, not far from Mount Gerizim. He had previously practiced magic in the city, and had gained a great reputation. He was commonly known as Simon Magus, and some people even began to think that he was divine and to call him the Great Power of God.

Philip accepted Simon's profession of faith as sincere, and allowed him to go around with him. The probability was, however, that Simon was so amazed by the miracles he saw performed by Philip that he just wanted to find out their secret.

This was confirmed when Peter and John came to his city. When Peter and John came, something else very wonderful happened, because as they laid their hands on the newly baptized persons and prayed for them the Holy Spirit fell upon them as had not happened before. When Simon Magus saw this he offered money to Peter and John to obtain the same power. Peter, however, recognized his perfidy immediately, and condemned him bluntly for trying to obtain God's gift with money.

"Your silver perish with you, because you thought you could obtain the gift of God with money!" said Peter.

All of that flashed back into Simon Peter's mind as he and John Mark stood in front of the statue on the Island of Tiberius in the middle of the river in Rome. The likeness was assuredly none other than that of Simon Magus, and the inscription hailed him as "the Holy God."

In the years since the event in Samaria, Peter had heard occasional reports concerning the further activities of Simon Magus. He had taken up, it was said, with a certain woman named Helena, who had formerly been a prostitute in Tyre of Phoenicia. Simon then explained his liaison by saying that Helena was the lost sheep, and he had come to redeem her. Talking like that about the lost sheep, Simon seemed to be using language he had learned from those who had told him about Jesus, and Peter wondered if Simon were still pretending to be one of the believers.

Now, at any rate, it was evident that Simon had already been in Rome, and had gained followers and been honored by them with this statue and its inscription.

It was not long afterward that Simon Peter was brought face to face, not just with the statue of the man he had forthrightly condemned earlier in Samaria, but with the person himself.

Simon Magus came back to Rome, learned that Peter was there and, being emboldened and confirmed in his high opinion of himself by the fact that he had not only so long survived Peter's curse but also so successfully attracted so many more adherents, challenged Peter to public debate. In this, Simon Magus maintained his pose of adherence to the community of believers in Jesus, and proposed that the disputation be held in the house of Clement.

Some of Peter's friends tried to dissuade him from accepting the challenge, and said: "We are anxious for you, and afraid lest, in such a contest with Simon, you should seem to be overmatched. For it very frequently happens that the one who defends the truth in a public debate does not gain the victory, since the hearers are either prejudiced, or have no great interest in the better cause. But over and above all of that, Simon himself is a most vehement orator, trained in the dialectic art and in the meshes of syllogisms. And what is worse than all, he is greatly skilled in the magic art. Therefore we fear lest he, being so strongly fortified on every side, shall be thought to be defending the truth, while he is in fact alleging falsehoods."

Peter, however, was of no mind to avoid the contest, and John Mark took some comfort in remembering, from his compendium, that Jesus had told his followers that in a time of testing they should not be anxious beforehand what they were to say, but what they should say would be given to them in the hour of need.

When the time came, a considerable company was gathered in the courtyard of the house of Clement, including friends of Peter, adherents of Simon Magus, and not a few outsiders, simply attracted by what they had heard was to take place.

Simon Magus entered with a flourish, a short stocky man, with heavy black hair and piercing eyes. Helena, his consort, was on his arm, and he showed her first to a seat. Then he strode to the center of the courtyard and raised his arms, striking his hands together as he did so. By one of his magic arts, as his hands touched, a sheet of flame arose from between them, and he glared through the flame balefully.

In spite of having made so dramatic an entrance, his opening words were disarmingly simple. He expressed appreciation for the opportunity of conducting a discussion with Peter on a subject which he assumed was of concern to all who were gathered there. Then he posed his first question.

"Will you please tell me, O Peter, if this statement is true? 'What God wishes to be is, and what he does not wish to be, is not.' "

Peter was more accustomed to telling in a simple way about the things he had seen Jesus do and heard him say, rather than engaging in a philosophical discussion such as, it now seemed evident, Simon Magus was intending to conduct. John Mark wondered whether Peter would be quite discomfited. He saw him bow his head deeply for a moment, then look up calmly, as if something had indeed been given him, from a higher source, to say.

"If I were to answer you, O Simon Magus," Peter began, "that what God wishes is, and what he wishes not is not, you would say that he then wishes the evil things to be, which are done in the world, since everything that he wishes is, and everything that he wishes not is not.

"But if I were to answer you that it is not so that what God wishes is, and what he wishes not is not, you would retort that God must then be powerless, since he cannot do what he wills.

"It is evident, therefore, that you have only contrived a logical trap, and do not truly and deeply desire to learn the truth. Let me only say that God's will is over all, but he has willed it to be so that men have it in their power to do things which they will, and he will not fail to visit them with rewards and punishments, according to their actions and their wills."

Simon Magus was obviously taken aback by the clarity of Peter's perception and presentation, but he glanced hastily at notes which he drew from a fold of his robe, and asked again: "Was God not able to make us all such that we should be good, and that we should not have it in our power to be otherwise?"

With the enunciation of this difficult question, Simon Magus again assumed a haughty appearance, as if he were quite confident that he was the master of the occasion. Again he was surprised by the forthright answer Peter made.

"This also is an absurd question," Peter said. "For if God had made us of an unchangeable nature and incapable of being moved away from good, we should not be really good, because we could not do anything else; and it would not be of our purpose that we were good; and what we did would not be ours, but of the necessity of our nature. But how can that be called good which is not done of purpose? It is for this reason—that souls may learn to desire the good—that the world goes through its long course until the visible heaven shall be rolled up like a scroll and that which is higher shall appear."

If Peter had stopped with his initial answer in this statement, Simon Magus might have been left with nothing to say, but Peter's mention of the visible heaven which, he said, is to be done away with gave Simon Magus an opening that he took quickly.

"If the visible heaven is, as you say, to be dissolved, why was it made at first?"

To this Peter made such a simple answer that Simon Magus felt he was in position to clinch his side of the argument by another set of questions which he thought would be truly unanswerable.

Peter said: "The visible heaven was made to overarch the present life of men, to declare to them the glory of God, and to remind them that, as our Master said, only the pure in heart shall see God."

"But," said Simon Magus, "if the Creator is good, and the world is good, how shall he who is good ever destroy that which is good? But if he shall dissolve and destroy it as evil, how shall he not appear to be evil, who has therefore made that which is evil?"

Again Peter bowed his head momentarily, then lifted his head and spoke calmly.

"If indeed that heaven which is visible and transient had been made for its own sake, there would have been some reason in what you say, that it ought not to be dissolved. But if it was made not for its own sake, but for the sake of something else, it must of necessity be dissolved, that that for which it was made may appear. In short, it is necessary that the condition of this world pass away, that the sublimer condition of the heavenly kingdom may shine forth."

Simon Magus looked momentarily blank, then grasped after something that Peter had said previously.

"You said that your Master taught that the pure in heart shall see God. But this is assuredly contrary to the law, for there it is written that God said, 'None shall see my face and live.' "

It was evident that Simon Magus had gained some knowledge of the Scriptures, but Peter was not baffled.

"There is no contradiction," he said, "for God is seen by the mind, not by the body, and by the spirit, not by the flesh. Wherefore our Master also said of the little children that it is their angels who in heaven always behold the face of the Father. Likewise he said that after the resurrection of the dead, they shall be made like the angels in heaven, and so they shall be able to see God. Thus my statement is not contrary to the law, neither is that which our Master said, 'Blessed are they of a pure heart, for they shall see God.' "

With several blustering oaths to cover his increasing confusion, Simon Magus cried: "Concerning one thing only render me a reason —whether the soul is immortal. But let it be tomorrow, for today it is late."

14

At the Pharos

On the morrow Simon Magus did not present an appearance, and it was eventually learned that he had departed again from Rome. Evidently after his excursion into philosophy, in which he had found that Peter, whom he had always judged a rather simpleminded Galilean, could answer very cogently, he had decided to return to his practices in the area of magic. Ultimately it was learned that he had perished in one of his own grandiose experiments.

In the meantime other persons reached Rome, whose arrival caused Simon Peter and John Mark greater pleasure. These were none other than Esther, the wife of Simon of Cyrene, and her son Rufus.

Mark remembered well the evening in Jerusalem when his mother and he had waited a long time for Simon and his family to come for the Passover meal, and how Simon had told them, greatly agitated, of his delay which had been occasioned by the strange events of the day, namely, that he had been constrained to carry the cross for Jesus, and had witnessed the crucifixion on the hill outside the city.

In due course, after that, Simon and his family had become members of the community of believers in Jesus in Jerusalem. Then Simon had died, Alexander, the older son, had returned to Cyrene, and now Rufus and his mother had come to Rome.

The talks which John Mark had with Rufus, now a fine young

man, and with his mother, reawakened his memories of Cyrene, where he too had lived in his earlier days. At the same time, Mark felt that Peter needed his services less than before, because he was more familiar himself now with the Gentile world, and also, of course, because Peter's wife had been free to come with them when they had come to Rome.

John Mark resolved to revisit Cyrene. When he spoke to Peter about it, he was pleased to find that Peter readily agreed. Not only that, but Peter suggested that he go on also to Egypt and to the great capital city of Alexandria.

"Rome, Alexandria, and Antioch are the three greatest cities of the world," he said, "and we must make sure that the story of Jesus is told also in Alexandria, since we have already been in Antioch and here in Rome."

It was in the third year of Claudius, and John Mark took his departure.

In Cyrene, although he was interested in being again at the scene of his boyhood, John Mark did not stay long. He found Alexander, son of Simon of Cyrene, and brought to him the greetings of his mother and of his brother, Rufus, in Rome. Through Alexander he also found and met with a small band of believers in Jesus, some of whom had been in Jerusalem on the Pentecost day when Peter had spoken. But a feeling which had grown stronger within him ever since he left Rome continued to increase. This was the feeling that he must press on to Alexandria, even as Peter had suggested.

John Mark strode down the road that descended the mountain from Cyrene to the seaport of Apollonia, and there embarked on a ship bound for the capital of Egypt.

✕

From the foredeck of the ship, John Mark gazed intently through the darkness. Finally he saw it, exactly as the master of the vessel had told him he would.

"The greatest sight as you come to Alexandria," said the master of the vessel, "is the lighthouse, which is one of the wonders of the world."

"Yes," said John Mark, "I have heard about it. Tell me what it looks like."

"Offshore at Alexandria," responded the master, "is the island which the Greeks call Pharos. It protects the harbors which lie behind it on either side, but it would be a great danger if one did not know it was there. So Sostratus and other architects, working for the first Ptolemies, designed the lighthouse.

"It stands in a colonnaded court, and towers up to a height of more than 250 cubits. The bottom story, half the height of the whole, is square and built of limestone. In it are the engines which lift the fuel to the higher levels. The middle tier is an octagon, made of marble, with a double spiral staircase within. The top story is circular, constructed of red-purple granite which was floated down the Nile all the way from Upper Egypt. It supports a cupola upon eight columns.

"In the cupola, visible far out across the sea, is a polished metal reflector. In the daytime this reflects the sunlight, and sends out messages. In the nighttime a fire of resinous wood burns in front of it, and can be seen as a light, almost like a star, from far away."

That was the way it looked when John Mark first caught sight of it. He could not be sure if it were a star or the lighthouse fire, but as the ship plowed steadily forward through the sea the light grew larger and he knew he was seeing the marker that would guide them into port.

When Mark awakened the next morning, his ship was lying at anchor in the Great Harbor which was the Eastern Harbor at Alexandria. The Pharos was not far away, the high tower of the great lighthouse rising from the island, and its high, polished reflector catching the brilliant light of the morning sun and sending it out far across the sea. The sunshine was also brilliantly illuminating all the buildings along the shore, these all being built of stone and covered with a gypsum stucco that was dazzlingly white.

The ship's master fell into conversation again with John Mark. It was plain that he took an almost proprietary interest in the great city to and from which his vessel regularly sailed, and that he actually knew a great deal about the history of the place.

"Just think," he said, "when the great Alexander first came here there was nothing but the island and on shore, on the hill, the old village of Rhakotis.

"Alexander was only twenty-five years old, and he was on his way to conquer the world. He went up to Memphis, and he came back down the Nile to Canopus"—here the captain gestured toward the coast as it stretched away toward the sunrising.

"He saw that this was a natural harbor, and that it could be connected by a canal with the Nile. There was fresh water, and a perfect climate, and limestone quarries, and gypsum along the coast" —here the speaker gestured toward the coast as it stretched away in the other direction.

"He ordered Dinocrates to build a magnificent Greek city. It would be the capital of his new Egyptian kingdom, and the metropolis of all of his kingdoms, even for the whole inhabited world."

"Dinocrates?" asked John Mark. "Who was that?"

"Oh," said the captain, "he was a very famous architect. Do you know what he did that first attracted Alexander's attention?"

Without waiting for an answer which was obviously out of the range of John Mark's experience, the ship's master went on.

"Alexander came from Macedonia, you know. Up there on the coast, three promontories extend into the sea like the prongs of a trident. The farthest, highest one is Mt. Athos, and it is more than a mile high above the sea. Dinocrates, therefore, proposed that he would carve the whole mountain into a statue of Alexander which, in its left hand, would hold a city of ten thousand inhabitants and, in its right hand, would pour forth a river running into the sea!"

John Mark expressed proper appreciation for the audacity of the conception of the architect of whom he had not heard before, and the ship's captain went on:

"So, when Alexander had great projects in mind he entrusted them to Dinocrates for execution. Here, between the sea and the lake" —and he gestured into the distance beyond the city—"he himself traced the boundaries of what he had in mind, and told Dinocrates to get on with building the metropolis of the inhabited earth.

"Never, I think," he continued reflectively, "did so small a village as Rhakotis become so great a city as Alexandria so soon, and, of course, the Ptolemies and even the Romans went on with the building until you see what you see here now."

Again the captain waved his arm expansively toward the gleaming city across the turquoise bay.

Not far away was the long narrow line of a mole which ran from the island to the shore.

"That," said the ship's master, "is the Heptastadion."

John Mark's Greek was adequate, and he murmured, "Seven stadia—well nigh a mile long. In this bright light it hardly looks that long."

"Yonder," the captain continued, "the city is laid out in a great rectangle. Through the middle, from one side to the other, runs Canopic Street, colonnaded and a hundred feet wide, and running across it from here to the lake, is the Street of the Soma."

"Of the Soma?" asked Mark puzzled. "The Street of the Body?"

"Yes," answered the captain, "the Soma is what they call the place where Alexander is buried, which is at the intersection of those two streets. You know Alexander came back from India and died in Babylon when he was not yet thirty-three years old. Then they brought his body all the way back to Memphis, but the high priest refused to receive him. 'Do not settle him here,' he cried, 'but at the city he has built at Rhakotis, for wherever this body must lie, the city will be uneasy, disturbed with wars and battles.' So he came back down the Nile once again, all wrapped in gold and protected by a coffin of glass, and was buried at the center of the city he had built.'

"Is it true," asked Mark, "that there have been wars and battles here ever since?"

"Well," said the captain thoughtfully, "there certainly have been plenty of tumults, and I think there will be more. There are so many different people living here that I suppose it cannot be otherwise. Over there in Rhakotis are the old-time Egyptians, here in the main part are the Greeks, and yonder in Delta are the Jews—and the Jews and the Greeks are always quarreling with each other, while the native Egyptians look down on both."

As the captain spoke, his arm had swept in gesture across the city from one side to the other, but John Mark was still puzzled as to what he meant by Delta where the Jews lived. Trying not to display too obvious an interest in his own people, Mark asked as to the meaning of the designation Delta.

"You see," responded the ship's master, "the whole city is built up in blocks and divided into five quarters which are called Alpha, Beta, Gamma, Delta, and Epsilon. Most of the Jews live in Delta."

John Mark made a mental note of the name Delta and of the direction of the captain's gesture toward the sunrising as he had spoken of the Jewish quarter.

The captain returned, in the explanation he was giving to John Mark about the city, to the Street of the Soma.

"If you go along the Street of the Soma you will see not only the burial places of Alexander and of some of the earlier Ptolemies, but also, not far away, the Museion and the Library. You remember I told you about Sostratus, who built the lighthouse here? Well, at about the time he was doing that, Euclid had been studying at the Museion, and Eratosthenes was head of the Library."

"There were many books in the Library?" asked John Mark doubtfully, for he was hearing of things which were far from his previous scope of knowledge.

"Half a million of them," said the ship's master triumphantly. "And that is only the Mother Library. In the Daughter Library, which is over there at the Serapeion"—he pointed toward the district of Rhakotis—"there are even more volumes. Also, when you go out beyond the city you will find yourself on the edge of the papyrus marshes; there is enough writing material there to go on writing books forever."

A saying from the Scriptures came to his mind, and John Mark quoted it, just attributing it to some unnamed wise man of whom he had heard: "Of making many books there is no end, and much study is a weariness of the flesh."

The captain smiled slightly, but it was plain that he was in much earnest in regard to all the things that he was telling about.

For his part, the conversation was beginning to recall to Mark's mind some things from his school days in Cyrene, and he thought of something he could say that would sound as if he were taking a more appreciative interest in what the captain was telling him than his somewhat disparaging quotation about "many books."

"I know that Eratosthenes, whom you mentioned as having once been the head of the Library here, was a great man. I remember that when I went to school long ago in Cyrene they often spoke of him, because that was where he had been born, and they were proud that he had become so famous. They said that he had even measured the earth, but I never understood how that was done."

"I think I can explain it to you, if you are interested," said the captain in a kindly way. "You see, in order to be the master of this ship I have to be a navigator, and so I have had to study a great deal about figures, and the stars, and the earth. Those are things that Eratosthenes knew more about than anybody else ever knew.

"As far as measuring the earth is concerned, he learned that in the summer when the sun comes closest our way it gets to be straight over Syene—up just below the First Cataract of the Nile—because there at that time it shines straight down a very deep well. So at that exact time he measured how much the sun lacked of being straight overhead here at Alexandria, and found that it was one-fiftieth of a great circle. So, he said to himself, the distance from Alexandria to Syene is also one-fiftieth of the distance around the earth. He knew that distance is 5,000 stadia, and he multiplied by fifty and got 250,000 stadia as the distance around the earth."

John Mark had done his best to follow this line of reasoning, which was in an area of thought not very familiar to him, and he commented respectfully: "With your own great knowledge of figures and the stars and the earth, I can see that you are well fitted to take your ship on long voyages. How far do you go?"

"Look," said the ship's master, with continued interest in all that he was telling and with appreciation for Mark's attention, "yonder on the far side of the Heptastadion is the Eunostos Harbor, the Harbor of Safe Return. If we should sail in there we could go on through a canal into Lake Mareotis behind the city, then through another canal all the way to the Nile at Memphis, and from there through a canal in the Valley of Tumilat to the Salt Lakes and on down into the Red Sea. Or we can go all the way up the Nile to Koptos, and then through a shorter canal across to the Red Sea. From there, we can sail all the way to India and back again, since we have learned that the winds blow toward that land in the summer and back again this way in the winter."

"Have you ever made that voyage yourself?" asked John Mark, greatly amazed at what he was hearing from the sea captain.

"Yes," he answered, "I have made one voyage there and back. And when you follow the Street of the Soma straight through the city you will come to the Lake Harbor, and there you may well see some ship that has even now come back from such a trip."

"Do some of the people of India come here too?" asked Mark.

"Ah, yes," replied the captain, "you will find everybody here— Greeks and Romans, Syrians and Jews, Libyans and Ethiopians, Arabs and Persians, Bactrians and Scythians, and Indians. This is the crossroads of the whole world, and here all manner of men mingle and become a kindred people."

"But I thought you said that the Egyptians and Greeks and Jews were always quarreling with one another," Mark ventured.

"Ah, yes," said the ship's master, "that is true too. I suppose the closer they all are together, the more they rub against each other and make trouble."

John Mark thought of his compendium of what Jesus had said and done, and recalled where Jesus had been asked for the great commandment and had replied with two—"You shall love the Lord your God. . . . You shall love your neighbor as yourself "—but he said nothing aloud, and the conversation came to an end.

15

Annianus

When John Mark was brought ashore from the ship, which rode at anchor in the Great Harbor, he landed at the head of the Street of the Soma. It would have been of interest to him to go along the famous street and see some of the monuments of which the ship's master had spoken in his eloquent description of the great city of Alexandria. Instead, however, he thought it necessary to place the concerns of his mission first. Presumably, it would be among his own people, who, according to the captain, were so numerous here, that he would find any who might have been in Jerusalem and might have heard something already about Jesus, perhaps even some who might have been there on that Pentecost day when Peter had spoken to so many from so many different lands.

Accordingly Mark turned to the left and toward the morning sun, in the general direction that the captain had indicated when he had mentioned the Delta quarter of the city, where most of the Jews lived. With an occasional discreet inquiry about Delta, he found his way without difficulty.

Proceeding generally parallel to the edge of the Great Harbor, he crossed the base of a cape which formed the eastern side of the harbor. He also crossed a canal, and then encountered a wall of the city which had the appearance of centuries of age. He wondered if this were

indeed where the great Alexander had traced the edge of his proposed
city, and where Dinocrates had built. The city stretched on before
him, however, and he went on, wondering if he were now in Delta.
Although the people about him were still speaking the Greek language, there were frequent Semitic words interspersed in what they
said, and it was soon evident to John Mark that he was in the midst
of his own people.

At that point a small incident took place which was to have
far-reaching results. The incident consisted in the fact that at that
moment the strap of one of Mark's sandals broke, and he sought for
the shop of a cobbler who might repair it for him.

Close by he found such a shop, and gave the sandal with the
broken strap to the cobbler. The cobbler, a man somewhat younger
than Mark, received the sandal in his left hand and, with his right
hand, took up a sharp awl with which to make holes for the resewing
that he had to do. It was the kind of a task that he must have done
many hundreds of times. This time, by one of those inexplicable
accidents in which a routine task is attended with sudden disaster, the
awl slipped, pierced the man's hand, and tore it badly.

"*Heis ho theos,*" cried the man in Greek, which means "God is
One."

It was of course an involuntary oath, but to John Mark it seemed
a sign that here was definitely a believer in the God of his people, with
whom he could make a beginning in telling in Alexandria about Jesus
as the Christ, sent by the One God.

Also Mark felt instant compassion for the man, for the grievous
wound in his hand would assuredly interfere with the practice of the
trade upon which he depended for his livelihood. John Mark had
often seen Simon Peter pray and lay his hands on some sick or
crippled person, with the result that a healing took place. He himself
had never supposed that he was authorized to undertake any such
thing, but now he was all alone in the great city, and here was a man
badly hurt, and hurt in the process of trying to perform a task for him.

Suddenly there came into his mind a passage which was in his own compendium of the things that Jesus had said and done. It was a short account of how Jesus had sent out some of his followers on their own, and had told them to drive out unclean spirits and heal diseases; it concluded, as Mark remembered it, with the report that they "anointed with oil many that were sick and healed them."

John Mark felt strongly moved to try to do for the wounded man in front of him what those earlier followers of Jesus had been able to do. He looked quickly about the small shop to see if any olive oil were at hand, but there was none. In lieu of that he did what he vaguely remembered having been told that even Jesus himself sometimes did. He stepped to the door, spat upon the ground, with the spittle made a small lump of clay, and placed it upon the wound in the man's hand.

With his own hand still pressing hard upon the clay and upon the man's hand, he looked up to heaven and said, "In the name of Jesus Christ the Son of God, be healed."

Instantly John Mark sensed that some kind of power was flowing through his hand, and he felt the hand of the wounded man tremble violently. Mark withdrew his hand, and carefully removed the clay he had applied. The profuse bleeding had stopped, and the flesh in the hand of the cobbler was whole and good.

The cobbler looked up into Mark's face and said to him with all earnestness: "I beg you, O man of God, to come today into the house of your servant, and we will eat bread together, because you have had pity on me today. First, however, I will complete the repair of your sandal."

At the house of the cobbler, John Mark learned that the man's name was Hannaniah or, in the Greek form which he used there in Alexandria, Annianus. Mark also met his wife and three small children.

After they had eaten together, the cobbler asked John Mark very respectfully: "O my father, I beg you to make known to me who you are, and whence comes this power that is in you whereby you have worked this great miracle for me."

John Mark replied by saying simply, "I am a servant of Jesus Christ, the Son of God."

Annianus exclaimed, "I wish that I could see him."

"I will tell you of him," said Mark, and he proceeded to recite several of the things that Jesus had done and said, as they were written in his compendium, and he also quoted several of the prophecies in the Scriptures about the Christ who would come.

"I know all too little of our Scriptures," said Annianus. "Here on the edge of Delta, where I live, many Greeks come to my shop and I hear them always talking about the books of their philosophers."

Mark remembered the attempts of Simon Magus to argue against Peter with philosophical questions, and he said: "If it be filled with pride, even the wisdom of the philosophers is vanity before God."

✕

Although John Mark went deeper into Delta to find lodging, he continued to visit Annianus. In the course of time the prophecies of Scripture and the testimonies about Jesus which the cobbler heard from Mark, together with the thought of the great miracle that he had seen Mark work on his hand, led Annianus to believe in Jesus whom Mark proclaimed as the Christ, and he and his household were baptized, together with several of his neighbors.

In Delta John Mark found also a synagogue of his people, and being present in the sabbath service and being recognized as a visitor from the homeland, he was invited to speak.

He began what he had to say with some of the words of the prophets, then went on to tell about Jesus and to declare that he was the Christ whom the prophets had taught them to expect. Afterward a few persons came to Mark to tell him that they had been in Jerusalem on the Pentecost day when Peter had first given his public message about Jesus, and that they had come back to Egypt as baptized believers. They were so few, however, that they had done nothing except continue to attend the synagogue services and there, in the silence of their own minds, confess that they believed in Jesus as the Christ and as risen from the dead.

John Mark now brought these persons, and a few others of the synagogue who showed an interest in what he said, together in a common gathering with the several believers at the house of Annianus. Other persons were soon attracted, and these included not only Jews but also Greeks—some of the latter being ones known to Annianus at his shop—and even Egyptians as well.

Although they came to the meetings together, John Mark could not help observing that there was a tendency toward animosity between the members of the several groups, and he remembered what the ship's captain had told him of the repeated disturbances between Greeks and Jews in Alexandria.

Therefore John Mark spent much time in talking with all the believers of how Jesus had stated that the great commandments were to love God and also to love one's neighbor as oneself. Gradually, he was pleased to see, a greater spirit of common understanding began to be manifest, and then the small community began to show power to attract much larger numbers of adherents—Jews, Greeks, and Egyptians all.

When baptisms were to be conducted, John Mark now had Annianus as his assistant. The latter always showed himself an eager student of everything pertaining to the message about Jesus, and even, on occasion, one through whom healing power flowed for the help of sick persons. So the work that was done in the name of Jesus in Alexandria prospered.

It was especially helpful to John Mark that in the course of his many conversations with members of the Jewish community he was able to point to passages in the Greek version of the Scriptures and remind them that this translation had been made right there in their midst. This fact was known to John Mark only as a general item of information, but as soon as he would mention it he would find on the part of at least many of the leaders of the Jewish community a very lively remembrance of what they had heard, passed down from their ancestors, about the origin of that remarkable work.

After the great Alexander, one of his generals, known as *ptolemaios,* or "warrior," had become ruler of Egypt and founder of a dynasty whose successive kings were each known as Ptolemy. He was hailed as *soter,* meaning "savior," a title he did not at all hesitate to accept, particularly inasmuch as his former master, Alexander, had himself been called a god by an Egyptian oracle and as the earlier kings of Egypt had also all claimed to be sons of the sun god. Ptolemy Soter was interested in literature, wrote a biography of Alexander, and was the one who established the Museion and the Library which the ship's captain had mentioned so proudly to John Mark. He appointed a Greek poet named Callimachus as chief librarian, and this man was the teacher of Eratosthenes, whom the ship's master had also spoken so much of. Ptolemy Soter also transferred many Jews from their homeland to Egypt; thus many of those with whom John Mark talked were descendants of persons who had come to live in Alexandria at that time.

The second Ptolemy was hardly ever mentioned without some reference also to his sister, Arsinoë, who also became his wife. He liked to call her *philadelphus,* meaning the one who loved her brother, and they reigned together as "brother-sister gods," the children of the "savior gods," the first Ptolemy and his wife. It was probably at the instigation of Arsinoë that Callimachus, still heading the Library, wrote a hymn in which he prophesied that Ptolemy would rule the world from the rising to the setting sun, while another poet described him as the greatest and wealthiest of kings, the master of 13,333 cities!

In spite of many features in his conduct which could hardly be regarded as other than objectionable by most members of the Jewish community, they usually spoke of the second Ptolemy with a considerable degree of respect and appreciation. He had encouraged more of their people to settle in Egypt, he had enlarged the first Library and started its "daughter" branch in Rhakotis, and for the Library he had desired to provide a translation of the Hebrew Scriptures into Greek.

This was what the Jewish leaders liked to tell John Mark about in greatest detail, when his use of a passage from the Greek version brought up the subject naturally. King Ptolemy actually wrote a letter, they said, to Eleazar, the high priest in Jerusalem, and asked him to send six elders from each tribe to Alexandria to make the translation. With the seventy-two translators the high priest sent precious parchment rolls in which the law was inscribed in Hebrew letters written in gold. For their work the king provided quarters free from disturbance on the island of Pharos, and there the translators carried out their task with remarkable speed and unanimity as to the appropriate rendering in Greek. Finally the entire community of the Jews was assembled at the place where the translation was executed, the finished work was read aloud to the entire gathering, and all accorded it the highest praise.

As leaders of the Jewish community in Alexandria from time to time told John Mark about these events of the past, it was evident that they were proud of the great translation of the law which had been made there among their ancestors and placed in the great Library in their city. The other books of their Scriptures, in addition to the books of the law proper, had also been rendered into Greek in due time, and when most of the people read in any of these books, or heard them read in the synagogue, it was the Greek which was used, because that was their usual language.

At the same time some of the scholars continued to devote themselves to the Hebrew text, as being the original, in preference to the Greek rendering. Furthermore, when John Mark would bring forth some Scripture text from the Greek translation and say that it had to do with Jesus as the Christ, they would look very carefully in the Hebrew and see if they could find some basis for arguing with Mark and controverting what he said.

On one occasion John Mark was engaged in a discussion with one of these scholars. He read to him from near the beginning of his compendium, where he quoted the prophet Isaiah in the words:

the voice of one crying in the wilderness:
Prepare the way of the Lord . . .

This was exactly the way the words read in the Greek translation of the book of the prophet Isaiah, and John Mark felt that he was on firm ground in saying, as he had often heard it said in the discussions in the community of the followers of Jesus in Jerusalem, that these words really described the work which John the Baptist did when he appeared in the wilderness of Judea and preached a baptism of repentance for the forgiveness of sins, and thus prepared the way for Jesus himself.

The scholar with whom John Mark was talking, however, found the same passage in his Hebrew scroll of Isaiah, and read:

A voice cries:
In the wilderness prepare the way of the Lord.

Then he almost thundered out his verdict: "The true text does not state that the voice cried in the wilderness. It is not allowable to say that this refers to the voice of John the Baptist because he preached in the wilderness of Judea. The true text simply states 'A voice cries'; that means the voice of the prophet, speaking in the Babylonian captivity. Also it says to prepare the way of the Lord in the wilderness, and that means that a way was to be made ready on which the Lord would lead his people home from exile across the wilderness between Babylonia and Jerusalem. That is what the true text says and means!"

×

It was, however, not so much differences of opinion about the use of the Greek and of the Hebrew texts of the Scriptures, or differences of opinion as to the proper interpretation of those texts, which led to a growing opposition on the part of the leaders and many of the members of the Jewish community to John Mark and those associated with him, as it was simple jealousy with respect to the growing success of the new movement. Some of the Jews found Mark's arguments from the Scriptures convincing, and his presentation of Jesus as the Christ, from his compendium of Jesus' deeds and sayings, attractive and compelling, and they continued to go over to the group that believed in Jesus; but far more Greeks, some of the Egyptians, and even some of the other peoples represented in Alexandria were now joining the movement.

In the course of time, therefore, the old animosities between the Jews and the Greeks in Alexandria, which often enough had erupted in actual violence, began to flare up again, now in the guise of opposition by the Jews to the growing community of the followers of Jesus, the majority of whom were now coming to be Greeks.

Finally this violence of opposition reached the point of actual riots which rocked the whole Delta quarter of the city. Excited to the point of frenzy, mobs rushed through the streets crying, *"Heis ho theos,"* "God is One"—the very words the utterance of which by Annianus had been associated with the first notable event in the work of John Mark in the city.

The city officials, however, being accustomed from long experience to outbreaks of this sort in the Delta quarter, acted quickly to bring the situation under control, and did so before any loss of life ensued.

In addition they sent a report, as was their custom, to the emperor in Rome. Claudius in turn, being well aware of the long history of troubles in Alexandria and being alarmed by this fresh outbreak, took occasion to include a sharp statement on the subject in his next official communication to Alexandria. This was a letter, composed in Latin and published in the city in Greek copies. The emperor began it in full formal style:

> Tiberius Claudius Caesar Augustus Germanicus Imperator, Pontifex Maximus, holder of the Tribunician Power, Consul designate, to the City of the Alexandrians, greeting.

Then, in due course, he took up a number of matters, such as
permission to the Alexandrians to erect certain statues in honor of
himself. After that he turned to the question of the disturbances. With
judicial impartiality he referred to the rights and privileges of the Jews
as residents of the city, rights and privileges which were under no
circumstance to be disallowed; then he admonished the Jews themselves not to cause trouble and, in particular, not to entertain itinerant
visitors who would foment disturbance. At this point the emperor
wrote:

> I warn the Jews not to introduce or invite into their midst
> Jews who sail down to Alexandria from Syria, thus compelling
> me to conceive great suspicion; otherwise I will by all means
> take vengeance on them as acting to assist in stirring up a
> plague which threatens the whole inhabited earth.

John Mark read a copy of the imperial communication
with mingled feelings.

On the one hand, he had no difficulty in recognizing that he
himself fitted the emperor's description of propagandists who came
down to Alexandria whose work resulted in the outbreak of disturbance. He had indeed come from Syria, since Jerusalem and Judea
were in the Roman province of that name and since he had in fact
started from Antioch of Syria on the journey which brought him
finally to Alexandria. His work had indeed, in spite of all he had done
to explain the teaching of Jesus about love of one's neighbor, resulted
in riots which had rocked the Delta quarter of Alexandria and had
come to the attention of the emperor. He wondered if similar troubles
had been breaking out in Rome because of Peter's preaching, since
Claudius seemed to refer to the movement connected with the name
of Christ as a pest which was endangering the whole inhabited earth,
and he knew that to the emperor the whole world was the same as
the Roman Empire.

On the other hand, Mark felt a sense of pride, as he read the emperor's communication, that the message about Jesus Christ had made a wide impact. Yet again he felt a sense of apprehension as to his own position and safety in Alexandria. He decided that the time had come to return, at least for a while, to Jerusalem.

16

Sarah

Sarah, who had looked at John Mark so admiringly on the night he left Jerusalem with Simon Peter, was now, some years later, a fully mature young lady. With black hair bound tightly about her head, and eyes that flashed with many lights, she was a striking figure, and to this John Mark was no longer blind. He had previously counted her one of his friends among the members of the community of believers in Jesus in Jerusalem; now the friendship deepened rapidly into a great mutual affection.

The community of believers also had grown stronger again. The crippling blows struck by Agrippa, which had included the execution of James the brother of John and the imprisonment of Simon Peter, and had led to the departure of Peter and John Mark, had come to an end with the death of the king some two years after those events.

It had come to pass, John Mark was told, that Agrippa had gone down to Caesarea to enjoy the games that were celebrated there every five years in honor of the founding of the city by Herod. On this occasion a throne was placed for Agrippa on the stage of the theater, which was a handsome structure, built in a curving hillside, looking out over the sea. On the second day of the spectacles Agrippa presented himself as a spectacle which outshone all the rest. He put on a royal robe which was woven completely of silver, and entered the theater at daybreak. There the silver, illumined by the touch of the first rays of the sun, shone like fire and by its glitter inspired fear and awe in the great crowd which gazed intently upon it. Looking toward this radiant figure, with the great sea behind it, some, who were either very willing to believe or very ready to take an occasion to flatter their ruler, cried out that the sun god was rising for them out of the sea. "May you be propitious to us," they said, "and if we have hitherto feared you as a man, yet henceforth we agree that you are more than mortal in your being."

Shortly thereafter, however, Agrippa looked up and saw a horned owl perched on a rope over his head. Immediately a scene flashed into his mind from a time long before.

He had been put in prison in Rome by Tiberius. Handcuffed to a centurion and standing in chains in front of the palace, together with many other prisoners, he leaned against a tree in his despondency. At that moment a horned owl alighted on the tree. One of the other prisoners, a German, asked the identity of Agrippa and, upon learning that he was a Jew and one of the most notable men of Judea, requested permission to approach and speak to him.

"Young man," he said, "I perceive that you are in despair at the swift reversal of your fortune, which has overwhelmed you at a single stroke. You will hardly credit the statement which interprets Divine Providence as intending your deliverance from your present difficulty. Yet the gods do assuredly tell me to tell you that you will very shortly be released from these chains and be advanced to the highest point of honor and of power. But remember also that when you see this bird again, your death will follow within five days."

As a youth Agrippa had concentrated on the first and favorable part of this remarkable prophecy, and it had indeed soon come to pass, when Gaius succeeded Tiberius and forthwith freed and elevated him.

But now it was the concluding and ominous part of the German's prophecy that came sharply back to Agrippa's mind. The horned owl was once again overhead, and he would die within five days. In fact, he was almost immediately smitten with an intense pain in his stomach.

Looking up at his friends, he cried, "I, who was called immortal by you, am now under sentence of death, and I must accept my lot as God wills it."

Even while he was speaking in this fashion, the pain became more acute, and he was carried off to his bedchamber in the palace. There, from the lofty window, he looked down upon his subjects who gathered in sackcloth to make supplication on his behalf. In exactly five days, utterly exhausted by the unremitting pain, he departed this life.

At his death Agrippa was survived but not succeeded by his son, then a youth of seventeen years. Claudius had not forgotten certain nationalistic gestures on the part of Agrippa, including his attempt, to which the emperor had put a stop, to build a new north wall of Jerusalem. Therefore he gave to the second Agrippa only certain adjacent territories, and once again sent out procurators directly from Rome to rule Judea, and now Samaria and Galilee as well.

With respect to the fortunes of the community of believers in Jesus, the presence of these immediate representatives of Roman rule was, perhaps surprisingly, of twofold benefit. For one thing, the procurators kept an iron hand upon everything in the land, and it was far less easy to stir up actions of violence against any particular group than it had been when the Pharisees were able, through Agrippa, to accomplish execution and imprisonment of leaders of the community of believers. For another thing, the ironhanded rule of the procurators was so harsh that the capacity of the people for animosity was largely channeled into an ever increasing hatred for the whole foreign domination to which they were subject, and less animosity, at least relatively speaking, was directed against the followers of Jesus.

But at the same time a new shadow fell over the land and, for the time being, it endangered the life of the community of believers in Jesus from an entirely different angle, and also seemed to John Mark and Sarah to preclude the making of plans for the future with any confidence. This was the shadow of a grievous famine.

It was in the spring of the year that the first of the new procurators, Cuspius Fadus, was succeeded by the second, Tiberius Alexander, the latter, interestingly enough, a distinguished Alexandrian Jew. With the springtime came the last chance of the year for rain. In the preceding autumn the rains had not materialized; during the winter clouds had gathered and the temperature had dropped low, but almost no moisture had fallen, and now the latter rains had failed utterly. Even the late planting, which could almost always count upon being nourished by the spring rains, would bring no fruit.

Food supplies were soon largely exhausted, and prices for anything that was available soared quite out of the reach of most of the people. Four days' wages was the cost of a double handful of grain. The same loaves of showbread stayed on the table in the Temple week after week, instead of being replaced every sabbath, and the priests dared not consume a crumb of them, lest they be attacked by the starving people.

In time, however, a measure of relief came for the main body of the people. It so happened that a famous queen of the East came to Jerusalem at this very time. This was Helena, Queen of Adiabene in Mesopotamia. In her homeland she had been instructed in the Law by a traveling Jewish merchant, and now she was on her first pilgrimage to the holy city of the faith which she had adopted, the city in which she chose ultimately to be buried in a handsome tomb which she constructed for herself and her family.

Coming now, at the height of the famine, Helena was greatly distressed by the want and misery that she saw on every side. Having provided herself with a very large sum of money for her journey, she immediately expended almost all of it for the relief of the hungry. The procurator Tiberius Alexander was in constant touch with Egypt, and knew that the famine, which had also been severe there in an earlier year, was now abated, and foodstuffs were again plentiful. Helena, accordingly, sent her attendants thither with adequate funds, and they returned with much grain.

This relief was not, however, shared with the community of

believers in Jesus, and there hunger continued. What little food she could obtain, Sarah shared with small children, and John Mark watched her grow thinner and paler every day.

Then a measure of help came also for this community, but not on the royal scale of the benefaction of Queen Helena. The help was brought by Barnabas and Saul from Antioch.

Barnabas, or Joseph Barnabas, to use his full name, was none other than Mark's own uncle, the younger brother of his father, the one that had gone off to Cyprus at the same time that Aristobulus, Mary, and John Mark had come to Jerusalem. Barnabas also had come eventually to Jerusalem, and also had become a member of the community of the followers of Jesus.

As a man of substantial means, Barnabas had acquired properties at Jerusalem, but in the community of believers he was among not a few who were poor, and he always shared generously with others. On one occasion of need he even sold one of his large fields outright and placed the entire proceeds at the disposition of the community.

In appreciation of such actions, the other members of the community made a slight play upon words and said that his name, Barnabas, really meant "Son of encouragement," and he now went most frequently by this name alone.

At an earlier period Barnabas had also gone for a time to the famous university city of Tarsus, and there in the school had become acquainted with a brilliant young man whose Hebrew and Roman names were euphoniously balanced in the forms of Saul and Paul. By a remarkable series of events Saul also came to Jerusalem, became an enemy of the movement of the followers of Jesus, and then, while on a trip to Damascus, saw Jesus alive after death and became a believer himself. When Saul came back to Jerusalem after that, the other believers were afraid of him, but Barnabas spoke for him and gained him a welcome.

Later Barnabas went to Antioch to work in the community of believers in that city. The number of the believers had continued to grow since the days Simon Peter and John Mark had been there, and feeling the need for help, Barnabas went off to Tarsus again and brought Saul back to assist.

Finally, when the famine came, several factors placed the Antioch community in a position where they were able to extend help to the Jerusalem community. The body of believers in Antioch was larger and better off than that in Jerusalem. When the first signs of the great drought were beginning to appear, a prophet named Agabus came to Antioch from Jerusalem and declared that there would be a famine in the whole land. While he probably meant only the whole land of Judea, the people in Antioch thought he meant the whole world, and began to lay by in store. Actually the famine was severest in Judea and, even at its height, Syria was little touched. Therefore the Antioch community was in a position to send relief to their brethren in Judea and Jerusalem and resolved to do so. The help was sent by Barnabas and Saul.

✕

While food would not be ample for a long time, the Jerusalem community was rescued from its direst straits by the relief from Antioch. As he watched a little color come back into the pale cheeks of his beloved Sarah, John Mark felt a sense of deep gratitude to his uncle Barnabas, the Son of encouragement.

It was also, therefore, with a sense of inescapable duty that John Mark listened when, at a somewhat later time, Barnabas said to him: "Mark, my nephew, I know that you have been doing valuable work in traveling with the message about Jesus and carrying with you the compendium you have made of the things that Jesus did and said.

"Now that the community at Antioch has carried out this present work of relief, of which Saul and I have been privileged to be the agents, I believe that they will be disposed toward other works that will reach out beyond themselves.

"When Saul and I return I shall propose that they send us off to Cyprus as their messengers to tell about Jesus. I know the island well, and there are already some scattered followers of Jesus there. I believe that we can rally them and win many more."

When Barnabas used the pronoun "we" he could have been referring simply to Saul and himself, but John Mark knew instinctively that the designation was intended more inclusively, that it was intended, in fact, to include himself.

"John Mark," said Barnabas, standing up to his impressive height, "I want you to go with us."

The mission which was thus laid upon John Mark had to be accepted, he felt, and the more so because of the help that Barnabas had brought to all of them, especially his dear Sarah. His parting from her was not without tears, partly because she was still weak from the long hunger and he felt so concerned about her.

The overland journey from Jerusalem to Antioch, the commissioning of Barnabas and Saul for the mission by the Antioch community, the voyage from the seaport at Seleucia to the harbor of Salamis on Cyprus, and the itineration across the island to the capital city of Paphos were all full of interest. Wherever they went, the impressive presence of Barnabas commanded attention, and the impetuous eloquence of Saul caused people to listen carefully if not always comprehendingly. As for Mark, with his carefully carried compendium of the deeds and sayings of Jesus, he found himself serving as a veritable officer of the message, handling the written word which was basic to the message they were presenting.

Much of the time, however, there also floated before the mind of John Mark, almost as if in a vision, the face of Sarah, and she moved also with a gentle grace through his dreams at night.

When he thought of Sarah and his love for her, however, he was also troubled by some of the things he heard Saul say.

In every address he gave, Saul told very movingly of how Jesus was killed and laid in a tomb, but was raised up from the dead and seen by many of his followers, and seen also, last of all, by himself. After that he would usually be asked by some of the listeners what they should do, and Saul would tell them to be baptized and wait for

Jesus to come again from heaven to deliver them from the wrath of the last judgment.

Then if someone asked what he should do in the time of waiting, Saul usually said, "In whatever state each was called, therein let him continue."

John Mark was not mistaken in what he thought Saul meant by that apodictic declaration. On one occasion a young man asked Saul if he should get married, and an older man asked about obtaining a divorce, and Saul answered flatly: "I think that in view of the coming end of the world, it is well for a person to remain as he is. If you are bound to a wife, do not seek to be free. If you are free from a wife, do not seek to be married."

Almost as an afterthought, Saul added: "But if you marry, you do not sin. Yet those who marry will have worldly troubles, and I would spare you that. Remember, the form of this world is passing away."

John Mark thought much about the problem. Both of the men with whom he was journeying had remained without marrying. As far as his uncle Barnabas was concerned, Mark suspected that it was simply a matter of circumstances. As far as Saul was concerned, it was evident that it was a matter of principle. Was the principle really correct, according to the teachings of Jesus?

Mark searched again in his compendium of sayings and deeds of Jesus. There it was, as he remembered it. Some Pharisees asked Jesus if it were lawful for a man to divorce his wife. Jesus asked them what the Law said, for he knew that they knew it perfectly well. They replied that Moses allowed a man to write a certificate of divorce. Jesus said that was an allowance for the sinful state of affairs in human life, but God's original purpose was shown in creation where he made male and female, and for that reason a man leaves his father and mother and is joined to his wife, and the two become one.

So, Mark concluded, it was not wrong that Sarah and he were so deeply drawn to each other. Saul's teaching was undoubtedly sincere and in accordance with what seemed to him a necessary principle.

It was not necessarily involved, however, in the fundamental principle enunciated by Jesus.

John Mark looked forward with eagerness, therefore, to the time when their work on Cyprus would be completed and, having finished the task for which they had set out, they would return to Antioch and to Jerusalem—which to him meant to return to Sarah.

The culmination of the work came in Paphos, the capital city, near the far end of the island. Here the Roman proconsul, Sergius Paulus by name, heard of the presence of the visitors, and summoned them to set forth what they had to say in his hearing.

As they entered the audience chamber of Sergius Paulus, Mark noticed a man standing at the right hand of the proconsul whose appearance somehow struck him as sinister. Although it was certainly a different person, Mark was irresistibly reminded of Simon Magus who had attempted to overcome Peter in Rome, and he managed to whisper to Saul, "Beware of the magician."

As it turned out, the sinister-appearing man was a Babylonian Jew whose name was Bar-Jesus in Aramaic and Elymas in Greek, and he was indeed a practitioner of the arts of the Magi. With a great knowledge of the stars and with many theories as to their influences in human life, he had interested the inquiring mind of Sergius Paulus, and with an unscrupulous use of an ability which he claimed to foretell events, he had put himself into an important advisory position with the proconsul. He was therefore immediately incensed when he saw that Sergius Paulus was taking an interest in what he heard from Saul, as the latter spoke on behalf of the visitors, and he launched into a violent denunciation of all that Saul said.

Saul in turn was greatly provoked, and cried out: "O son of salvation, as you claim by your name to be, you are really son of the devil, enemy of righteousness, and full of deceit and villainy. As the magicians Jannes and Jambres opposed Moses, so you oppose the word of the Lord. Behold, the hand of the Lord is upon you, and you shall be blind and unable to see the sun for a time."

No sooner were the words spoken, than Bar-Jesus began to grope in darkness; then, some days later, he regained his sight as suddenly as he had lost it.

In all, the proconsul was greatly impressed, both by what he saw happen and by what he heard from the visitors on the first occasion and also on several subsequent occasions, and he himself became a believer.

This accomplishment strengthened Saul in a conviction which had been growing within him, namely, that he was specially called to go to the Gentiles. He began to use almost exclusively his Roman name, Paul, and he looked toward further horizons in the Gentile world. The nearest adjacent areas lay across the sea to the north, including the regions of Pamphylia and Pisidia, and Paul proposed that they go thither.

All the way on the sea crossing John Mark wrestled with the problem of what he should do. He had felt that the invitation by Barnabas to go on the journey to Antioch and to Cyprus had a force he could not resist. His uncle, together with Saul, had brought the relief from Antioch to Jerusalem that had undoubtedly saved the life of Sarah. His uncle had asked his help for the expedition which he was planning.

But now Paul was replacing Barnabas in leadership and, as leader, was directing the party into an entirely different enterprise from that originally agreed upon and undertaken. Barnabas was indeed going along with the new plans, as he was quite free to do, but he did not exercise any pressure upon Mark to continue, and Mark did not feel the same responsibility to Paul as he did to Barnabas. Furthermore, he did have a strong tie in Jerusalem, and indeed a responsibility there too. He had projected with Sarah the approximate time that he would be away and the time that he might be expected to return, and that time was now somewhat more than up.

Although he realized that Paul would not be entirely pleased, Mark's mind was made up. When they landed at Perga in Pamphylia, he bade his companions of the Cyprus expedition farewell, and waited for the first ship by which he might sail to Caesarea and return to Jerusalem.

✕

In the house of Sarah, there was an almost deathly silence. John Mark was led quietly into the room of the girl he loved.

In the wake of the long famine, the plague had come to Jerusalem. Sarah, not yet fully strong, had come down with a fever.

The moment he saw her, lying upon her bed, John Mark remembered the fever by which his own father had died. He knew that Sarah did not have long to live.

She opened her eyes, and stretched a thin hand weakly toward him.

"I tried to wait until you came," she said.

In the time since the plague had struck and she had fallen ill, some power had kept her alive, waiting and waiting to see again the man she loved. Could that same power restore her now? In Alexandria John Mark had remembered the miracles of healing that had been wrought through Simon Peter and others, and he himself had prayed for Annianus and he had been healed.

During the days that followed, days which were like a dreadful nightmare, John Mark prayed for Sarah. He prayed aloud, with desperate supplication, in the solitude of his own chamber; he prayed silently, in the almost deathly silence of her room, with his hand upon the forehead of Sarah.

All was to no avail. Sarah had lived to see the return of the man she loved. Now she must go.

"Good night, my dear," she said to the man sitting beside her, squeezed his hand faintly, closed her eyes, and was gone.

17

The Gnostics

When Barnabas and Paul returned to Jerusalem to report upon the completion of their extended mission, John Mark was still going about the necessary affairs of his life, but only in a routine way. He believed that he would see Sarah again in the resurrection. Meanwhile the days were long.

Barnabas understood more than he said. He simply asked John Mark if he would wish to go with Paul and himself on the next mission journey which they were even then beginning to plan. There was no reason now why Mark could not do this, but when it was suggested to Paul, Paul refused. He had evidently felt that Mark's return from Perga to Jerusalem had involved a failure on Mark's part.

Barnabas and Mark, therefore, sailed off for Cyprus again, while Paul went another way. In the future, however, such misunderstanding as existed fell into the background, and both Barnabas and Mark had a number of further contacts with Paul which were entirely amicable.

From Cyprus John Mark soon went on by himself to Egypt again, for he more and more tended to think of that land as his own most proper place of labor, and he truly desired to see his friends there again and to learn how the community of believers had fared in his absence. Accordingly, Barnabas bade him farewell, and he was once more at sea and watching, after a few days, for the Pharos light at Alexandria.

In Alexandria he found that the community of the followers of Jesus had continued to grow and, proportionately, there was a larger increase in the numbers of Greeks and of Egyptians than of Jews.

The main meeting place of the community was still, however, in the Delta quarter of the city. Here there was a district of green hills not far from the seashore, which was still called Bucolia, or "pasture," because a herd of cattle had formerly pastured there. In the area, on one of the quiet streets, there was a large house which belonged to one of the members of the community, and he had allowed the larger part of it to be fitted out appropriately for the meetings.

From the street one entered by a small hallway into an open inner paved courtyard. Around this court was a series of rooms, while a covered stairway led to the flat roof above. Two of the largest rooms had been opened up together to make a hall of assembly which would accommodate a large number of people. At one end was a rostrum, and as John Mark was welcomed back into the community which owed its origin to his work, he often stood there to address the people or to read to them from his compendium of the doings and sayings of Jesus.

Another room of considerable size was arranged for a baptistery. Set partly into a niche at one end, and surmounted by an arched roof resting on pillars, was a sunken tank. Steps led down into this at either side, while terra-cotta pipes provided for letting water into the tank and draining it out. On either hand were rooms in which candidates for baptism undressed and dressed.

But the most interesting feature of the baptistery chapel was the wall paintings with which it was adorned. The use of painting and other forms of art in places of worship was of course very familiar to the Greek and Egyptian members of the community, while even those who had formerly been regular attenders of services in Jewish synagogues had been accustomed to seeing the walls painted with scenes from Scripture, particularly, as was natural here in this land, scenes of the ancient Exodus. So similar adornment was undertaken for the baptistery chapel.

On the end wall directly over the baptismal tank was a painting of the Good Shepherd carrying a lamb on his shoulders. Mark knew that such a figure was often portrayed by Greek artists, but he recognized that it was here intended to represent Jesus, and he smiled appreciatively as he remembered a statement in his own compendium that Jesus had compassion on a great crowd of people because "they were like sheep without a shepherd."

On the opposite wall were two small paintings, one showing Noah in his ark, the other the Israelites crossing the Red Sea. Mark decided that those had probably been copied from some synagogue, but he felt that they were appropriate also to suggest the final deliverance to which the followers of Jesus looked forward.

On one side wall, divided by the doorway by which one entered the chapel, was a large painting in two scenes. Mark looked upon it with some excitement as he recognized that it represented an event of which he had often read to the people out of his compendium.

In one of the two scenes a paralyzed man lay at full length on his side on a small bed. The bed had a coverlet with red fringes, and the man was dressed in a yellow tunic outlined in brown. Above the bed stood Jesus, clothed in tunic and mantle, in the act of stretching out his right hand toward the sick man.

In the scene on the other side of the doorway, the sick man, now healed, was walking away. He had turned his bed upside down, and was carrying it upon his back, holding it by the crisscross lacing.

"I say to you, rise, take up your bed, and go to your house," Mark quoted softly, as he remembered the words in his record.

On the other long wall, placed where one would see it first of all upon coming into the chapel, was yet another painting. Here there was a large sarcophagus and, standing beside it, three handsome, robed women.

John Mark had to stop and think a moment. Then he realized that this was a representation of the fact that Jesus was raised from the dead. The great sarcophagus did not look much like the tomb which Mark had found empty that morning long before, but he realized that it was the natural way for an artist in Egypt to depict a place of burial.

As for the three women, he quoted again to himself softly: "And when the sabbath was past, Mary Magdalene, and Mary the mother of James, and Salome, bought spices, so that they might go and anoint him."

As he gazed upon these pictures, John Mark was swept by two conflicting emotions. First, at the sight of the paralytic healed by Jesus, he felt a sense of rebellion. Why did not the Lord heal his Sarah, too? Then, in contemplation of the sarcophagus and the women who came to anoint the body of Jesus, he felt a sense of comfort. Jesus himself had been killed, but had been raised again. Perhaps Paul was right, after all. In whatever state one was, one had to wait for Jesus from heaven, to obtain the great deliverance.

As the word "deliverance" came into his mind, John Mark thought again of that day long before when he had stood with Peter and others of the Jerusalem community on the slope of the Mount of Olives and seen the simple cross mark, the Taw sign that stood for final deliverance, cut into the stone marking the burial place of James the son of Zebedee.

Now he suddenly realized that he was also seeing a cross mark which was placed in the corners or margins of some of the paintings in the baptistery chapel. It was like the Taw, and yet it was different. The difference consisted in the fact that the top of the cross was not a straight line, but a loop.

An Egyptian member of the community explained. "It is the *ankh*. Once upon a time it was only the knot in the lace of a sandal. Then it became the sign of life in our ancient writing. Now, because Jesus has been raised from the dead, it means life to come. We write it everywhere."

John Mark pondered the matter. The prophet Ezekiel had spoken of the Taw sign that was placed on the foreheads of those in

Jerusalem who would be delivered in the final time, and the community of believers in Jesus in Jerusalem had taken it as a mark to put on the tomb of James. The people of Egypt understood this cross with the loop as the sign of life, and the believers in Jesus here had taken it to stand for the life to come, which Jesus would give them. Surely the one usage was as well justified as the other.

This was the conclusion to which John Mark came in his reasoning about the matter, and the upshot of it was that he finally even began to wear one of the loop crosses on a cord about his neck as he saw other members of the community doing. This was what brought him into touch with the Gnostics.

✕

On the street one day John Mark was saluted by a passerby who also wore a loop cross on a cord about his neck. Although he failed to recognize the man, Mark supposed, by the sign he wore, that he must be a member, unknown to himself, of the community of believers in Jesus. He accepted the man's invitation, therefore, to tarry for conversation in a wayside inn.

"It is the sign of wisdom," said the man, fingering the loop cross at his throat and looking sharply at John Mark to see if he would reply in a way to indicate that he was also initiated into the mysteries.

Mark remembered something he had once heard Paul say, and replied, "Has not God made foolish the wisdom of the world?"

"But did not Jesus say that there is nothing hidden that shall not be revealed, and there is nothing covered that shall remain without being uncovered?" the man countered.

Mark made an affirmative movement with his head, for he remembered a saying of Jesus much like this which he had copied in his compendium.

Seizing quickly upon this measure of acquiescence, the man went on rapidly. "Jesus also said: 'Know what is in your sight, and what is hidden from you will be revealed to you. Know yourself, and then you will be known, and you will know that you are a son of the Living Father. But if you do not know yourself, then you are in poverty, and you are poverty.' "

John Mark was puzzled. The man had started out by quoting a saying of Jesus which he himself knew from his own compendium. Then the man had gone on to make Jesus speak like one of the Greek philosophers for, as Mark well knew, "know yourself" was a favorite statement of the philosophers.

The man evidently felt that Mark was showing interest in the teachings he was presenting, and he pressed on.

"Jesus said: 'Whoever has ears let him hear.' "

Again Mark nodded, and the man continued without pausing.

" 'Within a man of light there is light, and he lights the whole cosmos, but when he does not shine, there is darkness.' "

Abruptly Mark interrupted the affirmative movement of his head, and the look of puzzlement returned to his face. Jesus indeed, according to his remembrance of his own compendium, had spoken about putting a lamp on a lampstand, so that it might shine, but had he said the other words as the man gave them?

Still without stopping, the man went on, although Mark did not see what connection there was between the next words he uttered and those he had just spoken.

"Jesus said: 'I tell my mysteries to those who are worthy of my mysteries.' "

At that point the man seemed to have reached a sort of climax in what he wanted to say, and Mark ventured to ask, "Where have you learned these things which you say Jesus said?"

It was evident that the man did not know who John Mark was, and did not have any knowledge of his connection with the founding of the group of believers in Jesus in Alexandria, but only supposed him a person recently come to the city and recently associated with the group.

"I see from the loop cross at your throat," said the man, "that you have been with the group that call themselves followers of Jesus."

"You too?" asked Mark. "For I see that you wear the same sign."

"Yes," replied the man. "It was there that I first learned about Jesus, but now I belong to the group that has withdrawn in order to pursue the deeper mysteries. We wear the same sign of the loop cross, but to us it is above all the mark of the deeper wisdom. Come with me tonight, and you will hear."

The gathering into which the man introduced Mark that evening was held in an upper room lighted with many lamps. A white-robed man, with pale but calm face, was seated on a low platform, and a considerable number of persons sat about him on the floor.

"He is our teacher," Mark's companion whispered to him. "He has been in the place of rest, but he tarries with us until we too learn the mysteries of Jesus and find rest."

The speaker began with several affirmations, to which those seated about him made responses which they had evidently learned well.

"The good news of truth is joy."

"It is joy for those who know the mysteries of Jesus."

"He is the Savior who came forth from the fullness of the Father."

"He tells his mysteries to those who are worthy of his mysteries."

"He who has ears to hear, let him hear."

"So be it, and so be it."

After that preliminary the speaker launched into his discourse.

"The subject on which I shall speak to you tonight is that of ignorance and of wisdom.

"In the beginning was the fullness of the Father. From the fullness of the Father came forth the totality of being, but the totality of being was searching for him from whom it came forth.

"Because the totality of being was ignorant of the Father, there was anguish and terror, and anguish became dense like a fog, so no one could see. This fog condensed into matter, and error formed matter into the creature.

"But Jesus the Christ came from the fullness of the Father to enlighten those who by reason of forgetting were in the darkness. He enlightened them and indicated a path for them. And that path is the truth which he taught them.

"It was because of this that error became angry with him, persecuted him, oppressed him, and annihilated him. He was nailed to a tree of wood, and the tree became a tree of knowledge—knowledge of the Father—and those who eat of the fruit of the tree are caused to be joyful.

"But having divested himself of these perishable rags, the Savior clothed himself in incorruptibility, which it is impossible for anyone to take away from him.

"So those who receive his instruction and obtain the knowledge are beings from on high. Their names are written in the book of the living, and when their names are called, they hear, reply, and turn toward him who calls them, in order to reascend to him.

"There in the fullness of the Father they experience neither desire nor lamentation; no more is there death in them. But it is in him who is in repose that they repose, without striving or becoming entangled in the search for truth. They are themselves truth. And the Father is in them, and they are in the Father, being perfect and inseparable from that truly good Being. Such is the place of the blessed, such is their place of repose."

When all was finished and John Mark was walking away from the gathering with the man who had brought him, he found that he was thoroughly bewildered. In what he had heard there were certainly many echoes of what he knew in his own compendium of the sayings and deeds of Jesus, and of what he had heard from others in the company of believers in Jesus. There were also, however, many other elements which were strange to him, and all was transposed somehow into a different key. No longer were the teachings of Jesus related, it seemed, to the living of daily life and to the recognition of the kingdom of God in things round about one; rather, they were a sort of mysterious key for escaping from the flesh itself and finding a passionless peace in a realm of higher rest. Furthermore, everything depended not upon faith and repentance and baptism, but upon knowledge—and John Mark said the word over to himself several times in Greek, trying to comprehend what it meant: *gnosis, gnosis, gnosis.*

In spite of everything, Mark did not wish to fail to express appreciation to his companion for the invitation to the gathering.

"I can see," he said, "that your teacher is a holy man, and I found his teachings eloquently stated. But explain to me, please, if Jesus tells his mysteries to those who are worthy of his mysteries, how does one become worthy?"

The man, who had evidently advanced far in the teachings of his group, answered without hesitation. "You have heard that it was only through error that matter was formed into the creature. So the world of matter is all evil, and our souls are imprisoned in it. Therefore we must do everything possible to set ourselves free. We must restrain our appetites, deny our desires, refrain from marriage, and rule our bodies with an iron hand. The body, you know, is a tomb."

Speaking in Greek, the man had phrased his concluding aphorism in a way that constituted a play on words: "The *soma*, you know, is a *sema*."

John Mark thought of how Paul had also said that one should refrain from marriage, but for quite a different reason— simply that the time was short until the end. As to the body, Mark had heard him say not that a man should try to destroy it, but that he should present it as a living sacrifice to God, which would be an act of spiritual worship.

To his companion, John Mark only said: "Your teacher was pale and thin. I think he follows the teachings you have stated."

"I learned all these things only from him," said the man. "Will you come again and study further?"

Without committing himself, John Mark thanked his companion and, at the parting of their ways, walked on alone.

×

It was a number of nights later that another man, also previously unknown to him but also wearing a loop cross on a cord about his neck, came to the lodgings of John Mark.

"We know that you were recently in the gathering where the good news of the truth, as they call it, was set forth. But that is only the beginning of *gnosis.* Come with me, and you shall hear of deeper matters; you shall hear even the good news of the resurrection."

John Mark believed in the resurrection of Jesus. He wondered into what form this new group had perverted the doctrine. He decided, albeit not without misgivings, to accompany the man.

In a remote section of Alexandria, he was led down a spiral stairway into a subterranean meeting room, dimly lighted. Here he found himself listening to an address which, as he had gathered might be the case, sounded something like what he had heard in the previous meeting, but was much more complex in its phraseology and ideas.

"In the beginning was the fullness"—the speaker began with the identical words which John Mark had heard previously, but quickly went into more profound elucidations—"and in the fullness were the divine pairs, linked in union, the Inexpressible and the Silence, the Father and the Truth, the Word and the Life.

"But the offspring of the Word and the Life, who was Sophia, fell out of the fullness by reason of pride. She also gave birth to a son, and his name was Yah. He made the world and man out of evil matter, but Sophia breathed into man the breath of life. So the soul of man is from on high, but his body is from below. Accordingly, whatever is done in the body is of no consequence, and all that matters is that the soul should be illuminated and enabled to reascend to its home in the fullness. To this end the Christ, who was the Son of the Father and the Truth, came and dwelt in Jesus. In his resurrection we have the resurrection, and that resurrection is even here and now. Let us strip off the flesh and be free."

With these words the leader flung off his robes and stood out before the gathering completely unclothed, while most of the people did likewise, although some seemed embarrassed and did not comply.

John Mark perceived that the speaker, and the people who followed his example, intended a symbolic action. To die was, for the person instructed in these mysteries, to lay aside the garment of the flesh, and find the soul set free in the resurrection. To strip off every garment of clothing was to act out the resurrection even now.

John Mark shuddered, not at the nakedness of the people—for to him, as one who was very familiar with the world of the Greeks and who had himself often slept bare in the watchtower in the garden at Jerusalem and had exercised naked in the Xystus, this was not repugnant—but he shuddered at the nature of the teaching in which so crass a representation of the resurrection could be given, and in which so flagrant an allowance for any kind of bodily conduct could be recommended. He was to shudder even more at what followed.

The speaker was continuing. "Let us now practice our sacraments. The first is baptism."

In what he said next, John Mark recognized another play on words. The word for baptism meant "dip under," and also "dye."

"The cloth that is dyed keeps its color forever. The dyes of God are immortal, so those that are dipped under his water are colored for immortality."

With this explanation, and at the speaker's invitation, several of the persons who had not yet thrown off their clothing now did so, stepped forward, and were immersed in a tank of water with which the room was provided.

It was not this first sacrament which caused revulsion in John Mark, but the second and third sacraments.

"The second sacrament is the thanksgiving," said the leader.

At this juncture the people reclined at low tables and were served bread and a cup, over which the leader said certain words but, in this case, too softly for Mark to hear and understand. His guide explained: "It is the monthly blood of harlots which they drink."

"Our third sacrament is the bridechamber," said the leader, and Mark's companion whispered to him, "This is only for those who are being initiated into the highest order."

The speaker continued: "Baptism is the holy house, and the thanksgiving is the holy table, but the bridechamber is the holy of holies. Like unto the unions of the pairs above, so is the union of those who enter the bridechamber. If anyone becomes a son of the bridechamber he will receive the light. If anyone does not receive it while he is in this world, he will not receive it in the other place. Let those who have been prepared and certified for this step follow me."

The leader himself singled out a handsome woman in the group and led her to another chamber, while several other pairs, evidently qualified and obviously ready for their highest level of initiation, followed.

Dawn was lightening the sky when John Mark reached his lodgings again, and he breathed in the clean air of the morning with relief.

At the next meeting of the community of the followers of Jesus, he read to them from his compendium: "And Jesus began to say to them, 'Take heed that no one leads you astray. Many will come in my name, and they will lead many astray. But take heed; I have told you all things beforehand.' "

18

The Buddhist

Two things attracted the attention of John Mark to the man who was standing at the edge of a main street in Alexandria and speaking to a small group of listeners, namely, his appearance and certain words which Mark caught as he passed.

The event of a speaker on the street was not unusual, since the Stoic philosophers in particular often taught in this way and, indeed, usually presented exhortations the ethical character of which Mark heard gladly enough. But this man was definitely not one of the Stoic street preachers, being plainly distinguished by his saffron robe and shaven head.

Likewise, the words which John Mark caught might not have struck him so forcibly except for his recent experiences in the Gnostic groups. There he felt that he had seen the extremes—in the first group an ascetic denial of the flesh, in the second group a libertine encouragement of license in the flesh. The words which he now heard from the saffron-robed street speaker were "the middle way."

Thus it was that John Mark was interested, in due time, in making the acquaintance of the man, and in holding some long conversations with him. The man's name was Chunda, and he had recently come all the way from India on one of the sailing vessels whose voyages the ship captain had described to John Mark.

"Ever since the days of the great King Ashoka we who follow the teachings of the Buddha have been traveling abroad to spread the law of kindness," he said.

"Tell me of the great king," requested Mark, "for I know little of him, save that here in Alexandria I have sometimes heard his name, and I think that he must have been on the throne of your land at about the same time that Ptolemy, whom they call Philadelphus, was ruling here."

"That is correct," said Chunda. "After your great Alexander withdrew from the edge of our land, Chandragupta Maurya built an empire in the Valley of the Ganges, and Ashoka was his grandson.

"Like almost all kings, Ashoka set out to enlarge his dominions. He sent conquering armies all the way to the snow-covered mountains on the one hand and the warm seas on the other. In one land, on the edge of the sea toward the sunrising, he killed a hundred thousand persons, and carried away captive half again as many more. Of this you can read on the great stone pillars which he set up in many places in our land.

"But on those pillars you can read, too, of how the king was smitten with remorse for the slaughter, death, and carrying away captive which he had caused. In his profound sorrow and regret, he turned to the law of kindness which was taught by the Buddha, and henceforward made it his aim to promote security, self-control, peace of mind, and joyousness for all animate beings."

"Was that then what the Buddha had taught?" asked Mark.

"Yes, and about his teachings and his life I shall be pleased to tell you when next we talk," said Chunda courteously.

With equal courtesy John Mark expressed his interest in being so instructed.

When next they talked, it was evident that Chunda had occupied himself also in learning something of the teachings to which John Mark was committed.

"Even as you speak of Jesus and call him the Christ, which

means, I understand, the Anointed One," Chunda began, "so we speak of our teacher, Gautama, and call him the Buddha, which means the Enlightened One. It is the story of how he became the Enlightened One that is written in great detail in our sacred books, and that I will tell you in a few words.

"Like Ashoka, Gautama also had a royal upbringing, for he was the son of a prince whose land was at the foot of the snow-covered mountains. So his early years were filled with the pleasures of dancing and music, of drinking and making love, and, in due course, he was married and had a son.

"In those days he was completely shielded from the sadness of life, but finally, allowed to drive outside the palace and through the city, he saw an old man bent and feeble with years, a sick man convulsed and groaning with pain, and a corpse being carried by grieving mourners. For the first time Gautama confronted the inevitable realities of old age, sickness, and death, and he was filled with awe and horror. But on the way back he saw yet one other sight, namely an ascetic with shaven head and saffron robe, and on his face there was a look of peace.

"Gautama resolved to leave everything behind and go out to seek an answer to the tragedies of which he had, for the first time, become aware. He gazed fondly upon his sleeping wife and small son, then rode away into the night.

"His first endeavor was to emulate the peaceful ascetic whom he had seen, trying a way of life as extremely opposite as possible from his previous life of the pleasures of the senses. Practicing the most rigorous self-discipline, he starved himself to the point of great emaciation and final collapse.

"Then he knew that this was not the way either. He sat under a tree in deepest meditation—and then the great enlightenment came to him. After that, throughout the rest of his long life, he went about the land preaching and expressing goodwill to all beings."

"He went about doing good and healing all that were oppressed." John Mark found himself quoting a statement which he had often heard Simon Peter make concerning Jesus.

"But what did the Buddha really discover in his enlightenment, and what did he teach?" asked John Mark. "I have heard you speak of 'the middle way.' What is that?"

"He set it all forth," replied Chunda, "in his very first sermon in the Deer Park at Isipatana. What he said was called 'Setting in Motion the Wheel of Righteousness.'

"He said that there are two extremes: on the one hand, the habitual practice of self-expression, where every desire is given free rein and gratified, which leads to satiety and revulsion; on the other hand, the habitual practice of self-mortification, where the body is constantly punished and mistreated, which leads to the point where not even thought is any longer possible.

"Between these two extremes is the middle way. It is a way of right views, of right conduct, and of right mindfulness.

"To hold right views one must know that life is full of suffering, but suffering is caused by selfish personal craving, and so suffering can be destroyed by getting rid of selfish craving.

"To practice right conduct one must show goodwill toward all beings that live.

"To experience right mindfulness one must spend much time in meditation."

"If a man puts himself in the center of his own life, then," John Mark recapitulated, as he tried to grasp the doctrine that Chunda was enunciating, "he is bound to suffer. Only if he overcomes himself, can he find freedom and peace. Whoever seeks to save his life will lose it, but whoever loses his life will save it."

As the words poured out of his mouth it was John Mark's intention only to state in his own language what he had heard Chunda saying, but he realized after he finished that he had ended with a saying of Jesus out of his own compendium.

Another saying of Jesus from his own record came into his mind as he thought also of what Chunda had said about right conduct, namely, that it consisted in the showing of goodwill toward all beings. The saying of Jesus was one that he had quoted often in his talks in the community of believers, as he had tried to guide the Jewish, Greek, and Egyptian members into a greater spirit of consideration for each other: "You shall love your neighbor as yourself."

To Chunda he only said: "Can you tell me something more about the right conduct which the Buddha recommended?"

"What right conduct is can be seen best in the virtues of the Buddha himself," Chunda replied. "We have been taught that he brought ten qualities to perfection, and these are: almsgiving, to all beings impartially, whether they are good, bad, or indifferent; morality, especially in harmlessness to all other beings; renunciation, or freedom from sensual lust; wisdom, constantly more and more purified; energy, exerted in the effort to attain perfection and to assist the welfare of others; forbearance, which keeps the exercise of energy within limits; truth telling, which means never to break a promise; resolution, in working for the welfare of others; loving-kindness, shown to all; and equanimity, which expects nothing in return for any of its love or efforts."

As he heard these words, especially the closing ones, there came to Mark's mind yet another saying of Jesus which, although it was not incorporated in his own record, he had often heard repeated in the community at Jerusalem: "Do good, expecting nothing in return, and your reward will be great."

"Such qualities are attained," Chunda was continuing, "only by exercising loving-kindness, altruistic joy, and calm-mindedness. We must always be concerned about the welfare of all living beings, not tolerating the suffering of any being, always wishing long duration to the higher states of being, and being impartial and just to all creatures."

"Do you mean that other people, too, can attain the state of enlightenment which the Buddha attained?" asked John Mark.

"Yes," said Chunda, "but it will take a very long time. Indeed, the Buddha passed through many existences before he reached the goal."

"Do you teach that everybody will live many lives, one after the other?" asked Mark, struggling with an idea that was strange to him.

"Yes," said Chunda, "and it is from that weary round of going through all the sufferings of existence over and over again that we wish to be free. There is, of course, no soul, but as long as our desires attach us to existence, the elements of being reassemble, and we go again through the experiences of life."

"No soul?" thought Mark. Did not Jesus, according to the sayings in his own compendium, declare that his soul was sorrowful even to death, and tell his followers that it would not profit them anything to gain the whole world and lose their own soul?

But Chunda was going on. "We must therefore so meditate upon the elements of our life that we realize more and more vividly that everything is completely impermanent, full of suffering, and without true reality. These are the great liberating truths, the truths of the impermanence, the unsatisfactoriness, and the emptiness of all existence."

"You say," asked John Mark, "that meditation is the way to this realization?"

"Yes," Chunda said with strong emphasis, "it is the only way to attain right mindfulness."

John Mark remembered from his record that Jesus once went out to a desert place and there prayed, and again departed into a mountain to pray, and also exhorted his followers to watch and pray. "By meditation do you mean what we call prayer?" he asked.

Chunda answered with a certain measure of indirection, yet bluntly. "There are no gods," he said, "or, rather, they are themselves only beings on the way to the liberation which the Buddha has already achieved. Like the Buddha, each man must depend only upon himself for his liberation. It takes energy and effort. It is a hard way, and long.

"If you wish to practice meditation"—now Chunda made his reply more direct and specific—"you must prepare for it by obeying strictly the five precepts, which prohibit killing any living being, lying, stealing, drinking intoxicants, and having sexual intercourse."

John Mark remembered the libertine Gnostics who had exalted the last practice to mark the highest level of initiation into their esoteric doctrines, and thought how far away he was from them in the present conversation with the serene saffron-robed man.

"Then," Chunda continued, "you must withdraw your attention from everything outside, and concentrate upon some single point in your body, until you begin to feel glowing heat within."

John Mark remembered a statement in the Scriptures of his people, and pondered it momentarily: "While I was musing the fire burned."

"Your meditative concentration is beginning to burn up the impurities within," Chunda went on. "You are beginning to experience detachment. You will long more and more for utter peace. You have found that it is possible to escape from the weary round of rebirth, suffering, and death. You will attain tranquillity and equilibrium. In that state, undisturbed by likes and dislikes, freed from illusions and unclouded by ignorance, like sunlight that penetrates a quiet lake, supreme insight will arise. You will have a foretaste of Nirvana."

"Is that the name—Nirvana—which you give to the final goal?" asked Mark, as he strove to follow carefully each step in Chunda's presentation.

"Yes," replied Chunda. "The Buddha said that our quest is a search for that which is unborn, unaging, undecaying, undying, unsorrowing, and unstained—and he called that Nirvana."

"How do we know that we can reach that goal?" asked John Mark. "You have said that the way is long and hard."

"That is true," said Chunda. "The way is long and hard; indeed, longer and harder than we can even realize. But we know that the Buddha was a man, and he worked by his own human efforts alone, and he reached the goal and became the Enlightened One. That is how we know."

"He lived long ago, I think," said Mark, "even long before the

King Ashoka of whom you once spoke. Does the Buddha help men even now, today?"

"He did not worship the gods, the way many unenlightened people of my land do," replied Chunda, "and he did not wish anyone to worship him. One time a disciple followed him and looked at him constantly, and he said to him, 'What is this foul body that you see? He who sees the Law, sees me, and he who sees me sees the Law.' By the Law he meant the truth which he was setting forth, and he wanted his follower to look at that and not at himself."

John Mark remembered a saying he had heard quoted in the community at Jerusalem, according to which a woman had said adoringly to Jesus, "Blessed is your mother," and he had replied, "Blessed rather are those who hear the word of God and keep it!"

Chunda was continuing his statement. "Once again, just before the Buddha died, when his followers were very sorrowful that he was to leave them, he said that he would continue to be present with them in his teaching.

"So we reverence him as the supreme shower of the way. But he is not actually living now; he has entered Nirvana; he is beyond life and death, beyond space and time, beyond existence. We must work out our own salvation. Will you go this way too?"

John Mark did not make any commitment to the man who had spoken so eloquently and at the same time so serenely about the Buddha. Mark was deeply impressed by much that he had heard, but he was also puzzled by the statements that there is no soul, no one to whom to pray, and no real existence—as he understood it—for the Buddha in his Nirvana.

Mark also did not make any effort to persuade Chunda of the teachings to which he was himself committed. With what he supposed might have seemed to Chunda a stubborn clinging to the reality of a personal God and the fact of a continued personal existence, he affirmed again to himself the conviction that God had raised Jesus from the dead, and that Jesus had been seen alive, after his death, by some of his own companions. But in relation to Chunda, it seemed to Mark that he could only properly try to manifest the same kind of unselfseeking benevolence which Chunda had said was inculcated in his way of life, and which Mark felt was likewise implied in the command to which he himself subscribed, to love one's neighbor as oneself.

In addition to that, when John Mark spoke again in the gathering of his own community, the first passage that he read aloud from his own compendium was the one beginning "He that is not against us is for us."

19

The Priestess of Isis

Clea, priestess of Isis, surveyed the curve of her thigh approvingly. She had completed her bath and was lying back upon her couch while her serving girl worked carefully with the razor to make her body unshadowed anywhere. Clea was pleased that all her flesh was still firm and without blemish.

In the years of her service as the first lady of the chief goddess of Egypt, Clea's sharp wits and alluring body had combined to win many victories for her. She had no doubt that the acuity of her wits was unimpaired, but she watched every day lest any signs appear that the attractions of the flesh were diminishing. In the contest in which she was determined to engage next she knew that she would have to draw upon all of her resources if she were to win.

The times were surely propitious. While Claudius had lived and reigned it had not been so. In every struggle between the Greeks and the Jews, he had taken the side of the Jews. As a friend of the Jews, he had also tried to keep them from being disturbed by messianist agitators, a subject which he had included in an official letter to the city of Alexandria and a matter on which he had had to take action in Rome itself.

But when those who were going about proclaiming that a certain Jesus was the Messiah did not cause outright and obvious disturbances he quite overlooked them, and they, in fact, profited from the general friendliness that he showed to the Jews. Mark's former associate Paul even called Claudius "the one who restrains," with respect to the greater lawlessness which he feared might, under other circumstances, break out.

With the accession of Nero the restraint provided by law and order still prevailed to the benefit of the Jews, who were still legally accorded religious freedom, and this continued to redound to the benefit of the followers of Jesus too, who, in that regard, were not yet distinguished from the Jews, the people to whom not a few of them had originally belonged.

Otherwise, however, from the point of view of the priestess of Isis the situation had changed for the better. Nero was obviously a Hellenophile. He not only claimed for himself the title Son of Apollo, but he supported and encouraged everything that had the appearance of Hellenism throughout his empire. This obviously brought encouragement to the cult of Isis in Egypt, and to all connected with it. Was not Apollo, whose son Nero claimed to be, himself the son of the queen mother, Isis?

At the same time, to the continuing puzzlement and concern of the priestess, more and more of the adherents of the cult in which she served were going over to the community in which John Mark was now the rather widely known leader, the community which professed religious loyalty to none of the gods of Hellenism, but to a man who had died at Jerusalem not too long ago—and, they said, had been raised from the dead. What a parody it was, the priestess thought, of the doctrines of her own cult. She resolved that the next public ceremony in honor of her goddess should be the most impressive demonstration that had been seen, at least recently, in the streets of Alexandria.

The forthcoming occasion was not, indeed, the most important of the religious year of the goddess, but it was not without significance and interest. As the chief goddess of Egypt from ancient times and now a deity known throughout the Hellenistic world, Isis was naturally considered the goddess of the harbor at Alexandria, the founder of the practice of seafaring, and the guardian of those who ventured upon the several seas. So, at the opening of navigation in the spring, there was a public procession in honor of Isis of the Sea.

✕

The procession which John Mark watched as it moved along the Street of the Soma toward the Lake Harbor was indeed the most impressive he had seen in Alexandria. First came a band of pipers, sounding notes which stilled the gathering crowds of onlookers, and then a body of heralds who proclaimed the name of the event, the Day of Isis of the Sea.

A line of masqueraders followed, strikingly costumed to represent all the kinds of persons who had to do with the sea—sailors, masters of ships, astronomers, navigators, fishermen, merchants, warriors, and others. Musicians with pipes and flutes then preceded a chorus of chosen youths, clad in snowy white, chanting a hymn. More pipers followed, and then a great number of men and women with waxen tapers and other lights. These were those who thus signified their desire and intention to learn the mysteries of Isis. After them marched the long train of mystics, those already initiated into the several grades of the mysteries—men and women of all ages and conditions, luminous in pure white, the women with anointed hair covered with transparent veils, and the men with shiny, smooth-shaven heads. These all kept up a shrill jingling with sistra made of bronze, silver, and even of gold. These were curved devices which could be held in the hand and shaken, with loose rods and panels producing the noise, and with heads of Isis and her sister Nephthys hanging from the lower side. They were reputed to be instruments which would powerfully ward off and frighten Typhon, the evil one.

Then came many priests of Isis, in shining linen, carrying insignia of various sorts. The first carried a golden lamp; the second, models of altars; the third, a palm tree with golden leaves; the fourth, a golden vessel in the form of a woman's breast, from which he poured libations of milk upon the ground; the fifth, a winnowing-fan with thick golden branches; and another, an amphora. After these in the procession were a number of men who represented various deities, all in the guise of animals—the dog, the cat, the cow, the ibis, the jackal who was Anubis, the hawk who was Horus, and others.

Then, preceded by a single high-ranking priest with sistrum and crown of roses, there was carried a large but simple ark, representing the vessel in which the body of Osiris had crossed the sea to Byblos.

After that came many more women, robed in white, with flowers in their hair. The first of these sprinkled the street with balsam and unguent, the others carried mirrors behind them, held up to the face of the advancing goddess.

There she was, Isis of the Sea, in the person of her chief priestess, Clea, standing proudly in the prow of a ship carried by many men. The masts of the ship were stepped, the sails were billowing, oarsmen and helmsman were at their places, but it was the priestess portraying the goddess who attracted all eyes.

Clea again was glad that her flesh was still firm and her entire body, thanks to the razor used so expertly by her serving girl again that morning, was without a shadow anywhere. The hair of her head was bound up within a crown of gold, and there were sandals of gold on her feet. Otherwise she wore only a single garment, a dress of utterly transparent silk, and it was so knotted between her large firm breasts that they stood forward on either side like coral-tipped mounds of ivory. It pleased Clea to think that her appearance was not unworthy of the goddess she served.

It pleased her also to think that she had attracted the attention of John Mark. Her spies, circulating in the crowds as the procession moved along, had relayed the word to her that he was standing beside the Soma at the corner of Canopic Street, and had provided such a detailed description that she recognized him without fail. He was watching everything carefully, and he surveyed her calmly too, but as their eyes met for just a moment Clea was certain that she recognized in his eyes a look of loneliness. For the priestess it was enough. The first step had been taken.

✕

  The next step, and hopefully the decisive, destructive one, would be taken on the Mystic Night, but that would not come until the autumn. Of course, it was not only the Day of Isis of the Sea in the spring and the Mystic Night in the autumn which were important points in the year in respect to the goddess Isis. Almost the whole year was connected with her, and with those associated with her, in one way or another.

  Long ago the Egyptian astronomers had determined that the twelve months of the year, each of thirty days, did not fill out the annual circuit of the sun against the constellations of the heavens, and they had approximated a solution to the mathematical problem by instituting the practice of inserting an additional five days between the end of one year and the beginning of the next.

  These epagomenal or superadded days, as they were called, were promptly appropriated by the thinkers who wrought out the details of the mystery of the great goddess. Upon the first of the Epagomanae, Osiris was born, they said, begotten of the Sun, and accompanied at birth by a voice which cried, "The Lord of all things is now born." Upon the second day, Horus was born, son of the son of the Sun, whom some also called Apollo. Upon the third, Typhon broke roughly from the womb of his mother, displaying already the arrogance implied by his name as the "puffed up" one. For this reason the third of the Epagomenae remained always an inauspicious day. Upon the fourth day, Isis was born. Her name meant "throne," but to the Greeks it sounded like the word meaning "to know," while the name of a temple of Isis—Iseion—sounded to them as if it contained also the word for "true being," so they were persuaded that such a place was where the knowledge of true reality might be found. Upon the fifth day, Nephthys was born, sister of Isis.

That was the apportionment of the five epagomenal days by the thinkers of the cult of Isis, but the apportionment did not fully explain the relationships among the personages attached to the days, nor did it account for several other personages necessary to the complete unfolding of the mystery. To elucidate these matters it was necessary for the thinkers to explain further.

Osiris and Isis were both brother and sister and husband and wife, a dual relation not uncommon in Egypt and, in this case, a conjugal relation which was enjoyed by the two of them, it was said, even before they were born into this world. Horus was their son, and when he was little, with his finger in his mouth, they called him Harpocrates. Isis and Nephthys were sisters, and upon one occasion, Nephthys also lay with Osiris to become the mother of Anubis, the god who knows the way into the realm of darkness and of the dead. In more regular relationship, however, Nephthys was married to Typhon. Osiris and Typhon were brothers, some said, and the latter they called Set, too, without changing his arrogant and sinister character.

In celestial matters Isis was identified with the moon, and also with Sothis. Sothis was known also as Sirius and as the Dog Star, having its place in the constellation of the Greater Dog, and was the brightest star in the heavens. Osiris was identified with the sun, and also with Canopus—next to Sirius, the brightest fixed star. Horus also was associated with the sun and with the constellation Orion. Nephthys, sister of Isis, was the western horizon and the evening. Set or Typhon was the night. And Isis again was the eastern horizon and the dawn.

In terrestrial matters Osiris was all that is black and moist and seminal and, in particular, was the river Nile. Since Isis was Sirius and since the Dog Star appeared on the horizon with the morning sun to signal the annual inundation, she it was who summoned the life-giving waters to their height. She was also the earth which receives the overflowing waters and becomes fruitful, and one result of this amorous congress was the birth of Horus. Typhon, however, was all that was red and dry and dusty and productive of the drought; every part of nature that was hurtful or destructive belonged to him, and all events that were adventitious and tumultuous, as eclipses of the sun and disappearings of the moon, were his incursions and devastations.

With respect to animals, the Apis bull was sacred to Osiris, Isis was sometimes associated with the dog which represented her star, and Horus was the hawk that flies across the sky like the sun. But Typhon was assigned the ass and also the crocodile—since he once changed himself into a crocodile in order to escape from his rightful avenger, Horus; in short, all bad and noxious things—whether animals, plants, or passions—were considered to be the works, the members, and the motions of Typhon.

Finally, in physical matters, Isis was the embodiment of all feminine charms, and at once recognizable by the Greeks and Romans as none other than their own Aphrodite and Venus. By such charms she attracted Osiris to her irresistibly, received from him the seed of life, and became the mother of Horus. In this role Isis was the very embodiment of maternity, and was often pictured holding the infant Horus, or Harpocrates, to her breast and giving him to suck. As for Osiris, although he was the sun, he was represented everywhere in the form of a man, albeit ensconced in a flame-colored robe, and he was, moreover, shown most often with his private part erect, to betoken his faculty of generation. If his nakedness were hidden, this was not seldom with a fig leaf, this being imagined to bear some resemblance to the virilities of a man.

While all these details of identification and ramifications of relationship were assuredly kept clearly and correctly in mind only by the theologians of the Isis cult, and perhaps not always even by them, the story which they told about these personages was plain to all who heard it and much beloved by the masses.

Osiris, it seems, was the victim of a dastardly plot which was conceived and executed by his archenemy, Typhon, together with seventy-two accomplices who joined in the conspiracy. Having secretly taken the measure of Osiris' body and framed a curious ark, very finely carved and just the size of his body, Typhon brought this to a certain banquet. Inasmuch as all were wonderfully delighted with so rare a sight and admired it greatly, Typhon, in a sporting manner, promised that whoever of the company should find, by lying in the ark, that it was of the size of his body should have it for a present. As everyone present was eager to try, and as none fitted it, Osiris at last got into it himself, and lay down in it. Thereupon they that were present, being the accomplices of Typhon, ran to the ark, clapped the cover down upon it, fastened it with nails, and soldered it with melted lead. Then they carried it out to the river, cast it in, and let it float down to the sea at the Tanitic mouth of the Nile. This happened on the seventeenth day of the month Hathyr, which was in the fall of the year.

When Isis heard of what had happened to her brother and husband, she was devastated with sorrow. She wandered up and down the land, asking information of all she met. At last certain little children told her that they had seen the ark, and told her the mouth of the river by which it had gone into the sea.

Meanwhile, Isis also learned that Osiris had had intercourse with her sister as well as with herself, and that Nephthys, for fear of her husband, Typhon, had exposed the child who was born as soon as it was delivered. Isis was able to find the child, however, and it, being named Anubis, became her guardian and follower.

From Anubis, in due time, Isis had word that the ark, with Osiris in it, had been cast up by the sea upon the coasts of Byblos, and she went thither to recover it. Back in Egypt she and Nephthys opened the ark and mourned over the body of their lover, laying their cheeks upon his cheeks, embracing him, and weeping bitterly.

The wicked Typhon, however, managed to get possession of the body again, and scattered it about Egypt in fourteen parts. In the meantime Isis also gave birth to a son, Horus, and reared him secretly in the marshes. After long searching she finally succeeded in recovering and interring the dispersed members of Osiris, all save his most private part, which had been cast into the river and eaten by the fish.

As a replacement, Isis made an effigy of it, and this was the origin of the worship of the phallus by the Egyptians.

Finally, by the use of such powerful incantations as led to her thereafter being called "the mighty in magic," Isis brought together the scattered members, including the phallic effigy, and caused a complete body to lie upon a couch. Upon this she lowered herself in the position of love, the private part of the dead man came erect, and Osiris returned to life and to the embrace of Isis. After that he went to the western land to become a judge and god of the dead, while Horus grew up to avenge his father—although, after overcoming Typhon in battle, at the request of Isis, he spared his life.

Such was the story which was at the basis of the Isis cult, and the story which Clea, the priestess of Isis, looked forward to reenacting when once again the anniversary days came in the autumn. For every role her associates in the male and female priesthood would be sufficient, save for one. For the role of Osiris himself it was necessary that a new person be found every year, and that one a virgin male who did not know what would happen on the Mystic Night. Supposing that John Mark could be brought into that role, he would fall completely into the power of the priestess of Isis, and his leadership of the troublesome community, which was attracting so many of the former adherents of the cult of Isis, would be destroyed.

×

The man who had entered into long conversations of a deeply theological nature with John Mark wore garments of pure linen and had a completely shaved head. The latter feature reminded Mark of Chunda, whose very sincere expositions of the doctrines of the Buddha had elicited his own honest appreciation. Without realizing the effect of this similarity in appearance, Mark was unconsciously led to place undue trust in the new visitor.

Disarmingly, the man deprecated the significance of the external marks of his position as a priest of Isis. "For," said he, "as neither the nourishing of beards nor the wearing of mantles can render men philosophers, so neither will linen garments or shaved heads make priests to Isis; but he is a true priest of Isis who, after he has received from the traditions the knowledge of the representations and actions of the divine persons, next applies his reason to inquiry and speculation as to the truth contained in the same."

Mark gathered that the man wished to try to explain to him the inner significance of the various features in the story of Isis, a story which had indeed been of some interest to him ever since he had stood at the corner of the Soma and watched the elaborate procession of Isis of the Sea.

"You know," said the man, "that, according to the story, Osiris was tricked into lying down in the ark, and the cover was fastened tight. Now, since Osiris is to us the Nile and all the moisture which produces life, this closing up of Osiris in the chest really signifies to us the withdrawing and disappearing of the water. But since this was accomplished by Typhon, who is the dryness and the drought, we see that the one principle is contrary to the other, and that therewith the whole opposition of the evil to the good is set forth."

"I see," said Mark, "but in our Scriptures the Lord God says, 'I form light and create darkness,' hence I cannot allow that evil is a power equal with good, and quite able to overcome it."

The visiting priest was somewhat discomfited, but went on. "Furthermore, the fact that a chest containing the likeness of a dead man is carried in our ceremonies is not only to commemorate the disaster of Osiris, but also to encourage men to make use of and to enjoy the present things while they have them, since all men must quickly become such as they see there. For this reason the chest is brought even into feasts and revels."

"But is it not so," asked Mark, "that a man must also deny himself many present things, and perhaps even leave house and mother and lands, and be persecuted, and in the age to come receive everlasting life?" He spoke with especial firmness because he was giving the gist of a saying of Jesus, as he remembered it from his compendium.

The visitor seized upon the reference to the future life to press on with his elucidation.

"You know," he said, "that Osiris is the sun and Isis the moon. But Isis is also Sirius, the star that we call the Dog—that is why she is sometimes shown with a dog accompanying her, or sitting on the back of a dog.

"Well, on one morning at the beginning of the summer Sirius and the sun come up over the horizon together, and they are Isis and Osiris together. But at the same time there comes the great inundation of the Nile. The river rises twenty-eight cubits high between its narrow banks at Elephantine; ten days later it is fourteen cubits high in its broad valley at Memphis, and its waters spread out over all the fields. But that is Osiris, coming forth out of his chest of death, for when the ark was nailed shut it signified the withdrawal and disappearance of the water, and when the water returns it shows the deliverance of Osiris from the power of his enemy, and his return to life. Would you not also like to be delivered from the power of death, and be assured of immortality?"

As the man asked the climactic question, which embodied the essential appeal of the Isis cult to all men, he looked penetratingly at John Mark. Mark, however, said simply, "I do not believe that the things which are told of Isis and Osiris were really done as they are told, but I do believe that Jesus was really killed and raised from the dead, and seen again, living, by some of those who had companied with him."

Again the visitor laid hold upon Mark's words as a way of getting forward with his own purpose. "I believe," he said, with the appearance of greatest sincerity, "that you and your community and we in ours have much in common."

As he proceeded to work out what he meant, it was evident that he had already in some manner gained no little amount of information concerning the teachings and practices in the community of which

John Mark was the leader, the community which had come to appear so dangerous a rival to the cult of Isis that the priestess of the goddess was fully determined to win a victory over it that would be unmistakable to all.

"I think," said the priest, "that Isis suckling her baby, Horus, in the marshes, is much like your own Mary with the child Jesus."

Mark had nothing in his own compendium about the childhood of Jesus, but he knew that some of the members of the community in Jerusalem had been very much interested in gathering any information that they could from Mary his mother, and from other relatives and friends, about the earliest days of Jesus, and that some persons who had come from Jerusalem and were now in the community at Alexandria had themselves already commented on the similarity between Mary and her child, as they pictured them, and the representations they often saw of Isis with the infant Horus.

The man went on. "Like you we also believe in and long have taught"—at this point he was subtly suggesting the great antiquity, and presumably greater authority on this account, of the cult of Isis —"purification, communion, rebirth, and the immortality of the soul.

"You and we alike know how long mankind has been bound by the fear and horror of death"—here the man unconsciously admitted that the teachings of his ancient cult had not in fact been as effective as he liked to think, had indeed been more a statement of the problem and an expression of a deep longing than an answer. "Together our ancient story of how Osiris was brought back to life and your new account of how Jesus was raised from the dead can bring deliverance to many people."

John Mark was not disposed immediately to accept the logic of this conclusion, but he was not unmindful of many points of actual similarity between what was said and done in the cult of Isis and in the community of the followers of Jesus.

His visitor was not waiting for any comment, however, but pressing on toward the conclusion of his mission.

"On behalf of the priestess of Isis," he said solemnly, "I bid you

to accept our invitation. The greatest festival of the year approaches.
You may see the enactment of our doctrines as it is not permitted to
every outsider to see them. Afterward we shall ask you of your teachings too."

20

The Mystic Night

On the first day of the festival John Mark entered the Iseion with some trepidation. Was it right for him to venture into a pagan temple? Yet the messenger of the priestess of Isis who had brought the invitation had said that in sequence with this opportunity which they were extending to him to learn of the doctrines of the cult of Isis, they would also seek opportunity to learn of the teachings of the community of the followers of Jesus. Mark should not fail to enter any door that opened to him for the furtherance of his work; this door was potentially a very large one; it was also a very dangerous one.

The Iseion was a very large temple, being surpassed in size in Alexandria only by the Serapeion, another sanctuary of whose sinister character Mark would only come to have direct knowledge at a later date. High and impregnable walls enclosed the entire area of the Iseion and, for the festival now beginning, only the priesthood, the initiates, and those undergoing the long course of instruction in the mysteries, together with a few favored outsiders such as John Mark, were admitted. Some portions of the festival would be carried out, however, in the public streets of the city and on the seashore. The impact of the total event, therefore, both by what was seen in public and by such rumors as emanated from inside the walled compound of the temple itself, was very great.

While events connected with Osiris, Isis, and Horus took place at many and various times throughout the course of the entire year, and while the present fall festival was preceded by many preparatory doings and followed by yet others, the essential observance occupied four days. It was on the first of these four days that John Mark was now in the Iseion.

The first day was the day of the Searching. Osiris had been nailed into his ark and cast afloat upon the waters—so the reenactment supposed—and Isis was searching for him desperately everywhere. What was done to show this took place exclusively in the outermost courts of the temple. The large band of musicians and the chorus of singers were ranged in the colonnades, and their music had in it a note of frantic despair. On the spacious stage at the far side of the largest court the priestess of Isis led the simulation of the search. Her robes were torn—allowing provocative glimpses of the body of which she was proud—her long hair was loose and flying behind her, and her manner was distracted. She flung herself upon the ground in despair, she ran to various other actors in the drama and besought information from them. Anubis came out and joined her in her endeavors, while ultimately all the priests and initiates and neophytes also participated symbolically in the search.

The second day was the day of the Finding. Led by the priestess of Isis, now in the clothes of a traveler, a long procession made its way through the streets of the city to the seashore. There it was contrived that an ark was washed ashore, and this was retrieved and carried back through the city to the temple. The accompanying music was solemn, and the pace of the marchers was slow and sad.

The third day was the day of the Burying. According to the story the dead body of Osiris was obtained by Typhon, cut into pieces, and scattered throughout the land. Conducting the reenactment in the innermost courts of the temple, the priestess of Isis symbolically found the dismembered portions in their respective places, made for each in its own place a tomb, and made and entombed with special honor in the central inner court the effigy of the phallic member which could not be found. For all of this she wore clothes of darkest black, standing for the moon in full eclipse, beat upon her breasts, and uttered spoken lamentations to the accompaniment of dirges by the musicians and singers.

The fourth day was the day of the Raising Up. In the course of the day, to the accompaniment of music which began to carry a note of excitement and with the usual symbolic assistance of her many associates, the priestess of Isis, now simulating the person of the goddess who was the Mighty in Magic, gathered again the separately entombed members of the corpse of Osiris, transported them severally through the various rooms of the temple, and placed them together at last upon a couch in an innermost chamber, this final act being performed in solitude. At each phase in these proceedings, incantations were spoken, incense burned, potions concocted, and anointings of the members, especially of the phallic member, conducted.

Then all rested, awaiting the feast to be enjoyed at sunset, and the final festival of the Raising Up to be celebrated in the Mystic Night.

×

It was true that there was unassuageable loneliness in the eyes of John Mark—the same that had been there ever since the day that Sarah died—and this the priestess of Isis had seen aright on the first day that she had seen, to identify him, the leader of the community to oppose which she was, by her position, committed.

It was also the case—and this Clea had no way of knowing—that John Mark had only just completed, immediately prior to his receiving and acting upon the invitation to be present in the ceremonies of the fall festival of the cult of Isis, a series of special exercises.

The fact of which her intuitive perception had made her aware —that of Mark's loneliness—was what Clea counted on to bring her rival within her power. The fact of which the priestess was unaware was that which would deliver him, but only barely.

The latter fact, at least externally considered, might not have appeared significant even if it had been known. The series of special exercises in which John Mark had been engaged and which he had only just completed were hardly remarkable, at least in any visible way. The fact that Mark had undertaken the exercises was due to his encounter and long conversations with the man in the saffron robe, who had presented so earnestly the doctrines of the Buddha.

According to Chunda, right mindfulness was of the highest importance, and Mark was prepared to believe this, for he recalled that it was written in the Scriptures of his own people that as a man thinks within himself, so is he. Further, according to Chunda, the indispensable way to right mindfulness was the practice of meditation, and Mark's own Scriptures also supported this with the admonition "Be still, and know that I am God."

In describing the actual conduct of meditation, Chunda had specified that five precepts must be obeyed strictly. In their general form these precepts provided an outline of the basic moral requirements of the teachings of the Buddha and, as such, were incumbent upon all followers of those teachings. But for a monk always, and for anyone for a specific period of meditation, the requirements were heightened to an absolute form.

In their general statement the five precepts were that one should avoid killing, theft, falsehood, drinking of intoxicants or taking of drugs, and illicit sexual relationships. For a monk, and for anyone in an actual meditation period, the first precept was interpreted to forbid even the killing of an insect—although a poisonous creature might at least be repelled in a nonviolent way—and the fifth precept was heightened to prohibit all sexual intercourse, even of such sort as might otherwise, for a layman, be licit.

These precepts Mark compared in his mind with the words of the Scriptures which were his own ancestral heritage, and found them compatible.

The first precept prohibited the killing of any living being. Mark knew well from the Law of his own people the commandment "You shall not kill." He was quite willing to think it appropriate, at least during a period of special devotion, to consider that this applied to all living beings, the more so because Chunda had indicated that even if they were not to be killed, noxious creatures might at least, within the framework of the precept, be warded off.

The second and third precepts forbade stealing and lying, and the commandments of the Law similarly declared, "You shall not steal," and "You shall not bear false witness."

As to the fourth precept, which was against the drinking of intoxicants and the taking of drugs, Mark recalled how the Nazirites of his people, from the day of their separation to the special service of the Lord, forswore wine or strong drink, and how such abstinence had characterized great men among his people from Samuel to the John who had baptized Jesus.

The prohibition of all sexual intercourse during the time of meditation, which was called for by the absolute interpretation of the fifth precept, not only reminded Mark of the very strict commandment of the Law, "You shall not commit adultery," but also brought to his mind the case of divine punishment when the people, dwelling in Shittim, played the harlot with the daughters of Moab and were smitten with a plague in which twenty-four thousand died, and the example of the soldiers of Israel who would not even lie with their wives in time of critical battle.

It was, accordingly, not difficult for John Mark to affirm his own commitment to the principles of the five precepts, and to decide upon a period of strict concentration upon them and absolute adherence to them as the basis for an extended time of meditation according to the pattern prescribed by Chunda.

Day after day, during this period, Mark recited the precepts, took his position in solitude in a special cross-legged posture which Chunda had recommended, and concentrated upon a flickering candle before him, as Chunda had also said would be helpful. In the course of continued concentration, lights of many colors flashed before him, a burning heat was felt within his body, and, at times, a feeling of ineffable peace suffused him. On more than one occasion he felt that he was suspended far above his body, looking down upon it. Afterward he remembered how his onetime associate Paul had told of experiences in which he did not know if he were in the body or out of the body, and once felt himself even caught up to the third heaven. Probably the greatest effect for Mark, however, although he did not fully realize it at the time, was how, by the prolonged meditation, basic ideas to which he was already committed were rooted much more deeply than ever before in the lowest levels of his mind, whence they might emerge with elemental power even before the conscious processes of his thought might bring them into focus.

×

At sunset on the fourth day of the fall festival of the cult of Isis, John Mark presented himself, in accordance with his invitation, at the banquet which was to usher in the Mystic Night. To this, and to what was to follow, only the highest grades of initiates and the ranking priests and priestesses were admitted, and the allowance of the presence of one from entirely outside was considered the conferral of a distinct honor and privilege.

To preside at the dinner and to conduct the climactic ceremony of the night, Clea, being assisted by the usual serving girls, had groomed her handsome body with consummate care, anointed it with the most costly and fragrant unguents and perfumes, and drawn on her most beautiful wearing apparel. Her sandals were of gold, revealing painted toenails. Her arms and hands sparkled with jewelry. Her robe was white and flowing, but in places almost transparent, showing delicately tinted flesh beneath. On her head she wore the headdress of the horned moon, with the lotus of the resurrection rising on her forehead.

As on all four days of the ceremonies, Clea took no apparent notice whatsoever of the presence of John Mark.

The first course of the dinner progressed at a leisurely pace. In an interlude afterward there were ceremonies in the chapel of Horus. Paintings on the walls of this chapel showed the child suckled at the breast of his mother in the marshes, the youth studying the mysteries of the heavens, and the grown man fighting the battles of vengeance on behalf of his murdered father.

The second course of the dinner was eaten, and after that there were more observances in the chapel of Osiris. This was a cubical room, deep within the temple, and next to the chapel of Isis. Here, standing on the floor at the center of each of the four walls, was a life-size statue of Osiris as a handsome, muscular, ithyphallic man. The focus of attention of these statues of Osiris was a single figure of Isis in the center of the room.

The latter statue, and its position, were in fact the most remarkable feature of the room. In conjunction with the priests of the cult, the learned men of the Museion and their finest artisans had produced a result that was nothing less than amazing. Knowledge of the laws of magnetism and of the properties of metals had been combined. The figure of Isis was executed with the most delicate of craftsmanship, in the lightest of metals, and suspended in the very center of the room, equidistant from the floor, ceiling, and four walls, with no visible support, held in this mysterious position, floating in the air, by invisible waves of magnetism. In appearance the goddess looked very much as did her priestess, Clea, on that very night.

On the walls of this chapel were paintings which depicted the Apis bull, considered the image of Osiris' soul. He stood in virile majesty on a raised platform. Behind him was Isis, crowned with the moon, extending winged arms protectingly over him. In front of him a king offered gifts.

The participants in the banquet returned to the third and final course of the elaborate meal. It was time for the plan of the priestess of Isis to be put into effect. Large glasses of wine were at every place. John Mark lifted his glass with the others, set it down momentarily as he recalled the precept against drinking intoxicants which he had adhered to so strictly during his exercises of meditation, then picked it up again as he remembered that that period was over for now, and that he was not normally committed to the Nazirite vow of avoidance even of wine.

A voice was saying, "The first sip is a libation to the goddess. Let us drink."

This caused Mark to hesitate again.

No one could have anticipated the double hesitation which John Mark had exhibited, but that he would hesitate to take the first sip of the drink which was considered a libation to Isis had been foreseen and provided for in the plan.

The man carefully placed at table directly across from John Mark was none other than the priest who had visited him originally and had prevailed upon him, with carefully built-up argument, to accept the invitation to the dinner. He had lifted his glass simultaneously with John Mark and the others and had proceeded to take the first sip off the top forthwith. While Mark was still hesitating, the man quickly exchanged glasses with him, saying, "It is our custom."

Grateful for being relieved of his embarrassment about taking a libation sip from his own glass, John Mark accepted the proffered glass, lifted it to his lips, and drank deeply.

The priest had drunk an innocuous layer off the top; the balance of the glass, quaffed in full measure by Mark, contained a heavily drugged potion. Almost at the first taste Mark realized that he was drinking a drug, but it was too late. What he did not realize was that, in addition to the clever contrivance by which it was made possible for the priest to drink the top portion without harm, the drug itself was of such kind and measured in such precise quantity as to produce complete oblivion for a definite period of time and then, at a predetermined moment, to restore him to full awareness. The priestess of Isis had but to conduct the remaining affairs of the night to reach their climax at the predetermined point.

This she did, and brought the company from the banquet hall into the chapel of Isis at the planned time. This was the innermost sanctuary of the entire extensive temple complex. Here, earlier in the day, as all knew but as none had actually seen, since the ceremony was performed by herself alone, Clea had brought together in symbolic action the dismembered portions of the body of Osiris, including the phallic effigy, and had placed them together upon a couch, performing various magic spells over them.

This was what, in the story so often told in their cult recitals, Isis herself once had done, and the climax of the story was also portrayed in a large wall painting in this very chapel. Isis cast herself upon the corpse, the virile member of the deceased man came erect to meet her, and Osiris lived again. This was the climax of the Raising Up, the reenactment of which should mark the precise midnight hour of the Mystic Night.

X

The company which gathered in solemn excitement in the chapel of Isis in the moments before midnight was amazed to see, lying on the couch in the middle of the large chamber, the naked form of the guest who some time before had collapsed so suddenly and been carried from their banquet. Still a strong and handsome man, deep chested and well muscled, but utterly motionless and possibly, for all they knew, lifeless, this figure might well enough simulate the corpse of Osiris, but could hardly be expected to participate momentarily in any reenactment of the Raising Up of the slain one. That it was not only a drug-induced but also a time-limited state of oblivion in which John Mark lay, they had no way of knowing.

Clea took her stand at the foot of the couch, and proceeded with the ritual sentences which those who had experienced the symbolic ceremony on previous occasions knew well.

> O Osiris, Lord of all things, Son of the Sun, born on the first of the Epagomenae, brightness of Canopus, Apis incarnate, River of Egypt, Water of the world,
> I, Isis, Throne of the king, Lady of the Moon, Lady of Sirius,

born on the fourth of the Epagomenae, knower of all being,
mighty in magic, thy lover, receiver of thy sperm, mother of
thy child,
    have sought thee in all the world sorrowing,
    have gathered thy scattered members from all the land,
    have said over thy parts the mightiest spells,
    and do bid thee rise
    to be avenged by thy son,
    Horus, strong youth, mighty hawk, smiter of Typhon,
    and thyself to go hence to the land of the dead, there to judge
        and rule.
    Lord of life for evermore,
    to thee be joy, life, salvation, health!
    I cast myself upon thee.
    Do thou rise in thy virile strength to meet me.
    Rise, rise, rise!

As the priestess intoned the several sections of this liturgy she
also divested herself of all the items of her apparel, and she timed both
the words and the actions so that they were completed and she stood,
nude and waiting, in the presence of the company and at the foot of
the couch, precisely at the midnight hour.

    At the moment of midnight, in accordance with the
predetermined character of the potion with which he had been
drugged, John Mark came wide awake. At that moment the priestess
of Isis cast herself upon him.

The fragrance of her perfumes swept over him, the warmth of her
breasts pressed upon him, and the caresses of her hands moved over
his most sensitive parts. The response of his body was what the
priestess of Isis had counted upon, and she settled upon him with a
soft sigh. She had conquered, and henceforth he belonged to her.

So swiftly was all of this accomplished, in accordance with Clea's carefully contrived plan, that the physical reaction of John Mark's body preceded the full focusing of his mind upon what was happening. Had everything depended upon the functioning of his conscious mind, Mark would indeed have been lost in the depths of the scheming of the priestess of Isis. But deep below the level of his all-too-slowly-marshaled conscious thoughts were the concepts and convictions that had been more firmly implanted there, and made more instantaneously available from there, by the exercises of meditation in which he had so recently been engaged and in which he had so often impressed upon the deepest levels of his mind the five precepts of the doctrine of the Buddha, which agreed so well with the commands of his own Scriptures.

The absolute prohibition of all sexual intercourse whatsoever might not strictly apply any longer, inasmuch as he had concluded the series of meditations, but the general precept against illicit sexual relations, the commandment which forbade all adultery, and the example of the children of Israel sporting with the daughters of Moab and receiving the punishment of the plague—all these certainly did apply.

With strength born out of the deepest levels of his mind, and hardly yet knowing with his conscious mind what he did, John Mark doubled his powerful arms and compact hands beneath the breasts of the priestess of Isis and thrust her from him.

In the act he committed the sin of Onan. But that which in the case of Onan was displeasing to the Lord, according to his Scriptures, would surely in this case be pleasing to the same Lord, for he had left nothing of himself with the priestess who had schemed his downfall and therewith the crippling of his community—the community whose conviction of life to come was not based upon the restoration of earthly flesh to earthly function but upon the raising up of a life to that new level where, when they rise from the dead, as Mark's own compendium recorded the saying of Jesus, "they neither marry nor are given in marriage."

John Mark seized a linen cloth lying there, flung it about him, and rushed from the room. But as he ran from the temple, a guard snatched at him, and he left the linen cloth and ran away naked, as many years before he had run from a garden at Jerusalem.

21

The 30th Day of Pharmuthi

When John Mark repelled the advance of the priestess of Isis he changed what had been an opposition to the community he represented, mingled with an actual measure of attraction to himself, into a bitter personal animosity. By the failure of her scheme, however, Clea had reduced the effectiveness of her own leadership, and was not able further to proceed personally against Mark and the community of the followers of Jesus.

Her influence was still strong, however, with the priests of the cult of Serapis, and the leaders of this cult—closely related to her own in its origin and due to circumstances even more closely related than hers to the government—could, if they wished, act more directly and violently. The fact that, with all of its virtually official status, this cult was itself losing more and more of its adherents to the community of the followers of Jesus could be expected to lead, in the course of time, to such action.

Serapis was, in fact, none other than Osiris, but in a guise in which the ithyphallic god of the ancient Egyptians was more acceptable to the Hellenistic and Roman world. As far as his name was concerned, the ideas of ancient Egypt might have seemed to be still prevailing in full force, for the name itself incorporated the name of the animal with which Osiris was long connected. This was the Apis bull.

The bull was obviously a potent source of generative power and, as such, was worshiped from very early times. The cult of the bull, called the Apis, became especially prominent at Memphis and also here at Rhakotis, the village which became the nucleus of Alexandria. At both places, when an individual Apis died, the populace grieved and were anxious lest crops and childbearing should fail. Forthwith, with all the skill in the art which had been developed over many centuries, they proceeded to mummify the dead beast and bury it very ceremoniously in an enormous sarcophagus placed in an underground chamber. In the course of time, both at Memphis and at Rhakotis, there came to be long subterranean corridors with many chambers opening off on either side, each chamber being the burial place of an Apis.

No doubt because the ithyphallic Osiris was also himself the representative of generative force, it was appropriate that the bull be associated with him as, for other reasons, the dog was with Isis, the hawk with Horus, and so on among the figures of the ancient Egyptian pantheon. In some cases the Apis bull was even said to represent the soul of Osiris. Then, by a simple hyphenation, the name Osiris-Apis emerged and, with rapid pronunciation, this eventually became Serapis.

If the name of Serapis preserved primitive ideas from the earliest days of a literal animal worship, as might be seen in the numerous realistic statues of the Apis as a powerfully muscled, virilely endowed beast, the usual representation of Serapis showed that he was completely at home in the most sophisticated Hellenistic or Roman environment.

The usual statue of Serapis, the prototype of which was the colossal masterpiece in the innermost sanctuary of his temple at Rhakotis in Alexandria, showed the deity in the guise of a powerfully built man, seated in massive dignity upon a high-backed throne. Great locks of curly hair and a full beard framed his benign face, he wore flowing robes and sandals, and his upraised left hand held a tall staff of authority. Thus far, Osiris, sun god of Egypt, was, in the form of Serapis, appropriately enough equated with the highest god—Zeus of the Greeks, Jupiter of the Romans.

But on the head of Serapis was a basket or measure, a symbol of the fruitfulness of the earth and long known to the Greeks and Romans as a symbol of Hades or Pluto, the god of the underworld, while the right hand of Serapis rested upon a three-headed dog at his knee, and this was none other than Kerberos, watchdog of the entrance into the infernal regions. So Osiris, who was raised to new life to go to the other world as judge and god of the dead, was also appropriately enough recognized as the same as Hades or Pluto.

Combining these several meanings, the inscription on the base of the great statue in the temple at Alexandria read: One Zeus, One Hades, One Sun, that is Serapis.

The synthesis of so many elements in the one figure of Serapis, which made him at home almost everywhere, revealed the deliberate purpose with which the philosophers and priests of Alexandria, acting under the instruction of the first Ptolemy, had supervised not only the execution of the great statue, but even the introduction of Serapis himself as the new world god. To enhance his reign, unify his new kingdom, and recommend himself to the whole surrounding world as an enlightened man, Ptolemy needed such a god to hold sway over his state, and that was how he obtained him.

For this impressive deity an imposing central temple was also needed, and this Ptolemy had built in Greek style on the hill at Rhakotis, not far from where the long rows of the sarcophagi of the Apis bull rested in their subterranean chambers. Known as the Serapeion, the temple was enhanced with tall obelisks and adorned with marble columns. It was oriented toward the star Canopus, long sacred to Osiris. It was also arranged so that the window of its innermost sanctuary allowed the rays of the rising sun to fall on the face of the great statue of Serapis precisely on the spring morning of the 30th day of Pharmuthi, the birthday of the god. Thus the sun god in the skies greeted the sun god on earth.

As that date approached, in the eighth year of the emperor Nero, the priests of Serapis were taking counsel.

✕

Ever since the encounter in which he had resisted Clea, the priestess of Isis, John Mark had felt an occasional sense of foreboding. Even apart from anything he might have done to set up machinations against himself and his community in priestly and official circles, there appeared to be a growing disposition to actions of violence against the followers of Jesus in many places, a disposition certainly encouraged by the well-known predilection of the emperor Nero for everything Hellenistic.

These forebodings on the part of John Mark were not lessened by his experiences on several further trips in the East and to Rome. On two different occasions in Rome he found Paul in prison. There Mark was able to talk with Paul and even to be of some service to him, since the old misunderstanding of the time when Mark—with the vision of Sarah in his eyes—had gone back from Perga to Jerusalem had long since been overcome. He found Paul quite uncertain whether life or death would be the outcome, but quite reconciled to either. Mark found Peter engaged in sending correspondence to the followers of Jesus in provinces in the East, encouraging them to steadfastness and equanimity in view of expected suffering. Using Silas—who had been with Paul after Mark and Barnabas went to Cyprus—to write for him, Peter told them: "Even if you do suffer for righteousness' sake, you will be blessed. . . . If any one suffers as a Christian, let him not be ashamed."

Such thoughts of possible suffering—and such words of encouragement in the face of the worst that could happen—were in the mind of John Mark as he returned to Alexandria.

The thoughts which revolved about the apparently growing

probabilities of trouble for all the followers of Jesus everywhere led John Mark to have long conversations with Annianus about the future of the community in Alexandria. Obviously the very fact that many people were continuing to come into the community out of previous associations in the cults of Isis and of Serapis did not lessen the likelihood that the officials of those cults would try to promote actions against the community and its leader. Nevertheless Mark could not desist from his work, nor could the community decline to receive those who wished to associate themselves with it.

If the time should come when John Mark would no longer be present, he felt sure that the community would wish Annianus to assume its leadership. Annianus was Mark's own first convert, and he had been his good friend and associate ever since. Mark felt confident that such a selection would work for good.

He noticed also that another, much younger man, Abel or, in Greek, Avilus by name, likewise a believer in Jesus out of the background of the Jewish faith, was associating himself closely with Annianus, and he felt that Annianus would have assistance from him of the same kind that Annianus himself had given to Mark.

Finally, in the spring of the eighth year of Nero and not long before the community's annual observance of the festival of the resurrection of Jesus, Mark's foreboding concerning his personal fate reached an acute point, and he proceeded with a ceremony intended to secure to the community, under any circumstances, adequate future leadership. He laid his hands on and appointed to lead the community Annianus, with Avilus as his assistant. He likewise consecrated three presbyters, Milaion, Sabinon, and Cerdona, together with seven deacons, and eleven others for general service.

╳

This was also the time when, with the birthday of their god approaching, the priests of Serapis were taking counsel together. Their problem was the continuing increase in the number of persons defecting to the community of the followers of Jesus, and the corresponding continuing decline in the number of persons taking an interest in and giving support to the Serapeion. While their cult had the enormous benefit of a virtually official standing in the state, it nevertheless had never obtained the amount of influence on the daily life of the people which its leadership could have wished, and now the losses being suffered were embarrassing and discouraging. The cult of Isis, less officially supported, had wider popular support, and Clea, priestess of Isis, although actually facing the same problem in no small measure herself, made a special point of emphasizing to the priests of Serapis the character of their predicament.

Being fortified by such powerful official support as they always enjoyed, the priests of Serapis felt sure that even if they instigated actions of a sort which would ordinarily be considered as mob violence and quickly brought under control by the government, in this case what happened would be allowed to run its course and reach its goal before being stopped.

Public feeling on behalf of Serapis could be counted upon to reach its highest point at the time of the annual birthday celebration of the god, and this was now at hand. If the correct ideas were implanted in the minds of the crowd, the sentiment for Serapis could readily be combined with wrath against what was now the chief force working against him, that is, against the community of the followers of Jesus, and against the one who had long been known as its leader, John Mark.

Accordingly, the representatives of the priests of Serapis circulated among the always volatile pagan populace of Alexandria.

"Do you not see the wickedness of this sorcerer?" they asked. "He has done many evil deeds. He has gathered many people together. The sacrifices to the gods have been upset. The worship of Serapis has been hindered. The god will no longer look with favor upon our city unless we wipe out the evil. What will we do for the god on his birthday?"

The leaven worked rapidly among the populace. By the 29th day of Pharmuthi, the day before the birthday of the god, the priests judged the time was ripe.

"The name of the sorcerer is John Mark. The meeting place of the disturbers of our religion is in Bucolia in Delta." Thus the agents of the priests specified the objective.

In this year the 29th day of Pharmuthi fell upon the first day of the week and was the day of the festival of the resurrection among the followers of Jesus. The community was gathered in their usual meeting place on the quiet street in Bucolia in Delta, and John Mark was leading prayers in the assembly hall. He was saying:

> Let us stand nobly,
> Let us stand piously,
> Let us stand earnestly,
> Let us stand in peace,
> Let us stand with fear of God,
> and with trembling and contrition.

The angry shouts of the mob were heard approaching, and the defenseless community awaited the attack. John Mark knew that the time to which his forebodings had pointed was at hand.

Breaking into the assembly, the attackers concentrated their attention upon the leader. Rushing forward, they seized John Mark and fastened a rope about his throat.

"Drag the serpent through the pasture," they cried.

Partly dragging and partly carrying him, they went off with Mark and deposited him at last, bruised and bleeding, in a barren prison cell.

There in the middle of the night Mark saw Jesus standing in the cell with him, and saying, "Peace to you, Mark, my evangelist," and he was comforted.

In the morning, on the 30th day of Pharmuthi and the birthday of Serapis, the multitude came again, and again put a rope around Mark's neck. "Drag the serpent through the pasture," they cried again.

Mercifully, as they plunged down a series of steep steps toward the sea, dragging Mark behind them, his head struck a sharp corner of stone and his life was extinguished. But in the last moment he saw

Sarah stretching out her arms toward him, and the loneliness went out of his eyes, and John Mark died with a look of utter peace upon his face.

X

The representatives of the priests of Serapis then gathered wood from a nearby grove, with the intention of dishonoring the body of John Mark by burning it on the spot. There came, however, a swift storm from the sea, which deluged the place with rain, and the crowd dispersed, saying, "It is because it is the birthday of Serapis. Verily, the god has come to see the man who has been killed this day."

So the faithful people of the community of Jesus came and gathered the body of their leader and buried it close by on the grassy slope of Bucolia, not far from their place of assembly. Above the grave they put up a plain marker, and on one side they put the simple cross from Jerusalem which was the mark of deliverance, and on the other side the loop cross which was the mark of life to come.